T0198588

SHATTERED DREAMS

SHATTERED DREAMS

ANNA'S TOWN BOOK II

ROBERT COLEMAN

SHATTERED DREAMS
ANNA'S TOWN BOOK II

iUniverse books may be ordered through booksellers or by contacting:

iUniverse
1663 Liberty Drive
Bloomington, IN 47403
www.iuniverse.com
1-800-Authors (1-800-288-4677)

ISBN: 978-1-5320-9988-5 (sc)
ISBN: 978-1-5320-9987-8 (e)

Library of Congress Control Number: 2020912374

Print information available on the last page.

iUniverse rev. date: 07/27/2020

Prologue

A.C. CALLOWAY MOVED HIS family from Big Flat Mississippi to Tupelo in the fall of 1952. He had suffered through three years of poor crops from flooding and had sold just about everything he owned to pay out of debt. He, his wife, Allie, and two sons, Willy and Zack, had moved into a small house on the grounds of the Purnell Lumber and Supply company. Pappy, as the boys called him, took a job managing the lumber yard for his old friend, Wayne Purnell. He and Wayne had served together in the Navy, and were together when the Japanese bombed Pearl Harbor on December 7, 1941. Both were wounded and spent nearly six months in a military hospital where their friendship was cemented forever. Both were decorated veterans.

The move to Tupelo got off to a rough start for his two sons when they had to confront the two meanest boys in tupelo. It was at the Junior high school, where Zack met Annabelle Owens, one of the prettiest girls in school. In addition to being beautiful, she was also very smart and very brash. Their friendship quickly grew into something far more serious. The Calloway boys had become somewhat of heroes for teaching the McCullough's a lesson with a Louisville slugger bat. The McCullough's had been robbing students of their lunch money and striking fear into anyone who walked the streets around the school. The Calloway brothers had learned however, after their confrontation, that the McCullough's were desperate, and just trying to get enough money together to feed themselves and hire a doctor to see about their very sick mother. When Zack and Willy had learned why the boys were doing what they were doing, they wanted to help. When they went to Pappy to see if he could help Naught and Nate with their mother, a new friendship with the McCullough's began to develop.

AC had met Albert Davis, an old man who came to the lumber yard on a regular basis, and had befriended the old fellow who, was well into his eighties and in poor health. Albert had no family to take care of him and had no one to turn to when he fell ill. Momma and Pappy who had refused to let him go into a nursing facility, prepared a room for him and moved him into the house with the Calloway family. He soon became a part of the family and When the old man passed away, he left his entire estate to AC and Allie Calloway. The estate consisted of over a thousand acres of good farmland,

and over a half million dollars in cash. There were also nearly a hundred head of cattle as well. AC was now a very wealthy man, and when his friend Wayne, offered him a partnership in the business, AC accepted and the two men began an expansion of the business in Tupelo, and started two additional stores in West Point and Columbus. Tupelo was a thriving community, and they had also built a 36-unit apartment building on the west side of town.'

That Christmas Zack gave Anna a gold locket as their relationship grew more serious, then in the next year, Doctors at the center discovered that Anna had terminal cancer. When Anna learned that she was dying, she asked Zack to spend the night with her. That night they had their first sexual experienxe. Then, the Mysterious Doctor Luke appeared during the night and gave her medication. He also performed an ancient ritual on both Anna and Zack. The next morning when the Doctors checked on Anna, she had no sign of cancer. It had disappeared.

This presented problems for Anna and Zack, and for the hospital, for there was no Doctor Luke who worked at the hospital. Some legal proceeding followed, but with the help of Justin T. Webb, a local attorney, the problems were finally resolved, and Anna and Zack's bond grew stronger.

Nearly four years had passed now, and the expansion of the lumber business had been very successful. The future looked bright for the Calloway family, but no matter how much we plan for tomorrow, the future rarely unfolds as we Intend. Plans have a way of unraveling; Dreams turn to nightmares, and hopes, like grapes, sometimes wither on the vine.

"When you teach a child something you take away forever his chance of discovering it on his own."

-Jean Piaget

1

Grandpa's Store

Uncle Otto's Dog

I WAS FIVE YEARS old at my Grandpa's feet, in his old house in Big Flat as he slipped on his well-worn, smooth-toe shoes., They were ankle top, lace-ups with the metal hooks. I watched carefully as he wound the laces back and forth until he made the loop at the top of the shoe. There he stopped and said, "now do you want to try to tie it Zachery?" He was sitting in his ladderback rocker and was leaning forward to watch me.

I nodded, and then carefully began to try to make the bow, following grandpa's instruction on every move until he smiled and said, "good Job, Zack. Now tie the other one."

I followed his instruction, first a half bow then the loop and then the pull through, and after a dozen try's I finally got it right. He watched patiently until I finally made the bow and pulled it tight. Grandpa stood up, towering high above me, for he was well over six-foot-tall and to me, a five-year-old, he seemed like a giant. Grandpa was a lean man, old and weathered with a bushy handlebar mustache, thinning grey hair and a face like wrinkled old leather. When he stood, he was slightly forward bent, for he suffered from a stomach hernia and wore a truss. After he had slipped on his denim cotton jumper and a battered old brown fedora, he reached for his cane that was propped beside the brick fireplace. He looked down at me and smiled. His mustache curving upward

Grandpa always smelled of smoking tobacco for it seemed to me that he kept the old crooked-stem pipe lit all the time. It was just part of him being my grandpa. He reached on the mantel board and took the cap off a bottle of patent medicine and took two long swigs. I watched his Adams apple go up and down as he swallowed. He then wiped his mouth with his jumper sleeve and cleared his throat and shook his head as if it tasted awful. He replaced the bottle cap and stuck the half-empty bottle in the side pocket of his jumper. He Struck a match on the rock fireplace, touched it to his pipe and drew on it until he exhaled a puff of smoke.

"You ready to go Zack? Time for me to open up the store."

I never answered but ran ahead to open the door for the old man. It was a rare occasion when I could go with my Grandpa to his store in Big Flat. But Momma needed potatoes, {Grandpa called them spuds} and since we lived within sight of the old store, I would sometimes get to go with him as he opened for the day. We had lived in grandpa's old house in Big Flat all my life; Grandpa, Momma, Pappy, my brother Willy, and me.

It was barely daylight when we started down the dirt road, the rising sun was just breaking through the tall pine trees on the Eastern ridge just above Big Flat, and the old Hipp's house on the hill. Uncle Bud Lindsey, who had a small blacksmith shop across the road from Grandpa's house, was already pounding on his anvil, "probably sharpening plow points," grandpa allowed. The din of the hammer sent familiar echoes through the early morning stillness, as if this were the signal for the whole community to move. Grandpa said that Uncle Bud probably got a good cussin' every morning about that time. We could also smell the cinder smoke from his forge, wafting through the morning air. Grandpa always opened at five o'clock in the morning through spring and summer. After crops were harvested in the fall, he would open a little later. Grandpa was a partner with his brother Otto, and they took turns opening the store on a weekly rotation. Uncle Otto refused to open on any

Sunday, but Grandpa would. And on most Sundays. someone would come by the house, knock on the door, and ask grandpa if he would open for them to get some necessity. Grandpa never complained, for many of his customers were in the fields or at work at a sawmill six days a week and Sunday was their only chance to get to the store.

Grandpa took long strides and I had to run to keep up. I would occasionally jump to try to step in his tracks. His cane also made tiny round holes beside each right-handed footprint. Grandpa had made me a walking cane to replicate his, from wild cane that grew along the creeks and river bottoms. I would make holes right beside my tracks just like Grandpa. We passed Uncle Otto's house on the left side of the road, and the Baptist Church on the right, and then I could see the old *Lion Oil* Sign that stood as a landmark for Grandpa's store.

Across the road and on a narrow ridge stood the Big Flat School. It was a two story, building that sat smack in the middle of the little hamlet. At lunch time many of the older students would cross the dirt road and buy cold drinks and peanuts and candy if they had any money. Grandpa would also make bologna and cheese sandwiches for farmers and other workers who came by, slicing thick slabs from the long roll with a big butcher's knife.

As we neared the store Grandpa took a chain of keys from his belt and unlocked the front, and only, door to the building. It was not a large structure, but the Calloway store sold items that small farmers around Big Flat needed. From plow points, kegs of nails and fencing staples, nuts and bolts, overalls, and cotton sacks; there was a little bit of everything it seemed to me. He also carried a few canned goods and tobacco products as well as sugar, flour, and other staples. Grandpa said that he thought that every man in Big Flat either chewed, dipped or smoked, and some did all three. He said half the ladies did but only a few dared to be seen buying it openly, but he knew who they were, but he wasn't telling. He had one gas pump out in front of the store and a kerosene pump under the portico. There was no electricity in most of Big Flat, so people depended on kerosene for their lamps, but Grandpa's store and the school had been the first buildings in the village to get the electricity. It was also one of the first to get a telephone. Folks would come from all around to get grandpa to make phone calls for them to Doctors and often to soldiers that were away in the Army. The little store was also a message center. Things like, "If you see Tom Fowler, tell him his old bull has done jumped his fence and is hanging around with my milk cow." Grandpa would laugh at some of the messages he was asked to convey.

Nearly everybody in Big Flat had a charge account at Grandpa's store. Sometimes he did not get paid until crops were harvested and sold in the fall. However, the people around Big Flat were honest, hard-working folks who eventually paid their bills. I never heard Grandpa complain about anybody not paying what they owed. Accounts were kept in a simple sales book that the customer signed when they charged a purchase.

When Grandpa had turned on the lights, he went behind the counter to open the combination safe, where he kept the cash to operate the little store. The safe was large; head high to me, with a combination dial the size of a Big Ben alarm clock. The thing was probably fifty years old and bolted firmly to the floor. It must have weighed a ton. It fascinated me. Grandpa knelt in front of the big safe on one knee and I stood beside him to watch.

"How does it work, grandpa? How does that dial open the door?"

"Well, that's kind of hard to explain Zachery, but you know those jig-saw puzzles that your mother likes to put together, and how each little piece fits perfectly with other pieces and when all the pieces are finally in place how it creates a pretty picture."

I nodded and said I did, for momma would sometimes let me help her look for pieces. Sometimes she would help me find pieces and then let me put them in the right place.

"Well this old safe is kind of like that puzzle, only you can't see the pieces. They are all inside the door, but each part of the puzzle has a number and when you turn the dial to the right number a piece of the puzzle falls into place. You then go to the next number, and that piece falls into place. When you finally have the pieces in the right place the safe will be ready to open. This safe has five numbers to remember and only your uncle Otto and I know the numbers. Now I'm going to turn the dial to the first number, but first you must set the dial to zero, I know you have been learning your numbers so go on and set the dial to zero, and I will then turn the dial to the first number. Put your ear to the safe and listen, really hard, and you can hear when the first piece of the puzzle falls into place."

I put my ear to the safe door, and sure enough when grandpa got to the first number, I could hear a faint click. It was like magic. When grandpa had entered the last number and I heard the last piece of the puzzle fall into place grandpa said, "now pull the handle down."

I did as he said, and the big safe door sprung open. We both laughed.

Grandpa reached in and took a small cash box from the safe and told me to remember that instead of calling parts inside of the safe puzzle parts, they were called tumblers, he said. I didn't know if I would remember that or not, for I had never heard that word before.

When grandpa had retrieved the cash box, he took a paper sack from beneath the counter and put in four large red potatoes and told me to go on and take them to my momma. '" She'll be watching out the window for you, he said. So, don't piddle around."

I left the store and headed back up the dusty road toward grandpa's old house, the sun was now breaking over the tops of the big oak trees behind Uncle Bud's blacksmith shop along the Eastern hills, but I was back inside the store in a half minute.

"What are you doing back here at the store Zack? Your momma will be mad as a hornet if you don't get home with those potatoes, and I mean fast."

"I can't."

"What do you mean you can't? grandpa asked, his voice a little edgy."

"That goddamn dog of Uncle Otto's won't let me pass," I said.

"What did you say?"

"I said that goddamn dog……."

"I heard what you said! He interrupted. Who told you to say goddamn? That's a cuss word and your momma will surely wash your mouth out with soap if she hears you say that. You're not to use the Lords name in vain."

"That's what Willy calls him, I said. He said that goddamn dog is one mean, biting', sumbitch!"

"Willy huh? that's about what I figured. He's started to school and hasn't even learned to read, but apparently has got a pretty good education in cussin'. Your daddy is going to light up his britches. Come on I'll walk out with you. That dog wouldn't bite a biscuit, he said, just likes to bark and carry on. He's as dumb as a hoe handle; ain't good for nothing! If that dog bit somebody Otto would cut his tail off right behind his ears.

I tried to imaginate what a dog would look like with his tail cut off right behind his ears. I couldn't grasp such a thing, but it was like a picture that just wouldn't leave my head.

"Be a mighty short dog wouldn't he Grandpa? And he'd only have two legs."

"Yes, he would Zack and be mighty dead too. You're just wasting time Zachery, now come on, its time you got home."

Grandpa walked a little way from the store and when the dog came out and started barking, grandpa yelled at him one time, slapped his britches leg, and that was enough to send the mutt cowering back to his hiding place beneath Uncle Otto's house. I was still Leery though, for I could see the mutt's yellow eyes following me from beneath the darkness of his sanctuary as I passed by, as fast as I could run while carrying a sack of taters. I looked back one time and could see Grandpa still watching from the front of the store. He was grinning like a bear eating honey. I didn't find no humor in it though.

Momma met me at the door and said, "what have you been doing Zack? You know I told you not to tarry. Answer me Zack. Zack! Zack! Zack!"

I woke in a start from my reverie and sat up in my bed. I'd been dreaming.

"Breakfast is on the table Zack, you'll be late for school," Momma said.

"Sorry momma, I was having a dream of being back in Big Flat. Dreaming about grandpa and his old store."

Momma laughed. "I have those dreams too Zack, so you get ready for school. Your Daddy has already asked about you twice. Willy had to leave early; said he was going to pick up Jessie. He's driving our old truck. She's working part time at the drugstore. She helps them clean and get ready to open before she goes to school each morning. That girl has got Willy wrapped around her finger so tight, he doesn't know whether he's moving forward, or backing up."

"Yeah, I know. When he is not with her, he's over at the Guard unit studying for that Officers Candidate School. He's sure going to be disappointed if he doesn't make the grade, for he sure has his mind set on getting into flight school and being an Air Force Pilot."

Jessie and Anna and Penelope had been best friends since they started to school together in the first grade. The three, that some of the teachers called the triplets, were without a doubt the prettiest and smartest girls in the whole school. I don't know how Willy and I got so lucky. Beauty I have heard it said, is only skin deep, but ugly goes plumb to the bone. Both, thankfully, however, are in the eyes of the beholder. Anna was the boldest of the three and the others usually followed her lead. She was a loving person but was outspoken and didn't mind voicing her opinion even if her friends disagreed with her position. That ne was one of the things I admired about Annabelle Owens. She knew her own mind and would stick to what she believed.

2

School Promotions

Work at the law firm

IT HAD BEEN NEARLY four years now since our family had moved to Tupelo where Pappy took a job at the Purnell Lumber and Supply Company. I loved the town and its people. Tupelo was not an old town like many people suppose. There were no antebellum style columned homes, that lined brick paved streets like Oxford and Columbus. The town did, however, have its share of stately Magnolia tree. When the trees were in full blossom there was a sweetness that wafted on the evening winds. Momma called it the Magnolia wind.

The city was not even incorporated until after the Civil War. Until that time the area was known as Gum pond, but the Illinois-Mobile Railroad served as an Umbilical cord that connected the area with Memphis Tennessee to the north and Mobil Alabama to the South. The railroad became a major shipping platform for cattle and cotton being sold to markets in the North.

Then in 1936 a Tornado practically wiped the town off the face of the earth, destroying almost completely the area formerly known as Gum Pond. Dozens of Tupelo citizens were killed and hundreds more injured. Mississippians are Hickory tough people though, and soon began to rebuild. The area soon became a thriving industrial and banking area in North Mississippi. It had also become the chief medical center in Northern part of the state. "The Hospital on The Hill," as it was called was the very best and most modern medical facility that the state had to offer.

It had been over four years since Anna had been discharged from the hospital, and the ordeal that we had faced with the authorities after we had spent the night together and had sexual relations when we thought she was dying of cancer. We had not had intimate relations since that night, but Marie Owens kept rein on her daughter. I understood how she felt and so did Anna. We did not want to hurt her mother or disappoint my parents, but the wanting was still there.

Both my brother Willy and I had grown a good four inches in height and were both well over six foot and a good two inches taller than Pappy. Anna had just gotten prettier it seemed with each day and was the envy of every girl in Tupelo. I knew that other boys were asking her out, and that was a concern because I sure wasn't going to win any handsome contests. It was a pure mystery why she even liked me, but girls are funny about that sort of thing. While boys, it seemed were mostly influenced by eye appeal, girls were not nearly so shallow. I knew, however, that there was a lot more to Anna, Penny, and Jessie than just looks.

I had no interest in any of the other girls in school. Annabelle Owens was all I wanted. Pappy said I should play the field some, that I was too young to be serious about one girl. However, he had admitted that he had never dated other girls after he met our Momma and they had married at seventeen. Pappy said that picking a girl for a wife was a lot like picking a good pair if mules. "You don't want one that creates so much attention that somebody is always wanting to steal them from you, but you do want a pair that don't look bad pulling a wagon."

Pappy's philosophy didn't always make a lot of sense, but I got his meaning."

A lot had happened in the three years since then. Because of our excellent grades, both Anna and I had been tested at school and promoted to a higher grade. We were being tutored some to help with math and science, and we had also been given extra work to make sure we were getting what we needed. It was difficult to keep up with the extra work, but our grades were good, and we remained at the top of our class. I was still playing sports but Anna decided not to continue in the band program so she could spend more time on her studies. Willy and I were now only a grade apart in school and were both playing baseball for the same high school team because of our promotion, but with his determination to be a pilot, he was spending all of his spare time at the Air Guard Unit studying and preparing for the Officer Candidate School when he graduated in May. I had been working part-time for the Webb Law firm and when there was time Mr. Webb would tutor me on taking the Mississippi Bar Exam. He was a smart lawyer and he had started letting me watch and help when he was presenting cases in court. My days working and studying left little time for romance and that didn't set too well with me, but I felt it would pay off some day.

On some weekends, Willy and I would work on the farm, for there was always things to be done. Mrs. McCullough and her boys had moved into the old Davis house and had the place looking pretty good. Pappy had an indoor bathroom installed, and had the floors covered with new linoleum rugs. We had built new fences around the whole place and put a new roof on the barn. Little by little Pappy had turned the farm into a real showplace and a profitable one to boot. Pappy had hired Joe Webb to see to managing the farm and feeding the cattle and he loved the work. Pappy said Joe was well off financially and didn't need the money but wanted to work and still be free to hunt and fish. It was a great help to Pappy, for he did not have much time to work on the farm because of the expanding lumber business. joe always wore western boots that were well worn and run over at the heels. He had a handlebar mustache like our grandpa. He was tall and lanky and had a deep Mississippi drawl. I guess women would find him handsome in a rough-cut kind of way.

The McCullough boys had turned out to be good workers and they usually worked alongside of me and Willy as we cleared fence rows and put up hay for the cattle. Notch still cussed like a seasick sailor and had a fiery hot temper, but Naught had settled down, was able to keep Notch in line most of the time. Both boys were strong as an Ox, and both had slimmed down and put on muscles and the work in the sunshine had the boys deeply tanned. The girls at school had noticed too. Naught, however, had not yet gathered courage enough to ask any girl out.

Naught had been seen talking to Penelope Johnson on occasions and it was obvious he was smitten with her. Penelope liked Naught a lot, for she had told Anna that she thought he was handsome and wished he would just say what was on his mind. Naught had come to Penelope's aid when she was being accosted by two older boys at school, that were talking trashy stuff to her. He had dispatched them in a hurry and told them that they were not to speak to her again. She had smiled at him and took his arm for a moment. She had told Anna that his face had turned pink when she took his arm and could not speak another word. He was completely tongue-tied. Penelope, however, was still a little unsure about a romantic relationship with the boy who had once had a reputation of being one of the meanest boys in Tupelo. But Naught had really changed. He had turned out to be a good student and top-notch athlete and was a starting lineman for the football team. Because of his good grades, he too had been promoted to a higher grade. He was a year older than most of the students in his class, He had missed a lot of school when his mother was ill and he was trying to take care of her. His real interest, however, was not school, but in becoming a Marine. He was working hard on his studies in hopes that he could someday become an officer in his Guard unit and then eventually the regular marines. He said his goal was to make the military a career. Pappy had promised Mrs. McCullough that if her sons wanted to go to college, that the lumber company would see to it that their tuition was paid. Naught was a good prospect, but Notch, on the other hand was a better candidate for reform school. He had a chip on his shoulder the size of a chopping block and was prone to provoke trouble at every opportunity. He had been in trouble at school on more than one occasion. How brothers could be so different in temperament was a mystery to me.

Mrs. McCullough had proven to be an asset to the lumber company and was now running the entire lumber purchasing and distribution system as well as managing the contracting business. She was a beautiful lady and had an outgoing personality as well as an extra-ordinary capacity for numbers. She had plenty of would be suitors but showed little interest.

Pappy said he thought she was still married to Nate and Naught's father who had deserted them when the boys were small. She knew just how to be friendly with the customers but keep men at arm's length. She had her hands full with the raising of two tough boys and working a full-time job as well. She didn't complain though. She seemed grateful for the trust and responsibility Pappy had placed on her.

Anna who was getting ready to turn seventeen in a few weeks, spent most weekends working at the hospital as a clerk, answering the telephone and running errands for Doctor Little and the nurses. She was determined to be a Doctor and she loved the hospital work, but it sure weren't helping my romantic interests one bit.

Willy had turned seventeen and had joined the Air National Guard and spent one weekend each month at the Guard unit in Tupelo, and occasionally would spend a weekend at Columbus Air Force Base. They had not let him go up in a plane yet, but he was learning about the instruments and about military aircraft in general. Naught McCullough had joined the Marine reserves, and he too spent a great deal of his time at his Unit. Me and Willy and the McCullough boys would occasionally camp out on the pond at the Farm and fish for catfish and build bon fires on the levy and laugh and talk till morning, roasting wieners and boiling coffee over the fire. We would sit by the fire and make up ghost stories and tales about wild animals and big snakes eating people, and, of course, girls.

Me and Notch both hated snakes and sometimes we would get the jeebies and go and sleep in the house or the barn loft.

Squat was right there with us taking it all in. The big pond had a few snakes, but they would mostly disappear when we got in the water. I hated snakes of any kind but the big hound loved to catch them and would sometimes drag them up to the campfire and give me misery, but In the end we would agree that it was the best time ever.

One night, just after the McCullough's had moved into the Davis house, Joe Webb had heard us talking about camping at the pond that night, and decided to pull a prank on us. Joe fashioned a noise maker out of a big coffee can, and a waxed cord. He punched a hole in the bottom of the tin can and fed the waxed cord through the hole. When he would draw the cord back and forth through the hole, it sounded like a woman screaming. He hid in the brush and when we were all sitting around the fire talking, he pulled the cord through the can. We all had stick pokers in our hands poking at the fire, but when the first scream came, we all jumped up and threw our pokers in the fire.

"What to hell was that? Notch cried,' his eyes big as saucers.

When Joe shook the bushes, and the second scream came, Notch dang near trampled me to death heading for the house the rest of us right behind him in a cloud of dust. The third scream put us all inside the house almost crushing Mrs. McCullough as we all four were trying to get through the door at the same time.

"What's going on she asked. What is the matter with you boys? You look like you've seen a ghost?"

"There's something out there in the dark, in the bushes, Notch said, his eyes wide and big as goose eggs! Sounded like a panther or something."

"You boys are just imagining things," she said. There are no panthers around here, it was probably just a cat. You all go on back to your fire."

"I ain't about to be going back out there," Notch declared. Whatever that was that made that noise didn't sound like no normal, ordinary, animal.

We all four sat down on the couch and were just looking at each other when there was a loud bang on the door. Notch must have jumped a foot. And I dang near pissed my pants. We all came to our feet. Mrs. McCullough went to the door, shaking her head.

"What a brave bunch you boys are," Mrs. McCullough said, still shaking her head as she opened the door.

It was Joe Webb. He came in and sat at the dining table and accepted a cup of coffee from Mrs. McCullough.

"I saw that fire down on the levy, he said. Why aren't you boys down there? "he asked as he stepped inside.

"Something's out there in the brush, 'Naught said. It Sounded kind of like a woman screaming or a big wild animal. Its shore weren't no pussy cat."

Joe finished his coffee, got up to leave and said goodnight to Mrs. McCullough. "Probably just the wind blowing. He said, winking at her. Or, he added, there was that Circus that let some of their panthers get loose a few years ago. Thought they caught them all, but they were never quite sure. I know they let one of them old Boa Constrictors get loose and never did find him. Some said that old snake was twenty feet long and big around as a five-gallon bucket. That old rascal is still out there somewhere. You boys enjoy your camping, he said, with a grin as he left the house."

"Enjoy camping, my ass," Notch said. I might never go out after dark again. I shore don't want to get et by a Boa Contractor."

"Constrictor," Naught corrected.

"Whatever," Notch said.

We all four slept on Mrs. McCullough's floor till daylight. Mrs. McCullough made us a big breakfast the next morning and asked when we were planning another camping trip at the levy.

"When I get old enough to carry a bazooka," Naught declared.

Pappy had insisted that I limit the time that I spent with Annabelle, so we would usually go to see a movie or just meet on Saturday afternoons at the drugstore for a burger and milkshake. I would usually walk her home or just stroll around the streets of Tupelo. Even though I was now driving, Mrs. Owens would only on rare occasion let Anna go for a drive with me.

Anna didn't have much time for dating anyway. Sometimes she would kiss me when we went for a drive, and then sometimes she wouldn't. "I wondered what that was all about. Women were a mystery, and downright aggravating. It was confusion to no end—made me want to kick a stump sometimes. It was plain that what happened to Anna when she thought she was dying was not going to happen again. I was alright with that, for although I wanted her and thought of that night every day, I was willing to wait because I loved her and believed that she felt the same.

Pappy and Mr. Purnell were working hard on expanding the business and planning for the expansion of the Lumber company in West Point and Columbus. The new Tupelo showroom was nearly complete. They had bought twenty acres adjoining the property on the south side of the existing buildings and had purchased the city cleaners building along Main street and expanded the show room and hardware. They had also completed a new apartment complex on the West side of the Lumber Company and were looking for more property in Columbus and West Point to expand.

Pappy rarely came to my football games anymore, but Momma never missed a home game. Pappy hated that he could not be there with Momma, I knew he always loved to watch Willy and I play any kind of ball. The work was taking its toll on Pappy. His hair seemed to be getting grayer with each passing day, but he never complained. Momma was plainly worried about him though, for she knew that what Pappy really wanted was to be back home in Big Flat with Grandpa and his old friends.

It would be two more years before me and Willy graduated from high school, and she doubted Pappy would consider another move until they both finished. I wasn't sure that that was what momma wanted though. She and Bonnie and Mrs. McCullough had become very close and although she loved being around family. This was the first time she had developed close friendships beyond her kin. It would be hard to give that up.

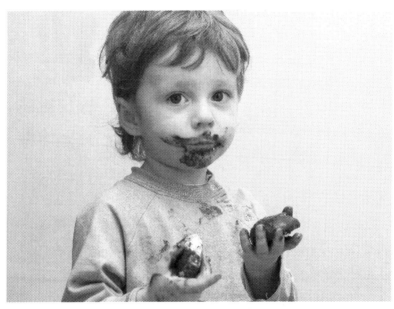

"Robert Calloway"

*"Children have never been very good at listening
but have never failed to imitate"*
                                                    -James Baldwin

3

The Letter

Family addition

SCHOOL HAD JUST STARTED back after the Christmas
holidays when Pappy received *the letter*. It was sent by
certified mail and the postman required his signature.
That was a strange event, for Pappy said he had never in
his life had to sign for a letter. He didn't open it until he
was home for supper that night, for he wanted Momma
to open it and read it to him. Pappy could read well
enough, but he always wanted Momma to read it to him.
It was like he was afraid he would miss something if he
read it himself.

The letter itself looked very official with big "Certified Mail" stamped in red letters across the front. It was from the Rosberg Law Firm in Indianola, Mississippi.

Me and Willy were all ears and wanted to hear every word. Momma read the letter slowly and carefully. Pappy always had a worried look on his face when he got letters. It was as if he was always expecting bad news. Momma, on the other hand, always smiled when she got a letter from anyone.

> *Dear Mr. Calloway,*
>
> *This letter is sent to inform you of the death of Mrs. Mary Louise Calloway, wife of your distant cousin, Herbert Lewis Calloway, deceased. Mrs. Calloway was married to the former Mr. Calloway for sixteen years until his death from cancer on November 25, 1951. Mrs. Calloway died from a similar disease on December 10th of this past year.*
>
> *Mr. and Mrs. Calloway gave my law firm instructions in their last will that we should contact you upon her passing. It was her wish that you take custody of her two children and raise them as your own if you are agreeable. There are no other living relatives that my firm has been able to locate. The two children are presently in custody of the Mississippi Department of Social welfare and will be put up for adoption if you do not agree to take custody of the children.*

The children are ages five and nine. Robert Lee is the youngest and Charlie Russell is the older. They are both bright and healthy and have been well cared for, but to be forthright with you, and according to Human services they are a "Handful," and will demand a strong and firm hand." Please respond to me by calling the number on the business card that I have enclosed

The Calloway's owned a home and small farm of eighty acres near Indianola and in accordance with her last Will and Testament, the property and farm equipment will be sold at public auction and the proceeds will be deposited into a trust along with a few thousand dollars on deposit at the Farmers and Merchants Bank of Indianola for the two children. If you agree to take custody of the children, you will have full control of the trust.

This is not an agreement to adopt the children, but rather an agreement to take custody. If you decide to adopt, that process will be determined and managed by the Department of Social Services.

Sincerely
Melvin Rosberg
Attorney at Law

Pappy looked across the kitchen table at Momma like he had just hit his thumb with a sledgehammer. A

27

painful wrinkle in his furrowed brow. He bit his lower lip, as he often did when he was in deep thought.

"Now don't that beat all, Pappy said. I haven't seen Herbert and Mary in fifteen years and I never have laid eyes on their children. They're distant cousins on top of that. Wonder why they would want us to raise those kids?"

A look at Momma and I could tell the wheels were already turning in her head, but there was no telling what she was thinking. I knew what I was thinking though, and Willy was probably thinking about the same thing. A pair of five and nine-year-old's in the house was downright scary. I wanted no part of it.

I knew Indianola was somewhere in the Mississippi Delta, and grandpa always had a low opinion of Delta people. That was good enough for me.

"I don't know, momma said, but looks like we have a big decision to be making. Those kids need a home."

"Decision, my hind leg, Pappy said, we got to tell them lawyers *no*! We don't need to be taking on them young'uns to raise. We still got two at home that's trouble enough he said, winking at Momma. We ought to ask them lawyers if they can put Zack and Willy out for adoption. We might get a good night's sleep every now and then."

"Well, Momma said, we have to give it some thought. They *are your relatives*, and those kids can't help being in the situation they're in. Besides that, how much trouble could they be?"

I could tell right off that Pappy *was not* going to have the final word on this subject, and that was trouble waiting to happen. Momma was a pure sucker when it came to kids. No telling how irrational she would be over two rag-tag orphans from the Delta. I had a notion our lives were fixing to change, and not for the better.

"Pretty much all the truth telling in the world
is done by children"
-Oliver Wendell Holmes

4

The Surprise

Charlie and Robert

ANNABELLE WAS WAITING FOR me the next morning
on the steps of the High School. Willy and I were now
going to the same school, so some mornings Willy would
meet Jessie at the Junior High and Anna and I would
sit on the steps of the school with them and talk until
we had to go to class. I told Anna about the letter that
Pappy had received, and that my folks were thinking on
the proposition.

"So. you might be getting brothers, Anna smiled."

Brothers? I suddenly had a sinking feeling in my
stomach. I thought I was going to be sick. One brother
was enough headache to tolerate. I had not thought

about it in that way, but that's what it would amount to, for I knew Momma and Pappy would treat them boys the same as they treated Me and Willy. Momma couldn't keep enough milk in the house now, and with two delta heathens in the family, I'd probably never get another full glass. I knew deep down that momma was going to take them kids in though. She couldn't help herself. That's just the way she was made. Women were definitely a mystery and men were just pure suckers. The thought of having two new brothers played on my mind the whole day so much I couldn't concentrate on my studies. I figured Willy was having to wrestle with the thoughts himself. I was wondering too what Pappy was thinking now. He was probably a train wreck. He might even be thinking of running away from home. I knew if Momma wanted to take those kids in, that's the way it would be. When it came to Momma, Pappy was like a catfish after a worm on a hook. He'd keep nibbling until he's got the whole hook in his mouth.

Next night at supper, Pappy announced the decision. Momma looked happy as a lark and Pappy looked like he had just had a tooth pulled with a pair of vice grips.

"We've decided to take the children in, so you boys are going to have to share a room again, and we'll put Robert and Charlie together, momma said."

Well, at least we were not going to have to share a room with those delta rattails. I think I would consider running off and joining a circus if I had to share a room with a five-year-old. I couldn't imagine what it would be like sharing a room with a nine-year-old too.

Pappy said he had called the attorneys in Indianola and they were going to arrange to bring the Children to Tupelo on Saturday, with papers and documents to sign to consummate the custody process."

Momma was already getting things ready for our new family members. She had bought new bed covers and was buying toys that would be appropriate for a five-year old. Pappy, as always, took everything in stride but I knew he had plenty of reservations about taking two children to raise. Momma and Miss Bonnie Purnell had been looking at larger houses in the neighborhood where the Purnell's lived. She had her eye on one that she liked a lot. I Knew Pappy was fixing to turn loose of some more cash. He didn't have a chance when Momma made her mind on something.

Me and Willy did not care one way or the other, the house we live in was plenty good enough to suit us. Pappy said that the house we lived in, didn't much matter, but how we lived in the house was what was important. The house we were living now was the best place Willy and I had ever lived in. Grandpa's old house in Big Flat was a large rambling structure but had no running water and indoor plumbing. Pappy was now having Grandpa's house plumbed for it would make life much easier for Aunt Zula And Grandpa. He had also bought them a new refrigerator and a cookstove. Pappy tried to give him a new television set, but grandpa said he was afraid he couldn't figure out how to operate the "frazzling thing," so Pappy bought him a new Zenith radio instead.

Grandpa said Aunt Zula had got plumb lazy since they got the radio. All she wanted to do was sit and listen to them folks talk all day long. Sometimes she would forget to fix his supper.

5

New Family Members

The Delta Kids

SATURDAY MORNING PAPPY GOT the call from Mr. Roseberg just before noon. He told Pappy that he was at the Lee County Court House and asked if he and momma could meet him there for, they both had papers to sign and that he would need to have them notarized and recorded there in Lee County.

Momma insisted that Willy and I go with them so that we could all get acquainted at the same time. Pappy took off from work and he and Momma drove over in Pappy's old truck, and Willy and I followed in the truck that Mr. Davis had left me in his Will. We parked along Broadway for all the parking places around the

Courthouse were filled. A grey-haired man in a dark suit and a woman and two children sat on a bench beneath magnolia trees at the walkway leading up to the East entrance to the courthouse. When Pappy and Momma walked up toward the entrance the man stood and removed his hat. "Are you, by Chance, Mr. A.C. Calloway?" The man asked.

"Yes, Sir I'm A.C. Calloway, Pappy answered, what can I do for you?"

"Mr. Calloway," the man said, offering his Hand to Pappy, "I'm Melvin Rosberg from the Rosberg Law Firm in Indianola and this lady here with me, is Miss Dorthy Nix, from the Department of Human Services, in Sunflower County. These youngsters `here, nodding toward the two children, are the young ones, of which I spoke to you about in the letter, Robert, and Charlie. "Mrs. Nix was appointed foster parent of the children at the death of Mrs. Calloway. They have been with her since the passing of Mrs. Calloway and as you can see, they've become quite attached to her. She lost her husband a few years ago and didn't think she would be able to care for the children on a permanent basis, but she was going to try if you did not want to take the children,"

Pappy looked like he had just seen Bigfoot and might take out running, for Charlie wasn't gonna be no brother, for sure, because Charlie was a *girl!*

"Who in their right mind would name their daughter Charlie Russell," I thought to myself. I looked at Willy and he looked at me, with eyes big as jaw breakers. We both looked at Momma and she was grinning like a mule eating sugar cane. Pappy had always said that he and Momma had both wanted a girl, but God had punished them by giving them two knot-headed boys. Well, now they had their girl!

Robert Lewis was a red-headed, freckled face, and blue-eyed kid that exuded trouble coming in batches. His hair was a mop that grew in every direction, and he wore bib overalls and new lace-up shoes. Charlie on the other hand, was pretty as a speckled pup. Big blue eyes and long red hair to her waist, and a smile that could light up the dark. She wore a new pinafore dress, new patent leather shoes and had a black ribbon in her hair. I knew that girl was going to be plenty of trouble too. She would have Pappy wrapped around her finger in two seconds. Shoot, Pappy would probably never have any time for me and Willy again, and Momma would likely forget she had sons at all. The Lord works in mysterious ways, they say. That's true I guess, and sometimes he works in ways that just seems to rub your fur in the wrong direction.

Robert Lewis held on to the hand of his sister and Mrs. Nix all the time that Pappy and Mr. Rosberg talked. He didn't say anything and kept his head bowed low most of the time. It was plain that Charlie oversaw her younger brother and she aimed to call the shots for the both of them. Pappy told Me and Willy to wait with Mrs. Nix at the bench, while he and Momma went inside the courthouse to get papers signed and they sat beside Mrs. Nix while we waited. It was plain as daylight that Mrs. Nix had formed a special attachment to the Children as they peppered her with questions.

"Will we ever get to see you again Mrs. Nix?" Robert asked.

"Well That will be up to Mr. and Mrs. Calloway," she answered, but I don't see why not.

"I don't want to live in this place. I don't like Tupelo. I want to stay with you," Robert said rubbing back tears from his eyes.

Mrs. Nix pulled the child near her and kissed his head. With teardrops glistening she said," Now Robert Lewis, we have already talked about this, and you know that this is what your Momma wanted. She knew that this would be the best for you and your sister."

"Well, if that didn't beat the band," I thought. Here me and Willy was not wanting those kids in our family, and they didn't want to be there either. The kids were scared to death to be in their situation. Everything in their life had been turned upside down and inside out and they were, no doubt, just plain scared. Their parents were dead, and they were about to be given to strangers that they had never even seen before this day. I had heard Pappy say many times that life was not always fair. Well he was dang sure right about that. Life had sure not been fair to Robert and Charlie. Momma and Pappy were trying the only way they knew to help correct that. I could see that now. Willy and I would have to do our part too.

Pappy, Momma and Mr. Rosberg were gone for nearly a half an hour before they returned to the bench where we were waiting. Mr. Rosberg told Pappy that he had parked on Court Street down past the Lyric Theater and that he had several boxes and a suitcase in the trunk of his car and if he would drive by where he was parked, he would unload the children's possessions into his truck. Pappy made a loop around the courthouse and followed. We pulled up beside Mr. Rosberg's Lincoln. Mr. Rosberg got out and opened the trunk. The trunk of the big car was filled with boxes and packages.

"These are the belongings of the children, Mr. Rosberg said.

Pappy and Mr. Rosberg began loading the boxes into Pappy's truck while Mrs. Nix and the two children stood on the sidewalk and looked on. They were about the sadist looking people I had ever seen. Robert kept rubbing the teardrops from his eyes, while Charlie just looked defiant.

Mr. Rosberg and Mrs. Nix shook hands with Momma and Pappy. Mrs. Nix Knelt on her knees before Robert, pulled him to her bosom, and kissed and hugged him. She then hugged Charlie and then walked swiftly from the children with her face in her hands, obviously crying. She got into the passenger door of the car. Mr. Rosberg got into the car, put it into gear and drove away. Willy and I watched as Momma took Roberts hand and his sister took the other. Pappy opened the door to the old truck, the children crawled in and Momma and pappy got in with the children between them. Pappy drove off and Willy and I followed. We could barely see the tops of the children's heads through the back window of the truck as they turned on Broadway and down to Main and toward home.

Squat the big Black and Tan Hound bounded from beneath the house when we drove into the yard, barking to announce our arrival. Squat was a full-grown hound, now, standing a good twenty inches tall. He was sleek and shiny.

"Is that hound a biter? Charlie asked. I don't like biters, "She said.

"Nothing but biscuits," Pappy replied."

Willy and I carried the boxes and suitcases to the front porch and Momma and Charlie carried them inside; Charlie's mouth running like a leaky faucet. She was telling Momma about what she and Robert liked to eat and was asking if we had any books to read. She never gave Momma a chance to answer until she had another question or was offering information. Momma was a patient woman though and would nod and answer with a smile when she got a chance.

Robert sat on the front steps and Squat had his nose in his face. Soon he had his head in the boy's lap and Robert had his head laying on the dog's back. Squat had found a new friend and it was plain as day they were going to be big pals.

Momma had talked to Charlie about sleeping arrangements and learned that the two had shared a room all their lives and the same bed too, since their mother had taken sick. Charlie didn't think Robert would take to beings separated from her very well. Momma agreed that the arrangement would be ok for the time being, but she said that very soon she would have to find a different arrangement. A girl needs her privacy, Momma had said, and it was going to be difficult in a house full of boys.

Momma had let it be known that she had been thinking about a bigger place since they had decided to take the children and she thought she knew exactly the right place. She said that there was a four-bedroom house for sale in the neighborhood where the Purnell's lived. and Bonnie had been trying to get her to have Pappy look at it. It was two houses down the street from their own. Bonnie and Allie had become almost like sisters and talked every day, and sometimes on Saturday afternoon they would take walks together around Tupelo. If they moved in that neighborhood, I figured that she would probably have Bonnie's husband Wayne for breakfast every morning for he and Pappy were best of friends too.

When Momma had told Bonnie about the new additions to their family, she said that Bonnie seemed as excited as She was. I knew how Momma operated. When she made up her mind about something, she would suggest it to Pappy at night after supper. Pappy was a pushover where she was concerned, and she knew it, but she always tried to make him believe that major decisions were his idea. Sometimes, she said, he just needed the right kind of suggestion. Momma had plenty of tools in her toolbox and she knew how to use them all.

Momma cooked fried chicken and skillet fried potatoes for supper along with milk gravy and hot biscuits and chocolate pudding for dessert. She always cooked eight large biscuits for our family: two each for Pappy, Willy, and Me and one for Momma and an extra one for Squat. Tonight, she had cooked ten. One for Robert and one for Charlie. Charlie had fixed Robert's plate when we sat down to eat. That Robert had eaten his biscuit and gravy before you could spit, and had gravy from ear to ear, and had finished off a glass of milk before the rest of us had taken more than two bites.

"Robert you are such a pig, Charlie scolded, wipe your face and use your manners!"

"Can I have More Milk Miss Allie? Robert asked.

Momma started to get up to get more milk, but Charlie said, "No Robert; no more Milk!"

"He pees the bed Ms. Allie," Charlie offered."

"I don't either, you're lying! Robert said," pounding the table. Plates and silverware bounced.

Momma must have jumped a foot!

"You piss like a racehorse, and you know it, said Charlie."

Willie had just taken a mouth full if biscuit and gravy and when Charlie came out with that statement, he almost spewed it across the table.

"I don't piss like no racehorse either, I just have accidents, every now and then Miss Dot says, and she don't lie," Robert shouted.

"Pappy said woah now! You two just hold on. If Robert wets the bed every now and then, that's no big deal, we can handle that. Allie has a sure-fire cure for bed wetting,"

"Only way to stop his bed wetting is to cut his wiener off! Let's cut his wiener off Pappy!" Charlie blurted, slapping her hands on the table.

"You ain't cutting my wiener off. Don't let'um cut off my wiener Momma Calloway!" Cried Robert.

"No Robert, she's just pulling your leg—she's just kidding. Nothing is going to happen if you have an accident."

Momma looked like she had swallowed a horse fly sideways and Pappy spilled his coffee. Me and Willy were about to burst to laugh but knew better.

"Ms. Dot washed sheets nearly every day, Charlie offered, and I've slept on the floor nearly every night to keep from smelling like a pee pot.

"You ain't going to cut my wiener off!" Robert yelled.

'OK, Pappy said, raising his voice. That's enough, you two eat your supper and we'll handle the bed wetting problem. Nearly all kids wet the bed from time to time. They outgrow it."

Me and Willy looked at each other holding back outright laughter, Pappy winked at us. This was going to be a pair of Delta heathens that tested every nerve and value that this family ever had. We finished our supper without further conversation, but I couldn't hardly wait for breakfast in the morning to see what would happen. There were no biscuits left for Squat. Robert finished off the last biscuit and sopped up the last bit of the gravy. This was going to be better than watching a circus parade.

Momma put Robert and Charlie to bed at eight o'clock and sat on the bed after tucking them in. She talked to the children in low tones but with the door open, Me and willy could hear most of her conversation with the children.

"I know how you both miss your mother, Momma began, and your daddy and Miss Dot. I know We can never replace your momma and daddy or Miss Dot, but if you give us a chance, we will all love you and care for you and the boys will look out for you just as if you were their own brother and sister. If you have trouble at school the boys will be there looking out for you. Later, if you and Robert want to adopt us, we will make you a full fledge members of our family. We do have some rules, and one rule is that we don't use profanity. No cussing in this house. That will get you in trouble. Another rule is no name calling; you must treat everyone with respect. If you have a problem, you can always come to me or Pappy." Momma hugged both children and turned out the lamp beside their bed and left the room.

I wondered what those kids were thinking right now.

There's no mention of bed wetting in the scriptures,
So, I reckon that means it's ain't a sin. Just
an aggravation- even to the Saints.

- Unknown Source

6

Robert Lewis

Bed Wetting

AT BREAKFAST THE NEXT morning, Robert was the
first at the table, waiting for momma to get the eggs and
biscuits on the table. Charlie came in fresh as a daisy and
fully dressed and animated, and ready for school.

"How'd you get him not to pee the bed?" Charlie
asked.

"Now that's a little secret between Robert and Me,"
Momma answered.

Both Charlie and Robert looked at Momma as
if confused, but neither pursued the issue. I wanted
to know the answer to that question too. Pappy just

grinned. Like he and Momma knew how to stop bed wetting that was their secret and was going to remain so.

Pappy told Charlie that she would be going to her new school today.

"It's a little far for walking, so Miss Bonnie Purnell is going to drive you over. Momma Allie wants to meet your principal and take all your records from Indianola. Miss Bonnie is a nice lady. I think you will like her a lot. You behave yourself, and she might treat you to ice cream after you are finished at school."

"Robert do you have any questions?" Pappy asked

Robert looked at Pappy, with gravy from ear to ear. "Do Girls fart?"

Pappy didn't crack a smile; Just nodded his head as he chewed his food, and said, "Pretty sure they do Rob, why do you ask."

"Never heard a girl fart. Just wondered." Willy told me that there was a girl back in Big Flat farted like a steam engine."

Momma looked at Willy like she might just choke a fart or two out it him. Willy turned red.

Charlie rolled her eyes and just shook her head and looked like she wanted to hit her brother with a rolling pin. Minutes later, a horn honked in the front yard, and Momma Exclaimed, "Bonnie is here, go wash your faces while I get your record, Robert gave a swipe at his face, and was leaving the bathroom when Momma caught his arm and pulled him back. She took a bath cloth and washed his face good and clean and took a comb to his hair, with him pulling away with every swipe. She released his arm and he was out the door and bounding down the steps to the car. Mrs. Purnell stood by the back door to the Ford sedan and Robert jumped inside.

"You Miss Bonnie?" Robert asked. Sliding across the seat.

"I am, Bonnie said, and I'm guessing you're Robert"

"Yeah, did you know I was an Orphan, but I am not now?"

"You're so lucky to be staying with the Calloway family."

"I guess! Robert sighed, but I miss Missis Nix".

Seconds later Momma and Charlie came to the car, Charlie wore a new pinafore dress and black and white Saddle Oxfords she carried a satchel across her slender shoulders-- she was pretty as a bird dog puppy. Momma carried a large brown envelope with the school records.

I wanted Anna to meet the kids and I was hoping some of her gentler personality traits might rub off on Charlie and kind of smooth out some of her rough edges. I phoned her house hoping she had not already left for school. Mrs. Owens answered the phone. I asked her if I could pick up Anna and bring her by to meet Charlie after school. I told her I thought Anna could help her adjust, for she had no friends or other family in Tupelo.

"I tell you what, Mrs. Owens said, why don't you bring Charlie here for dinner tonight. That way I can get to know her too, I`ll have to check with my folks, but I'm pretty sure they will say ok. I have to go out to the farm with Mr. Webb after school to help him gather up some cows that Pappy is selling, but I can be there by seven," I explained.

"Seven will be fine. Hope she likes Spaghetti, for Anna is making dinner and she wanted spaghetti, Mrs. Owens added.

"I feel that I must warn you, Mrs. Owens, that Charlie is a brash talker and is prone to say whatever comes to her mind."

"Don't worry Zack, I've got plenty of experience with a headstrong girl. It will be fine."

"I wouldn't put no money on that," I said.

Anna and I did not see much of each other at school anymore, for she was loaded with science and math classes, while I was focused on the social sciences, namely political science, economics, and History. She and I were blessed to have good and smart teachers. The paddle was used to enforce discipline and the thought of a paddling worked well. There were few disruptions except for a few fist fights bow and then. Most of those kinds of issues were settled off the school grounds.

I had spent most Saturday mornings and other spare time working for the Webb law firm and had decided I wanted to study law instead of medicine. Anna, however, had never wavered from her dream; she knew that she wanted to be a doctor and she was dedicated to that singular purpose. She worked any spare time she had at the Tupelo Medical Complex, often working with Dr. Little who also tutored her as much as his time would allow. She had learned a lot too. She began using medical terms that I had never heard of and talked about the children that Doctor Little had seen as if they were her responsibility too.

Sometimes I felt she was slipping away from me and becoming a different person. I knew she still cared for me, but she never talked about our future much anymore. That sometimes caused me to feel a little confused and often downright scared. Those feelings would pass as soon as she put her arms around me and kissed me, which was not nearly often enough to mitigate my fears.

Dr. Little was a great teacher, Anna said, and would often take her on hospital rounds with him so that she could understand how important it was to treat each patient as a special person. I knew Anna was going to be a great doctor for she had all the same caring qualities that Doctor little exhibited. If I had a concern about her it was that she was likely to get too close to her patients. Anna could not help herself though, she was naturally a loving, caring person. I knew she would be a great doctor.

"I went to see Anna on my first date
I wasn't early and I wasn't late
That first-time date was sure no game
When she opened the door, I forgot her name"
                              Robert Coleman

7

The Farm Work

Naught gets a date

PAPPY HAD BOUGHT FOUR cutting horses for the farm, three mares and a stud. He also bought a pair of big black Georgia mules. The horses were gentle animals and were great for herding and rounding up cattle. My favorite was a dapple grey we called sparky. Sparky had plenty of pep and liked a good run and he was ready for a ride when We had him saddled. Pappy would sell off a few dozen head of cattle every year, so the pastures didn't become over grazed. After school was out in the afternoon on Wednesday, I met Mr. Joe Webb at the barn. He had three horses saddled and waiting. He was, as usual wearing an old felt fedora hat that looked like it might have been through the Civil War. He also wore western boots that were run over at the heels. Mr. Webb was a fine hand with horses and cattle. He always seemed to be smiling,

"How was school, he asked off-handed like.

"School is school, I said, getting educated ain't much fun."

"I can see school has done wonders for your English! He laughed. Well, you could always quit and start picking cotton," he added."

"Nope, guess I'll stick to trying to be a lawyer."

"Good Idea, although We've already got too many bad lawyers and not enough good cotton pickers. However, if I needed a lawyer for anything, I'd want my brother. We don't agree on too much, but I know he is a top-notch attorney."

"Why three horses? I asked.

'Naught will be here in a bit to help us. Your dad wants us to bring up fifty head, from the lower pasture, down by the highway. He's only going to sell about thirty head, but he wants to pick them himself. Your pappy has a good eye for livestock, and he sure knows how to bargain with those cattle buyers. All his livestock is in great shape and will bring top dollar."

Pappy bought pure bred Herford brood cows and registered Angus bulls and was raising a strand of cattle that beef packing houses would pay top dollar for.

We didn't wait for Naught but headed for the lower pasture at a good lope. Sparky hadn't been ridden for a few days and was enjoying the ride. Mr. Webb began calling the cattle before we reached the medal gate that separated the open fields of ankle-high grass. Nearly a hundred head had gathered at the gate by the time we rode up.

"You've really got them trained, Mr. Webb." I told him.

"Don't take long, he said. This is where I've fed them all winter."

I got off the grey and unlatched and opened the metal gate. The cattle began pouring through the opening.

Naught joined us as soon as we opened the gate. I tried to count as the herd came through the gate but lost count quickly, for they were crowded together. Mr. Webb had dismounted and when he thought we had enough, he closed the gate leaving a whole herd poking their noses between the rails of the fence and mooing.

The three of us drove the herd to the catch pen by the barn with little trouble. Mr. Webb told us to put out ten bales of hay and a salt block and make sure there was water in the barrels for them to drink. When that was done, Mr. Webb told us that the cattle buyer would be by the next day to make an offer on the cows. He wrote down our time in a little notebook he took from his back pocket. The whole thing took no more than an hour, but Mr. Webb was a stickler for detail, and he wrote it down in minutes. Pappy would decide what to pay. He told us we were free to go.

Naught had developed a strong crush on Penelope King, and she liked him a lot, but had not agreed to go out with him on a date. She was not sure about dating a boy that had once been considered the meanest boy in Tupelo, but today he was smiling like a cat with a fur ball.

"Well. He said as we were taking the saddles off the horses, she finally did it.

"Did what? Who did what?" I asked.

"Penelope, finally said she would meet me for a movie."

"No kidding? I said. She must be plumb nuts. That girl needs to see a shrink," I laughed.

"I know," he grinned. I can't believe it either. I've never had a girlfriend; I'll probably make a fool of myself. I can't hardly remember my own name when I'm around her; she is so dang pretty and smart."

"Yeah, you probably will," I said but I knew how he felt, for I had those same feelings when I first met Annabelle Owens, but I was not about to make it easy for him.'

"I was kind of hoping that you and Annabelle would go with us and you could kind of help me along. I like her and don't want her to be embarrassed by me," Naught said, with sad eyes.

"Just try *not* to be yourself," I panned. I could see fear and desperation in his face and decided I better ease off for I remember how I felt the first time I went out with Anna. "Don't worry Naught, you'll do fine, but I'll ask Anna if she can go out. What night did you make the date for?

"Saturday afternoon. We're to meet at the drugstore at two o'clock and go on to the movie at three."

"That sounds like a good plan. I'm going to see Anna and have dinner with her and her mother tonight; I'll ask."

He Smiled. "Thanks," he said, how much money you think I'll need?" he asked.

"Well, I said, let me think? Two milkshakes for you and Penelope, two for me and Annabelle, four movie tickets two popcorns, and four Cokes. Oh. I reckon about ten dollars ought to do it-- you don't want to look like a tightwad."

"Ten Dollars! Are you nuts? I don't have half that much. Besides that, I ain't buying you no milk shakes or movie tickets or popcorn or nothing, "he yelled!

"Well, I guess you're on your own, Good luck!"

"What? You are a butt head you know."

"Ok, I laughed, just kidding, three dollars ought to be plenty," I laughed.

"He looked like he was ready to run me through with a pitchfork. He grinned and then said. "Could you loan me a dollar."

Heck no, I ain't loaning you a cent. Don't know if I'm going to be able to pay for me and Anna." We then turned the horses back into the catch-pen, for Pappy might use them if he was not satisfied with the herd that Joe Webb had selected to sell. We put feed out for the horses, took the saddles to the tack room and said goodbye to Mr. Webb.

Mrs. McCullough came out on the porch when Naught and I walked up to my old truck.

"Got Supper on the table Zack. You're welcome to stay and eat if you want," she shouted.

"No Mrs. McCullough, but thanks, it sure sounds good. Charlie and I are having dinner with Anna, and I am already running late."

I jumped into the truck and headed down the dusty road toward the highway. The sun was just barely above the tree line in the western sky when I turned onto the highway toward Tupelo.

Charlie would be driving Momma crazy, asking her when I was coming to pick her up. Charlie was a hyperactive little girl and her face would turn beet red when her patience ran thin. She was also prone to cussing when she was frustrated. She was probably purple by now and silently calling me every cuss word she could think of.

8

Dinner with Anna

Charlie meets Anna

IT WAS A LITTLE before seven when I stopped at the house to pick up Charlie. Momma and Pappy were setting in the big rockers on the front porch, Robert was sitting astraddle of Momma's legs with his back on her breast, his left hand in Momma's hair; his index finger twisted in her hair. Momma had him covered with a quilt for it had really turned much cooler. Pappy liked sitting on the porch for a while after supper and sometimes smoke a pipe in the cool night air. Robert was sound asleep. Charlie was using Pappy's knees for a bench, her hands moving in every direction and her mouth running like a thrashing machine.

"Didn't take long for them to make their selves at home," I thought.

Momma had Charlie dressed in her best clothes and hair brushed back in a long ponytail. She was an absolutely beautiful little girl. I ran to the house to wash up a little and change into a clean shirt. Charlie had followed me into the house and was telling me to hurry.

"Where you been so long. I'm starved, she said."

"Had to work. But I'm hungry too," I said"

When I came out the door, Charlie was bounding down the steps toward the old truck. She opened the door and slid inside. I climbed in under the steering wheel and closed the door and started the engine. Charlie slid across the seat pressing her little frame against me.

"What are you doing I said, trying to move her over with my elbow."

"I'm practicing," she said.

"Practicing what?" I asked. Looking down at her.

"Practicing what I'm going to do when I go on a date with a boy."

"You're nine! For Christ's sake!"

"I won't always be though," she said, looking at me like I was an idiot.

I said, "You aren't going on a date for years. Now move over by the door where you're supposed to stay on your first date. Momma may not let you out of the house until you're thirty!" She held her ground though and never moved away from me. I just shook my head.

I pulled into Anna's driveway a little after seven. Anna and her mother were sitting in the porch swing even though the weather had turned much cooler. They had a blanket spread across their legs. Charlie was out of the truck as soon as I stopped the engine, bounding toward the porch.

"Hey there, she yelled. I'm Charlie, are you Annabelle, Zacks sweetheart?"

"I'm Annabelle, and this my mother, Marie. I've been hearing about you a lot," Anna replied.

"Probably wasn't much good if you heard it from Zack." she said. He doesn't like me much."

"That's not true," I said looking at Anna. Why would you say such a thing?

"You wouldn't let me sit close to you coming over here tonight," She countered.

"Well you were wanting to act like you were on a date, and you're too young for that.

Now Anna and her mother both were taking joy watching me squirm. Finally, Anna said, "Let's have dinner and then maybe we can walk down to the drugstore."

"That sounds good to me, anxious to get off the subject of Charlie." I had noticed that Anna had not admitted that She was my sweetheart, and that troubled me some, but my stomach was overruling any other thoughts at the present time. We went to the dinner table. When I was ready to sit down, Charlie rushed to sit beside Anna. Leaving me to sit at one end of the table and Mrs. Owens at the other. Anna then got up and went to the stove and helped each of our plates with a pile of spaghetti. She sat a plate in front of each of us along with a green salad of tomatoes lettuce, onion, and sweet peppers. There was a bowl of salad dressing and a bowl of grated white cheese on the table as well. She then sat beside Charlie and passed the salad dressing around. She then passed the Parmesan cheese. I had never had Parmesan before and only took a little. Charlie, however, covered her spaghetti entirely as Mrs. Owens and Anna watched in awe.

When she took a big bite of the spaghetti, she gagged.

"Oh puke! She said, what is that God awful stuff." Spitting it back in her plate.

"I take it you don't like Parmesan cheese," Anna laughed. I'll get you some just plain spaghetti."

I was embarrassed but didn't comment. Mrs. Owens just seemed amused. She asked Charlie about her day at school, and what she like to do for fun. Charlie was, as usual animated and never stopped talking, asking one question after another. Finally, Mrs. Owens suggested that if we were going for a walk we needed to go. It was getting late and we couldn't keep Charlie out too late.

We walked from Anna's house over to Court Street and down to Broadway. Although it was after eight o'clock the City Drugstore was still busy with customers and nearly all the tables were full. I had told the girls that I would buy Cokes for everyone. Charlie. However, insisted on having a root beer. And she wanted to sit on the stools at the counter. We sat down, taking a stool between Anna and me and Charlie began spinning back and forth.

''I've never been in a store like this. She said. In Indianola we had a drugstore, but they didn't have Ice Cream and cold drinks''

When we had finished our drinks, we walked down to Main Street for a block or two and then back to Broadway. We walked past the jewelry store, where I had bought the Locket for Anna the first Christmas we were in Tupelo. I wondered if she still wore it but didn't ask. We took Broadway down by the theater and around the Courthouse. The movie "Shane" was playing at the Lyric, but it was the '*COMING SOON*' poster of "Peter Pan" that caught Charlie's eye.

"Will you bring me to see that Charlie said bouncing up and down on the sidewalk. Robert will want to see it too—Please Zack, you've got to bring me, please?"

That's when Anna took my hand. I knew it meant something but wasn't sure what. Anna looked at me and gave a slight nod."

"Ok. I said. If it's ok with Momma and Pappy."

"Will you come with us Anna she ran putting her arm around Anna."

"Zack hasn't asked me," she replied, turning her head, and looking up at me with a little grin.

"He's not very thoughtful, Charlie said, throwing up her hands but I know he wants you to." He's a knucklehead if he doesn't."

"Of course, I want her to come with us. How do you know so much about how I feel?"

"Plain as daylight that you're crazy about her, and I think she really likes you a lot, though I don't see why she would," Charlie declared.

"You're mean!" I said.

"Well, you're dumb as a rock about girls!"

She was sure right about that! I didn't comment.

The three of us walked back to the Owen's house and we sat in the porch swing for a while. Charlie between us her mouth going full blast and every part of her body in constant motion."

We left Anna's with not so much as a handshake from Annabelle by nine o'clock as momma had instructed, for Charlie had to be in bed by nine and be ready for school the next day. We climbed into the truck, and Charlie moved next to me. This time I did not try to push her away. By the time we reached Main Street she was fast asleep. Her head resting against me. Her motor had finally run out of gas. I held her tiny frame with my arm to keep her from falling. When we pulled into the drive, she did not wake up so, I carried her in my arms to her room, Momma took over, then and tucked her into her bed beside Robert. Momma was not happy that we were not back by nine as I promised, but she didn't say anything. I knew she would later though.

"It was kind of nice having a little Sister to look out for," Charlie was really a special kid. It had been a good day, I thought that night as I closed my eyes to sleep.

9

Movie with the Kids

Jason Wilbanks

Pappy had plenty of work on the farm to be done and on Friday he paid me four dollars. Pappy sure didn't over-pay his sons. But Anna had called and left a message with Momma that she wouldn't be able to go to the movies the next day, that she would be working at the hospital. I was disappointed, of course, but Naught was going to be livid and a wreck to boot. I went to the lumber yard and told his mother to let him know of the developments. She laughed.

"That boy may have a nervous breakdown she joked, but It will be fine. He needs to handle that situation on his own, anyway, she added.

I Went to the Webb Law firm as usual on Saturday morning, for that was the busiest day of the week for the firm, and he had plenty of deliveries and errands for me to run and besides that, he paid a lot better than Pappy. He usually gave me two dollars and a lot of free advice for my half-day's work. Since I could not take Anna, to the movie, I decided to ask Momma if I could take Robert and Charlie. I think she thought I must be losing my mind, the way she looked at me.

"You think you can handle both by yourself?" She asked, shaking her head, and smiling.

"Sure, I said, no problem. If they give me any trouble, I'll just leave them. Somebody's Momma will surely take them."

Momma threw a towel at me. "Ok, she said but you bring them straight home once the show is over, and don't fill them up with junk! She went to her purse and took out two one-dollar bills and handed me the money. Hope that's enough, she said, it's all I have in my purse."

When I told Charlie and Robert that I was taking them to see a movie I thought they would pee their pants from excitement. Just before two o'clock we loaded into the old truck and headed for the theater. I parked a block away on Main Street and down toward the theater. When Charlie saw the drugstore sign, she leaped for joy, "Can we get a Root Beer, Zack, she begged. Robert said nothing but his eyes were big as saucers.

"You got a nickel? I joked.

"No, but you do. I saw Momma Allie give you some money when we left!"

"Ok, Ok, I said as we pushed through a crowd of people on the street and went inside.

"When we were inside, Charlie shouted, Look Zack there's Anna, and ran to her table, but Anna was not alone. When I looked toward the table, she removed her hand from the arm of a young man in a white jacket. He wore a Hospital patch on his sleeve. He was blond headed, tall, and thin and handsome to boot. Anna looked stunned. I probably looked worse. My heart sank and was racing. I could hardly speak but managed to tell Charlie to come on and leave Anna and her friend alone, we had to get our drinks and go. I was still holding on to Roberts hand and didn't realize it until he yelled, owh! You're squeezing my hand. Charlie reached to hug Anna, but I caught her hand and pulled her away. I turned and pulled them from the Drugstore. Anna called after me, but I did not answer but hurried to the door.

"Are we not going to get a Root Beer.?" Charlie pleaded.

"No! We'll get one at the theater, and popcorn too if you want, I said. I was mad as a hornet but tried my best not to let the kids know. Had Anna deliberately lied to me about having to work? Did she have a new boyfriend she was seeing? How could she do that? Many questions flooded my jealous mind. I had to get myself under control, I had the two children with me, and they had nothing but the movie and a good time on their mind and I wasn't going to allow myself to ruin the day for them. There was a line of people waiting outside the theater, including Naught and Penelope up a head of us. They were laughing and talking and Naught was grinning like someone had given him a hundred dollars. Penelope was hanging on his arm. They saw me and waved but were not about to lose their place in the long line. to come back and say hello. A few minutes later they opened the doors to allow people to exit the show that had just ended. Ushers came out and put up a braided rope to restrain the crowd from blocking the entrance as a huge crowd exited the theater.

When the theater lobby was finally cleared, the ushers removed the braided rope and the line moved forward. Two lines then began to form around the ticket booth as we approached the entrance, and the lobby was soon filled. I had bought tickets for Charlie and myself, but Robert Lewis being under six got in free.

The sound of popping popcorn and the aroma of hamburgers frying on the grill aroused my hunger senses. I had not eaten lunch and was starved. I wanted a burger but didn't have enough money to buy one for the kids too. It angered my hunger senses. Charlie could barely contain herself, but Robert held tight to me and seemed a little frightened by the throng of people around us, afraid that he might get separated from us. Finally, I hoisted him to my shoulders so that he could see over the crowded room. He laughed and he was happy when we reached the concession and ordered our Root Beer and popcorn.

We then moved inside the theater and were ushered to our seats by a young boy in a tall theater hat. Robert had to share the seat with his sister and was ok with that until the movie started. When the movie started to roll, he crawled into my lap and both the kids were clapping when the show began. The Movie "Shane" was the featured film, but there were cartoons before that and both the children laughed and clapped loudly at the antics of Buggs Bunny and Elmer Fudd... My thoughts were still on the scene I had just witnessed in the City Drugstore. Annabelle Owens, the girl I loved, with another boy! My stomach rolled. I was Jealous, plain, and simple. I was angry at Anna, and my heart ached for her all at the same time. How I could hurt so much and love Anna so much, at the same time, was beyond my understanding. But it was what it was, as Pappy would say.

> *"There is no greater glory than love nor any greater punishment than jealousy"*
> *- Lope de Vega*

10

The Green-Eyed Dragon

Anna with another boy

THE TRIP TO THE movie was a huge treat for the kids, even though my own heart was aching. I was building a bond with the children that would prove to be everlasting. I did not understand just how fragile our most precious relationships could be, until I saw Anna with another Boy.

What would I do without Anna? I could not imagine the answer to that question. Charlie was a smart kid and the many disappointments she had experienced in her young life had equipped her with instincts far beyond her nine years of living. She knew that something was askew between me and Anna and voiced her concern on the way home from the show.

"You mad at Anna, she asked?" Looking directly into my eyes.

"Maybe, I said. She was with another boy!"

I saw that but that's no reason to be mad at her. You don't own her."

"No, I said, but I thought I owned her heart. Complicated! It's hard to explain!"

"Nothing hard about that! You feel what you feel, you love who you love, and you want what you want, but sometimes you don't get what you want, and you can't do nothing about It, she said with head now bowed, and her eyes downcast."

I knew she was telling me something very important about her own life in order to try to make me feel better. She had lived a lot in nine years, losing both parents and then being thrown among stranger that she had never even seen before, suddenly my troubles seemed small compared to the hurt that Charlie had known. I was glad that she had come to our home and into our lives. I hoped we could make her life better. I suddenly realized that I loved Charlie as much as I did my own brother.

Robert was asleep between me and Charlie when we pulled into the drive, Momma and Pappy were sitting in the ladderback rockers on the front porch. I carried Robert to the porch and deposited him in Momma's lap. Charlie went to Pappy's knees and started telling him all about the day. I went inside. Willy was home from guard duty sitting at the kitchen table and eating crackers and cheese with a half empty milk jug in front of him. I took a glass from the cabinet, pulled out a chair and sat down and ate with him.

"How was the movie?" He asked, making conversation.

"Very good I said, you ought to take Jessie."

"Think I'll ask her—maybe you and Anna could go with us. Maybe grab a bite to eat."

"Don't guess that will happen, I said.

Willy stopped chewing and looked straight at me. "What's going on between you and Anna, he asked?'

"Don't know, I said. She was with another boy at the drugstore today, when she told me she would be working at the hospital."

"Oh, shit! That is not good. Have you talked to her?"

"No. Don't aim to either," I said flatly.

"Well I hate to hear that brother, but I never could see what she saw in you anyhow."

"Thanks for your sympathy, I said leaving the table and going to our room. I turned on the radio and listened for a while to the grand Ole Opry out of Nashville and went to sleep listening to The Carter Family singing *"I'm thinking tonight of my blue eyes"* and thinking of Annabelle Owens. Love is definitely a complicated business, I thought, and it seemed that mine was bankrupt.

11

Annabelle's Trouble

Danger for Anna

ANNABELLE SAT ALONE ON the steps to the porch of their home. A blanket across her shoulders, her face in her hands, her head on her knees. She was crying. "What have I done?"

It had been three weeks since she had first met Jason Wilbanks, a medical student from Tennessee who was receiving some training in the Radiology lab at the Medical Center. He was smart and handsome, funny and he had been drawn to her immediately. She at first rejected his attention but he was persistent in taking every opportunity to flatter her whenever she was working at the hospital, even bringing her a single red rose one day.

Although he said he was twenty and she was only sixteen, the age difference did not seem to matter to him, and he had asked her out after only knowing her for a week. She said no that her mother would never allow her to go out with someone that much older than her. She did not tell him that she already had a boyfriend, and she knew there were rules about the professional staff fraternizing with students. She should have known that this would be a big problem. However, she was infatuated with his forwardness and not prepared to deal with his charming ways. Now she was disgusted that she had not told him that she had a boyfriend and with her own behavior in general.

She had finally agreed to go with him to the Drug Store for a soda. She never gave a thought that day that she might See Zack or even that she had lied to him until he walked into the drugstore. It was not until Zack had left the drugstore, visibly upset, at seeing her with Jason, and with the kids in tow that she finally realized what a foolish girl she had been.

She told Jason she needed to go back to work and this upset him visibly, but he paid for the drinks and they left for his car—a new Corvette convertible that was a gift from his father-- a wealthy Nashville banker. He had given Jason the sports car at the beginning of his Medical School in the late summer of 1953, it was one of only a few hundred produced that year. He had paid the princely sum of 3200.00 dollars for the car. Jason then asked Anna to go to his room at the apartment where he was staying so, they could be alone—she emphatically said no! He then tried to force a kiss on her when they had got into his car to drive back to the Med Center. He had cursed her even slapped her and even tried to hold her forcibly trying to fondle her breast, but she was able to get out of his car and run back to the safety of the drugstore. Jason drove off. She was shaken to her core and crying. She thought he was going to rape her. She called her mother from the drugstore and asked her to come and pick her up.

"Why are you at the drugstore, her mother asked. You were supposed to be working this afternoon; and how did you get to the drugstore? You are supposed to be at work until I pick you up."

"I know, but I'm not feeling too good. A coworker brought me here. Just come and get me she pleaded; I'll tell you about it when I get home."

"I'll be there as soon as I can."

Now all she could think of was Zack and the look on his face when he had seen her with Jason. She longed to see Zack right now and let him hold her close. "I don't deserve his love," she thought.'

The next morning Anna waited on the steps of the school, still shaken from the events of the night before, hoping she would see Zack and she could beg him to forgive her, but he never came. She did not blame him. She went through her classes all day, but her mind was not on her studies. She was scheduled to work with Doctor Little at the medical center that afternoon, but she did not want any further contact with Jason Wilbanks She was afraid of him now and there was no one she could talk to about it. Her mother would not understand that much she was sure off. Doctor Little would understand but it might jeopardize her future at the hospital. She had to tell someone, and Jessie was the only other person in the world she could trust to silence. She made up her mind that she would talk to Jessie today after school. She knew too that Doctor Little needed to know about Jason Wilbanks's behavior toward her, but she did not know how to handle it. Maybe Jessie could help her figure out what to do.

"You've got to tell Zack, Jessie said flatly. If you love him, you have got to tell him what happened! He is smart and will know what to do—but most of all he is crazy about you. If you do not tell him now, you may lose him forever."

Anna had called and asked Jessie to come by after school. Jessie could tell that she was crying and very upset, so she went right over. The girls sat in the porch swing and talked. Anna went through the entire sordid ordeal while Jessie held her hand and shed tears with her.

"Now listen to me Anna. Let me call Willy and ask him and Zack to come right now. We will tell them both what happened maybe they'll know how to handle Jason. They may want to kill him." They both laughed.

"Ok, if you think Zack will come," Anna finally said. He probably hates me!

"He'll come. I'll tell Willy it's extremely important."

Jessie used the phone to call for Willy. Allie answered the phone and called for Willy. He came to the phone and minutes later he shouted for Zack who had stretched out across his bed and was helping Charlie with her math.

"Need to go help Jesse with moving some furniture. We won't be long momma", Willy shouted as they started for Zack's old truck.

"You two better not be late for supper; Robert don't leave leftovers"

Willy and Zack pulled into the drive at the Owen's house five minutes later.

"What are you doing, why are you stopping here? Anna don't want to see me."

"Yes, she does, and you're going to talk to her. If I must drag you in there, feet first. She asked Jessie to get me to bring you. She has something important to tell you."

"Yeah, she's probably going to tell me she's engaged to that boy she was with."

"Don't think so, Jessie sounded as if it was some kind of trouble."

They got out of the truck and Anna met Zack before he could take step. She threw her arms around him and whispered. "Thank you for coming Zack, I was afraid you wouldn't. I'm sorry for what I did and don't blame you for being mad at me,"

"Not mad at you Anna. Truth is I love you more than ever, but I was disappointed for I thought you loved me too."

"Oh, Zack. I do love you and I made a terrible mistake. Come to the porch, I have lots that I need to tell you."

Anna took his arm and led him to the porch with tears streaming down her face.

12

Zack Hires a Lawyer

Zack gets help

With Willy and Jessica, Zack and Anna sat at the kitchen table, and Anna laid out what had happened, beginning with the day that Jason Wilbanks had started his training at the Medical Center in Tupelo. Anna left out nothing. She was crying by the time she had gone through the Jason's trying to force himself on her. Zack put his hand on her arm to comfort her, but she was so distraught that she could not seem to stop crying.

"I don't know what to do Anna said, through sobs. I am afraid of him and can't stand the thought of going back to the hospital as long as he's there. I love working there with Doctor Little, but I do not want to get him involved in my problems. Zack and I have had problems with the hospital before and I know that we do not want that to come up again either.

Zack had said nothing while Anna told her story, but his mind was working full speed, and though seemingly calm, he was raging inside. Finally, he spoke.

"I think I can handle Mr. Jason Wilbanks," Zack said.

Everyone looked at him, with mouths open.

"What are you going to do brother? Kill him?"

"That's my second option, he panned!"

"Don't joke like that Zack, I don't want you to get into trouble," Anna said.

"I've got another Idea," he said. One thing you said that he told you that strikes me as not adding up, but I want to talk to my Attorney."

"Your attorney? Willy laughed. You don't have five dollars, Brother, how you going to hire an attorney."

"Just got a couple of questions for him, and I've got connections," Zack answered.

"You guys have got to go! Anna said, Mother will be here soon, and she might just kill me if she finds the two of you here." Before you go Zack, I want you to do something for me, Anna said.

"What's that" I asked.

"Kiss me," she said standing and putting her arms around him.

I took her in my arms and held her to my body, then kissed her with my brother and Jessica watching. I felt no embarrassment—only love for Anna.

Willy and I headed back toward home and left Anna and Jessica standing on the front porch. it was nearing five o'clock, but I told Willy to drop me off at the Webb Law Firm, that I had an errand to run.

"Tell Momma and Pappy I had a job to do and that I'll be late for supper."

Willy dropped me off at the curb in front of the law offices of Justin T. Webb and I took the stairs to the second floor. The office staff was gone for the day, but the door was open, and I made my way down the hallway to the Lawyer's office. I knocked on the big mahogany door.

"Come in! Mr. Webb yelled."

I entered. The room was heavy with cigar smoke. Mr. Webb loved cigars but rarely smoked in his office out of respect for his staff. They all despised the smoke. When they left, however, he would light up as soon as they were out of the building. Mr. Webb had his desk covered with law books and papers. His jacket draped across one of the two client chairs in the office-- he wore a crisp white shirt—his tie loosened at the collar. He looked over the top of his eyeglasses when I entered the room,

"Zack? What are you doing here at this time of day.?"

"I want to hire you to be my lawyer to answer some questions for me."

"You don't have to pay me to do that. You work here."

"I know, but I think it's best that I pay you, Zack said, taking three crumpled one-dollar bills from his pocket and laying them on the desk in front of Mr. Webb.

"You want a receipt?" Mr. Webb laughed.

"Yep, I said, if you don't mind."

Mr. Webb's facial features turned from smiling to real concern. "This must really be important for you to want to hire me."

"I want to know if you're now my lawyer?"

"Why sure. You just hired me! I will 'have Margarette write you a receipt tomorrow."

"Thanks Mr. Webb. I don't want any question about our conversation being private."

I had learned something about Lawyer Client privilege from working at the law firm.

"Because what I'm going to tell you must be kept confidential, and what I say can't be discussed with anyone except those I approve; It involves Anna," I added.

"I understand. You haven't committed a crime have you Zack?"

"No nothing like that, but I think someone else may have and I want you to pass some information to someone and I don't want anything I tell you to get into the public."

"Tell me what you want.

For the next twenty minutes I went through the details of what Anna had experienced. With Mr. Webb listening intently.

'' What exactly do you think I can do?"

"I think he may have lied about his age for one thing, He told her he was twenty and I think he may be much older, even though he looks very young. He told her he had finished pre-med and was now in Med School at Tennessee. I think it takes about four years to finish pre-med and he has been at Tennessee for at least two years.

"Secondly, I would like to know if he has tried this before with other girls, and finally, if any of this is true, I want him away from Anna."

"I'll see what I can do. It is easy enough to see if he has prior arrests or complaints against him, and the hospital should have his true age. If he tried to assault Anna, though, he should be charged with a crime, but it would be her word against his and she would, of course, have to testify against him in court. I know lying about your age is not a crime. If it were most of the women in Mississippi would be felons, he joked. But, if he lied about it in order get Anna to go with him so he could assault her, that's another issue."

"No, we don't want Anna to have to testify in court. There must be another way to handle this, I said.

"I'll see what I can do. Dr. Little is a close friend of mine. Give me a day or two and come by and I will give you an update. "I can't promise you anything,"

I thanked the lawyer and left the office. I was worried, but I felt much better now that Mr. Webb was now helping. I had done all I could do for the time being, but I was still wondering where Anna's heart really was. How had she really felt about Jason Wilburn. I drove home and Momma had a plate sitting on the table. The rest of the family had eaten. I expected to be scolded by Pappy, but he said nothing, Pappy was always able to read my feelings and he knew something was boiling inside me. I finished my supper and went to my room where Willy had his head in a book, but lay it aside when I entered,

"Well, what gives, brother?" He asked.

"Don't know much. Talked with Mr. Webb; he is going to help if he can. I feel better about the situation, but I dang sure am not thrilled about her being with him, in the first place."

Willy laughed. "Girls have a way of making you want to bite a nail sometimes."

"Yeah, I know. Right now, I could chew a railroad spike!"

13

Jason is Dismissed

Troubled mind

THE NEXT DAY DOCTOR Little sat in his office, surrounded with medical books and charts, at the Medical center. The Hospital administrator, Dr. James Bell sat in a padded visitor's chair beside him. Doctor Little wore his normal white duster, while Doctor Bell was dressed in a typical blue business suit and tie. Doctor Little spoke to his nurse: "Miss Perkins, would you ask Mr. Wilbanks to come in the office and have a seat?"

Jason Wilbanks had been summoned to come to the office at two o'clock. It was a bit after two o'clock in the afternoon, and he was curious as to why the Administrator wanted to see him, but he knew better than to ask. If the administrator wanted to see you, -you did as he ordered. He entered the office when the nurse asked him to come in. Doctor Little asked him to be seated.

"What can I do for you Doctor?" Jason asked.

"Well it's probably just a misunderstanding of some sort, Dr. Little said in his smooth and calming Southern Drawl. But something has come to our attention that we need to discuss with you"

"'What kind of misunderstanding? Jason asked.

"Dr. Bell will explain that to you," Dr. Little offered.

"I'm sure you have read and understand the hospital rules handbook concerning employee's interaction with students or subordinates, who work here at the Center," Dr. Bell began, we have several high school students who work here, and there is talk that you have been seen fraternizing with one of the students. That behavior is absolutely prohibited, and in some cases, it may be a crime if you are over the age of twenty-one and the person you are fraternizing with is a minor. The hospital does not tolerate this kind of behavior by its professional staff. I noticed that your application to the training program gives your age as twenty- four, and you were overheard by other employees that you told one of the students you were apparently pursuing, that you were twenty. It is further stated in the complaint that you may have tried to seduce the person. If that is true…well, you know the consequences of that."

"If what is alleged is true, it would be very embarrassing for you and for this institution. We have two choices as I see it. You can withdraw from the training program and go elsewhere, or I can give this information to the State Police and the Mississippi Medical Board where it is likely to get very ugly. I will need your decision first thing tomorrow, if you choose to leave the program that will be the end of the matter. If you choose to stay, we have no choice about what is required of us. We will immediately report the incident to the medical boards in Mississippi and Tennessee."

I am sorry to say that part of this is true, Jason said, but in fairness, I didn't know she was a minor and I meant her no harm. I swear," His face red with anger.

"Apparently the young lady thought otherwise, Jason. Again. I will need your decision first thing tomorrow, and you are not to speak with any of the students."

Jason stood and left the office without comment. He never went back to his duty lab, but tossed his lab coat across the nurses' station, as he left the building, went directly to the parking area and climbed behind the seat of his Corvette and headed to his apartment. Twenty minutes later he had his possessions loaded into his car, took highway78 toward Memphis and said goodbye to Tupelo.

Doctor Little called Attorney Webb the next evening for him to tell me that Jason had not reported to work, and that he had called Jason's contact number at his apartment, and was told that he had taken all his possessions and left town around midnight and left a message for his landlord that he would not be back. He told Zack to tell Anna to come back to work when she was ready.

Webb told Doctor Little that they had run a background check on Jason Wilbanks and had learned that he had had one other report of assault, but charges had been dropped, when the girl in question had suddenly decided that she did not want to testify. The only other issues were a couple of speeding tickets.

I drove directly to Anna's when I got the news so I could tell her in person. Her mother came to the door when I knocked. She looked surprised to see him.

"Zack! I was not expecting you. You know that Anna doesn't go out on weeknights."

"I know, Mrs. Owens, I Just had something I needed to tell her in person."

"She's on the phone, I'll get her. Have a seat in the swing."

I liked Mrs. Owens and I felt that she liked me too, but it seemed she would never forgive me for what Anna and I had done a year before, and I really didn't blame her for being so protective of her only daughter. I hoped that somehow, someway I could regain her trust and she could put it all behind her.

Moments later, Anna came through the door and I stood up. Anna came to me and embraced me with a tender hug. "What's going on Zack?"

"Got good news. Mr. Webb called, and said that you could come back to work when you were ready. Jason is no longer at the Medical Center. He's left town and took all his possessions with him."

She hugged me again and then gave me a quick kiss. "I don't know why you even like me anymore, I know I don't deserve you."

"A very wise person told me two days ago that "You can't help what you want, and you can't help who you love, but sometimes you can't have what you want, and there's nothing in the world you can do about it. I was afraid you loved someone else and there was nothing I could do about it."

"I'm guessing that it was your father that told you that," Anna said.

"No not Pappy, I said. It was Charlie."

"Well, I don't know what you did but I am so thankful that Jason is gone, and I won't have to be around him ever again."

"Me too, but I've got a question I have to ask!"

"What's that Zack?"

"Did you ever have feelings for him?"

"Not like my feelings for you., Zack."

"I don't know what that means Anna! I stammered. If you do not want me around, just tell me now. I do not want to have to compete for your love."

"No Zack, it's not like that, Anna cried. I cannot explain why I did it. I'm sorry."

"I have to go, I said, just wanted to let you know that your problem was over with him if you want it to be. I think you should talk to your mother about what happened. She loves you and deserves no secrets from you."

I went to my truck and left Anna standing on the porch—her arms folded tight in a cross over her stomach. My mind was filled with doubt and confusion.

Anna was wondering if she would ever regain Zack's complete trust again. She realized how she had hurt him, and she loved him so much she could barely breathe. Tears again flowed down her pretty face. Zack's question had struck a nerve and her heart was breaking.

"Charlie Calloway"

"I could never be angry with a little girl"

-RC

14

Girls Will Be Girls

Charlie in trouble

ON FRIDAY, OF THE next week, Pappy, Momma Mr. and Mrs. Purnell left on a trip to Indianola. They took Robert Lewis along with them, but Charlie was in school and could not go, because of mandatory testing that day. Momma left Me and Willy in charge. Charlie was mad as a wet hen when she learned that she could not make the trip to her former home and Robert was getting to go.

The reason for the trip was that the property of Pappy's cousin Herbert Calloway, was to be auctioned off at the Sunflower County Courthouse the next day at ten. Pappy wanted to be sure that the property brought a fair price. There were eighty acers of good delta farmland, with a not so good farmhouse, and several pieces of farm equipment, as well as household Items.

Pappy had asked Bonnie's friends in the Real Estate business to look into the value of the property in Sunflower County, and they estimated that good farmland would bring three- hundred dollars per Acre, and the value of the farm house was put at two thousand dollars

After they had driven out to look at the property on Friday. Pappy decided to enter a minimum bid of twenty-six thousand dollars, but he hoped someone else would pay more, for he really did not want to own any delta farmland. He had enough to oversee now. Pappy did not like the delta country along the river. He loved the small farms and the rolling hills in the northern part of the state. He said the flatland of black gumbo delta was rich soil and good for growing cotton, and not much else. He said most of the farms down there did not even have a decent shade tree.

Momma had called Charlie's school and left word at the school to call me or Willy if Charlie need someone to pick her up or there was an emergency.

Well, there was an emergency. Coy Johnson, the Principal at her school called the High School at eleven o'clock for me or Willy to come to the elementary. Charlie was giving them trouble. I went to the office and told the principal at my school that I would have to leave to see what was going on with Charlie and that I was in charge while my parents were out of town. He signed me out and I walked down to the curb to my old truck and sped over to the Elementary school. I went up the steps where I had first met Anabelle Owens, through the double doors and down the wide hallway to the Principals office. Through the glass enclosure I could see Charlie sitting in a folding chair with her arms crossed over her chest and her face red in defiance. The Principal was standing in front of his desk with his finger pointed toward Charlie. He was obviously scolding her. I tapped on the door and he motioned me inside. Charlie did not move from her seat, But I could tell was glad I was there.

"What is wrong, I asked. What's the problem?"

"Well," Mr. Johnson said, shaking his head," this young lady has punched another student in the face, blooding her nose at lunch and then kicked her in the rear. I told her she would have to take a paddling, but she said NO SHE WOULD NOT! "

I asked the principal if I could have a minute to talk to Charlie alone, and he consented. I went and sat down beside Charlie in another folding chair after the Principal had stepped outside. I asked her what happened,"

"Adel Lee started it, she said. She pushed me down and got my new dress all dirty and wet, and she called me a dirty little Delta hussy. I didn't know what a hussy was, but I knew it was not nothing good. She had two friends with her, and they were laughing at me too, so

I punched Adel in the nose and knocked her flat and when she started to get up, I kicked her in her skinny ass! I was a fixing to punch them other two, but they ran like scared chickens to the principal's office. Now he wants to whoop me. I told him if he did, I'd get me a lawyer"

"Charlie, you can't be fighting and threatening the Principal., I said. That will just make things worse, But I do not blame you for punching that girl, I pulled Charlie to me and hugged her and told her to not antagonize the principal. I was going to talk to him. I motioned through the window for the principal to come back in. When he entered the office, he took a seat behind his desk.

"Charlie told me what happened, I explained and although I think the other girls are as responsible for what happened as she was-- she told me she would not do it again and Charlie doesn't lie. In fact, I don't think you could make her lie. But beyond that, the whole thing is all my fault anyhow, because I told her that there was always people who would try to bully a new kid at school, and for her not to let them get away with it—to punch them in the nose if she had too. She was just doing what I told her to do. Charlie looked at me with her mouth open and tears forming in those blue eyes. If you must paddle someone, Mr. Coy, paddle me instead. I will take the whipping for I'm the one to blame.

Mr. Johnson was silent, and stone faced for a minute, his hands folded into a steeple under his chin—his elbows propped on his desk.

"Well, he said one thing is perfectly clear here. You love this girl. There will be no paddling this time.

"Yes, I do love her—she's my sister!"

Charlie ran to me and grabbed me. I knelt and took her into my arms and kissed her head. I whispered to her to tell Mr. Coy you are sorry for causing trouble and next time you'll come to him if you have a problem.

Mr. Coy told her to return to class. And as she left his office, she told him that the next time she would talk to him before she punched somebody! Mr. Coy just shook his head and grinned. There was no way Coy Johnson was ever going to paddle that child.

I walked with Charlie down the hallway to her classroom. She held my hand all the way. The school had the familiar smell of sweaty children. The hallway was covered with bulletin boards, all with various themes. Charlie stopped by the one beside her classroom and showed me a picture she had drawn. I was impressed and told her so. When we got to her classroom she turned and hugged me again.

"Are you gonna tell Momma Allie and Pappy Calloway about the trouble I caused today?

She asked.

"What trouble, I asked, grinning at her. She smiled.

"No, this is just between the two of us."

She gave me another hug and went into her classroom. I hoped that one day I would have a daughter just like Charlie.

I left Charlie and returned to school feeling more like a parent than an older brother. Charlie was a tough little girl and she was not prone to settle differences by diplomacy. She felt a "Big Stick" was better than big words. I figured she was right more times than not. I figured she would love the same way. When she grew into womanhood, she would be someone who loved unconditionally and would except nothing but the same in return.

15

A Talk with Anna

Anna in danger

I did not see Annabelle all day and I wanted to talk to her but thought it best that I gave her a chance to talk to her mother. And if she didn't talk to her, I would have to really consider what I should do. Momma and Pappy would not return until the next day so when school was out, I drove over to pick up Charlie. Willy was driving Pappy's old truck, and he was home when I got there. Charlie was hungry so we ate peanut butter and saltines and drank milk before we started homework. Charlie was a quick study and had no trouble with anything she had to do. She loved math and sciences classes but did not care much for English and History. When she

SHATTERED DREAMS

finished her work, she wanted to know what we were going to do for Supper.

"What would you like? I asked.

"Hamburger and fries at the drugstore and a root beer," she answered. I looked at Willy and he nodded his accent. An hour later we were loading in my old truck and headed for the drugstore with Charlie sitting between us clapping hands and singing some silly song she had learned at school. We were all three laughing. Willy was earning a little money from the Air Guard and with what he earned from working on the farm, he seemed to always have money in his pocket. That was good because I rarely had any.

The drugstore was crowded, so we sat at the counter on stools, and, as usual, Charlie was like a spinning top until our food arrived. She ate most of her burger and half of her fries. She drank her root beer and wanted another, but I said no."

"Tightwad." She said.

"Spendthrift!" I countered.

She laughed.

I laughed.

Another Root Beer later, we left for home. The phone was ringing when we walked through the door. It was Momma calling to check on Charlie and see what we had fed her for dinner.

"Candy and potato chips and a grape soda, I winked at Willy.

"You two boys will have that girl rotten by the time I get home,": Momma fussed.

Charlie wanted to talk to momma, so she took the phone and rambled on about her day and asking bout Robert and what all they did. Did they see Miss Nix? Did they see their old house? And on and on she talked until Momma finally said she had to go. Charlie hung up and went to the bathroom for her bath and got dressed for bed. She said that this was the first time she had slept all by herself since Robert was a year old.

Willy and I sat in the rockers on the front porch and talked about how things had changed since the Kids had moved in. We were getting accustomed to the new routines and the rhythms and rattles of the new family and Momma and Pappy seemed to have renewed energy since they came. The new additions at the lumber yard was moving along at a nice pace. Finally, we headed to our room but both of us stopped by to check on Charlie. She was propped up on her pillow reading "The Ransom of the Red Chief" a short story by O Henry. We sat down on the bed beside her.

"Everything ok, Sis? I asked. That is heavy reading there," I said.

"Peachy," she said. "The book reminds me of Robert though. I've been reading it to him. It makes him laugh."

"Ok then, if you need us just call—we'll leave the door open." We got up to leave.

"There is one thing," she said.

We turned and I asked, "What's that Kiddo."

"Momma Allie always tucks us in and kisses us goodnight."

"Well, we don't want to leave anything undone. I went to her bed and tasseled her hair and kissed her on the head and tucked the covers around her. Willy gave her a hug and we went to our room."

The next morning was Saturday, so we got to sleep later than usual, although I had to go to the Webb law Firm by nine o'clock. Willy was to look out after Charlie until noon when I would be off work. When I awoke, Charlie was lying cuddled beside me, her favorite bear cradled in her arms and she was sleeping peacefully. I eased from the bed grabbed clothes and headed to the bathroom for a quick wash off. Pappy had the bathroom plumbed for a shower, so I showered off, combed my hair, and went to the kitchen for a peanut butter sandwich and a glass of milk. Willy followed me into the kitchen. I poured each of us a glass of milk and we sat at the table and ate.

"I see we had a visitor last night," Willy commented.

"Yeah, she's a prize," I said.

I hoped Momma and Pappy would get back early, raising kids was a chore. I had to admit, though that having the kids in the house had given me a different perspective on what was really important to me, and our family had been given a burst of new life from two knot heads from the Delta.

16

Charlie and Anna

Snow in Tupelo

I WAS ABOUT TO walk out the door when the phone rang. It was Anna. I was glad to hear her voice but was still unsure of exactly what I felt. "Zack Ok, I know you are still upset with me, and I don't blame you for that, but I was wondering if Charlie would want to come over and spend the morning with me. I know your parents are out of town. Mom and I am not working today, if she wants to, she can stay with me until you get off work.

"I know she would like that. If you are sure your mother would approve. I will have Willy drop her off. She's still sleeping now and hasn't had breakfast, but I'll get her up and Willy can drop her off about nine."

"Thanks Anna. I will pick her up as soon as I get off work.:

"Can we talk a little, Anna asked."

"I'd like that'. I said.

I explained everything to Willy and went to wake Charlie. She was elated that she would be spending time with Anna. I was happy too.

"Made you a grilled cheese sandwich, I said, as she followed me into the kitchen. Eat your breakfast and drink your milk. Willy will drop you at Anna's. Put in a good word for me, I winked."

"I don't tell lies," she said, grinning.

At Noon I left the law firm and drove to Anna's house. She and Charlie were in the swing covered with a blanket for the temperature had dropped drastically, and the sky was overcast, and it was beginning to spit a little snow.

"What are you two doing sitting out here in the cold, it's freezing, I asked stepping up on the porch."

"Watching it snow, Charlie said, isn't it pretty?"

"It sure is", I said looking straight at Anna.

"Come sit in the swing with us, she said, we've been having hot chocolate with marshmallows, it was delicious."

"To my surprise Anna threw back the blanket and patted the swing for me to sit beside her. I sat down and she covered the three of us with the blanket. The warmth of her body beside me was like a lightning strike. With her hand beneath the blanket she took my hand and squeezed it. I wanted to kiss her. I wondered if she had talked to her mother about what had happened to her. For some reason I felt that she had to discuss the matter with her mother before things between us would ever be right,

Suddenly, Mrs. Owens came through the door with a full cup of hot chocolate. She was even smiling as she handed me the cup. Marie Owens was a mirror of her daughter. The same beautiful face and just a little more mature figure. From the back, one would be hard pressed to tell which was which.

"I thought you might like some hot coco, she said, And I want to thank you for what you did for Anna. She looked at Anna and then at me again. And thanks for bringing Charlie by. Bring her any time."

"You mean you actually enjoy having her around? I said, winking at Mrs. Owens." We'll give her to you If you want her."

"Zack! You're mean, Anna said, hitting me with a tap on the shoulder."

"He don't mean it Anna, I know he loves me! Charlie said shaking her head and throwing back the cover and coming to me and giving me a hug. He offered to take a paddling yesterday for something I did." "Nobody has ever loved me more than Zack. I always feel safe when I'm with Zack" she said to Anna.

"Tears formed in Anna's eyes. I feel that way too Charlie, Anna said.

"And so do I, Mrs. Owens said, looking straight into my eyes, she had teared up too.

Maybe she is finally warming up to me a little, I thought.

The snow began to fall in heavy flurries, the wind was picking up, and the ground was beginning to get a white coating. I told Charlie we had to go and get home before the streets became coated and slick. Anna told me to take the blanket to cover Charlie until she got to the truck. We said goodbye and ran for the truck,

Pappy's old truck was parked under the big Oak tree when we drove into the yard. Momma was standing in the doorway waiting for us when we ran up the steps to the porch. Squat came out from beneath the house and followed us up the steps to the porch but then turned and went back to his warm lair under the house.

"Where have you two been? Momma asked with her hands on her hips. We were worried to death about you in this weather."

"Charlie spent the day with Anna and her mother today. I think they have taken to Charlie, although I don't know why, I said winking at Momma. That's when Charlie jumped on my back, and Robert grabbed me round the knees."

"You take that back Zack Calloway. You know you love me." I picked her up and held her in my arms and squeezed her. She kissed me on the cheek. I carried her to Pappy who was sitting at the table sipping on a cup of hot coffee. Pappy took her from me, and they both wrapped up Pappy. It was plain as day that Pappy was a sucker for the kids, and they loved him in return. Momma just looked on and shook her head, smiling from ear to ear.

Momma or Pappy had not mentioned adoption of the kids to me or Willy since they had taken custody, but there was no doubt in my mind that they were already discussing it. I felt that they wanted to be sure that the children were feeling at home and wanted to be part of the family. They had been through a lot and Momma knew that they needed stability in their lives. When we sat down for supper, Momma said that before we started eating, there was something she wanted to talk about. She smiled at Pappy before she began.

"It's been a few weeks now since Charlie and Robert joined our family. And we want them to be full members of our family. We love you and Charlie, nodding at Robert and then to Charlie and we would like to start the process of adoption process, if it's agreeable to everyone."

"What does that mean?" Robert asked. We are not going to have to leave here are we?

"No Momma said, it just means that you will be a legal member of this family. Willy and Zack will be your full brothers, and Pappy and I will be your legal parents. What it does not mean, however, is that we could ever take the place in your hearts of your real Mother and Daddy. But it does mean that we will have total responsibility for your welfare."

Robert looked like he did not know what Momma was talking about. "Is Charlie still going to be my sister.

Charlie looked at Robert, rolling her eyes. "Unfortunately, you're still going to be my brother. And we do want to be a part of this family, adopted or not. "Don't know why you'd want Robert though. He acts so stupid at times and he eats like a horse.

"Well then we'll ask Mr. Webb to start the process of adoption. That may take a few months but nothing about the way we will love and care for you."

17

Trouble for Anna

Losing control

JASON WILBANKS WAS ANGRY. No, it was more than just anger. He was irate! He had been rejected by a sixteen-year-old high school student. "What was she thinking? He was wealthy, handsome, and very smart he thought to himself. He had been the pride of Pike River High school, a star athlete graduating at the top of his class and then a year in France to study European History, and language; four years of pre-med at Tennessee, graduating with Honors. Now this." He hated Mississippi and despised being sent there for a part of his Medical training. He hated their drawl and their everlasting friendliness. They were backward and cultureless country bumpkins. Annabelle Owens, however, was a prize he was determined to take.

Annabelle Owens the student he wanted to bed had rejected him. She was the cause of his troubles and he knew it. There were other young girls at the Medical Center that he wanted but non as beautiful as Annabelle Owens. Of course, he had been in trouble before—many times, but his father with all his money and political connections, had always been able to settle all his indiscretions. This was different. His father had warned him if he got in trouble with underage girls again, that he would be on his own. And if the authorities got word of this situation, that would end his future as a Doctor of Medicine. He simply could not let that happen. Annabelle Owens had to be dealt with. It simply could not get out that he was twenty-four years old and had tried to force himself on a high school student. He knew there were strict rules of conduct for Doctors and the med school could dismiss him without giving a reason if they got wind of any improprieties. He could not let that happen. His whole future was at stake and the reputation of his family in Nashville.

If she had just not rejected his advances, things would be fine, but she had; and now it was too late for her to make amends. He was not accustomed to being rejected, and from a tart from Tupelo. She would pay dearly for that mistake.

He had left the Medical center and picked up his possessions at the Apartment where he was staying and headed North from Tupelo on Highway 78 toward Memphis. There was little traffic He stopped a mile out of Holly Springs at the Hitching Post Café, an all-night eatery that was a favorite of truckers and night travelers. He needed a drink. He drank gin nearly every day. He carried a small flask and would mix it with his coffee or soda during breaks at the hospital. He preferred beer, but it was difficult to hide the smell of beer on his breath. He had been addicted to alcohol since high school, and only a few of his closest friends knew of his problem. He had no more gin now, his flask was empty, and he would not be able to buy any until he crossed the State line into Tennessee.

He ate for the first time that day. He stopped again in the small town of Olive Branch and filled up with gas. A half hour later he crossed the state line into Tennessee. Five miles across the border he found a Motel that advertised rooms on their Marque for eight dollars a night. and decided to stay there for the night. He bought a six pack of beer at an all-night gas station that was next door to the motel. His addiction was at a point now that he could not go a day without it. He rented the room for two nights. He needed time to think about how he was going to deal with Annabelle Owens.

He registered under the name of Gene Durant, paid the night clerk the sixteen dollars and went to his room.

It was a sparsely furnished, drab room with only a dresser and a nightstand. He found a bottle opener by the sink and opened the bottle and guzzled the entire bottle. He lay down across the bed and lit a cigarette and inhaled deeply. His nerves were shot, he thought. He downed another beer and finally slept. His last thought was that he would make Annabelle Owens regret the day she was born.

A thunderstorm passed through the city just after midnight, dropping heavy rain. Jason was awakened by the heavy thunder and went to the window. The motel parking lot was flooded, and lightening flashed across the night sky. Jason cursed under his breath, opened a warm beer, and lit his last cigarette. He studied his city map again and then slept again. He awoke several times during the night shivering from the cold and the need for more alcohol.

When morning came Jason drove to the edge of town and ate breakfast at café along the highway. He was starved and his eyes had dark circles and he had not shaved in three days. He was twenty-four years old but looked forty. His hands were shaking as he tried to hold his coffee cup. He had to calm himself and prepare himself for the mission that lay ahead.

"Truth has no regard for anyone's feelings"
                              --Katherine Dunn

18

New Home for the Family

Lessons on lying

ROBERT LEWIS, AS USUAL. Was the first at the breakfast table. Momma had a platter of eggs and bacon on the table. There was also a big bowl of milk gravy and a dozen home-made biscuits. She and Pappy drank coffee and there was milk for the rest of the family. Charlie fixed Robert a plate and told him to mind his manners. He paid her no attention and started eating before momma got seated. Once she was seated, she told us that she and pappy had an announcement. We all looked directly at her.

"I'm so happy to tell you that we are going to be moving into a new house," she said.

Robert Lewis stopped chewing and asked "why? I like this house," he said.

"I know, momma said, I like it too, but the lumber company wants the house and lot to further expand the business, and the family has grown, and we need more space. We will be moving into the new house when the school year is over in May. Do not worry Robert, you will like the new place. We will take everyone over to take a look on Saturday afternoon. Charlie will have her own room, and so will you Robert. Zack and Willy will continue to share a room, but it will be larger than the one they have now."

"You mean I won't be sharing a room with Charlie anymore? Robert asked," his big eyes wide.

That's right Robert, it is time Charlie had her own room. She is a girl and needs her privacy.

"What does that mean, "he asked.

"It means that she needs a room to herself," Momma said.

Robert did not comment, further, but from the look on his face, it was plain that it frightened him a little.

"Are we taking Squat with us" Robert asked.

"Pappy said "sure, the new place has a fenced yard and plenty of room under the house for shelter."

Robert Lewis seemed to be ok with the announcement and started back on his biscuit and gravy.

"Pappy asked if everybody was ok with the prospect of a new place to live. We will be just two houses down from Miss Bonnie and Wayne and only a block over from where the Owen's live—Annabelle and her mother. Any Questions? he asked.

Charlie spoke up. "Is it ever ok to lie, Pappy Calloway?"

Everyone stopped eating and looked at Pappy to see what his answer would be."

After a moment of silence Pappy said, "I think it is sometimes alright to lie."

Momma dropped he fork in her plate and it was so loud everybody nearly jumped out of their chairs. She looked like she was ready to break a platter over Pappy's head.

"There are different kinds of lies, Pappy said. There are lies to deceive, this is usually very wrong. For example, he continued, if Robert Lewis here, nodding toward Robert, told Momma he had washed his hands before eating and he had just wiped them on a towel, that would be a lie to deceive—not good."

Robert looked suddenly at his hands, it was plain he had not washed his hands, but pappy did not call attention to the dirt on his hands and arms up to his elbows.

"There are also lies to protect people's feeling," Pappy continued. Let us say Charlie's friend got a new dress, but it was about the ugliest dress Charlie had ever seen. Let's say that if the friend asked Charlie if she thought her new dress looked pretty. Should she tell the truth and tell her friend that it's the ugliest dress she ever saw and hurt the feelings of her best friend and maybe lose her as a friend, or should she just tell her the dress looks great. We are all faced with similar situations all the time. Most of us do not want to hurt a friend's feelings so we tell this kind of lie. We call these white lies, but they are still lying, Pappy said. Never lie to deceive. You will usually be found out; The Bible teaches us not to bear false witness against our neighbors. Many people think that this means "Never Lie." But I take it to mean we should not tell lies about anyone or say things that are not true that might cause them harm."

Momma didn't look all that happy about the lesson on lying that Pappy just gave us, but everyone, including momma took the measure. We ate the rest of the meal in silence, everyone contemplating the subject of lying. I wondered what Momma and Pappy had ever lied about. No, I probably did not want to know.

"I knew that there were other times when people lied but didn't mean to lie. Things happened that were unavoidable that could cause people's plans to change and keep them from fulfilling a promise. I could not get Anna's lie to me out of my mind. Had she lied to deceive or was it a lie to protect my feelings? Lying was a complex subject and a sin, I calculated, of which we are all guilty. I had lied when I told Anna I was not mad at her when I was mad enough to kick a stump.

Jason had lied to Anna about his age and his intentions—clearly a lie of deception. Anna had lied to me and to her mother for a number of reasons. Charlie was the only person that I knew that was completely honest. She saw no need to lie about anything. She said exactly what she felt. She spoke the truth from her heart, even if it might hurt those around her. I hoped she would not change. Robert, on the other hand at five had already got a good start on stretching the truth to get what he wanted. His cute and innocent face soon had my Momma Wrapped around his finger, but beneath that exterior was a bundle of trouble. While he had Momma fooled, Pappy saw right through him and kept a tight rein on the boy. The kid loved Pappy though and would talk momma into walking with him down to the lumber yard nearly every day to eat lunch with Pappy. Momma would pack a lunch for him, and Pappy and Robert would sit on a stack of lumber and eat while Momma would talk to Mrs. McCullough or Bonnie Purnell. Sometimes Pappy would buy peanuts and an RC Cola for lunch doe himself and for Robert. He showed Robert how to pour the peanuts in his drink and they would laugh and talk as they drank and ate the salty mixture. That had been one of the true pleasures Willy and I had shared with Pappy, many times.

Robert had stopped his bed wetting. I had finally learned Momma and Pappy's secret to solving bed wetting. One night when Willy and I had stayed up late listening to the Cardinals baseball game on the radio. I had just turned off the radio when I heard momma talking in whispers to Robert. I went to the door and watched as momma pulled him from the bed and took him to the bathroom and stood him in front of the commode. Momma whispered, coaxing him to pee. She turned the water in in the sink and Robert peed a stream we could hear from our room. Charlie was right, he pissed like a racehorse. When he was finished, she picked him up and tucked him back in bed. He never woke up completely and I confronted momma about it the next morning, and she admitted that her and pappy had been taking nightly turns of taking Robert to pee every night, and Robert was so near asleep that he wouldn't remember it the next day. So much for a magic formula to cure bed wetting.

Saturday evening, Pappy took off from work and we drove across town to see the new house that pappy had purchased. It was a nice red brick with a front porch that spanned the front. There were four tall windows across the front. White pillars supported the porch. The floors were of high gloss oak and there were four bedrooms and two complete bathrooms. The kitchen and dining area were huge. With the house empty of furniture our voices echoed through the cavernous rooms. The ceilings were ten feet high causing the large house to seem even larger. There were closets in every room. We had never lived in a house with a closet. There was also an attic fan, to cool the house during the hot Mississippi summers. Attic fans were a true luxury, and only the better homes were equipped.

The house sat on a large corner lot with shrubs and flower beds along the sidewalk. To the left of the house was a workshop that set back from the rear of the house about thirty feet, and a garage and a storage area in the rear. There were two large pecan trees in the front yard and two more in the rear that would provide plenty of shade in the hot summers. To momma it must have seemed like a mansion, Pride showed on momma's face. Pappy looked unimpressed. To him it was just a house. To Pappy, home was where Momma and the kids were. The two children were in awe of their new home. The drive back home was in silence as we all contemplated on living in the new place.

19

Jason Leaves Tupelo

Anger takes control

JASON WILBANKS HAD STEWED for two days in his anger at Annabelle Owen. For two days he drank beer and smoked cigarettes hardly leaving his room. He needed cash and was afraid to call his father for extra money. He knew his father, Gordon Wilbanks, would ask questions and might even call the Medical Center if he suspected that he was being lied too, He would surely stop sending money if he learned he had been ousted at the Medical Center. He got a deposit in his bank from his father each week to pay his expenses while in school and he did not want that to stop.

Jason was an alcoholic but would never admit it. He had started drinking in high school and had been able to hide that fact from his friends and his family, though some of his closest friends suspected he was an addict. He could barely make it through the day, now, without liquor. His preference was beer, but it was hard to hide the smell of beer on his breath. He always carried a small flask of gin to sip on through the day. He had been able to keep his secret through medical school, because in Nashville liquor was readily available and everyone in his family drank some.

In Mississippi, however, managing his drinking had become more difficult. He would usually head for the State Line on weekends and buy enough beer to last him all week. Mississippi was a dry state, and no one drank openly.

Just before noon he decided on a plan. He would see how much he could get from selling the car. He carried the title in the glove compartment. It was an expensive car and he needed to get enough cash to buy a cheap vehicle and have enough money to carry out the plan, and then get out of Mississippi for good.

There were dozens of car lots and dealers along the highway advertising that they paid cash for cars. He finally bargained to sell the car for eighteen-hundred dollars and then bought a beat up six-year-old ford for two hundred cash. Next, he stopped at a pawn shop and paid the owner twenty dollars for a twenty- two caliber snub nose revolver and a box of shells. It was lite and easy to conceal. Although he knew nothing about guns himself, the shop owner assured him that it was plenty powerful enough to provide protection. He shoved the gun in the glove box of the ford and left for the motel. There he showered and shaved and put on a clean shirt and headed south. An hour later he was outside the little village of Red Banks in Mississippi. It was desolate country of red clay hills and scrub oaks. He pulled off the main road onto a dirt lane a half mile east of the Red Banks Country Store. He took the pistol from the glove box, loaded the weapon and picked out a target on the side of the road, and fired at it until the chamber was empty, reloaded and moved closer to the target and fired until the gun was empty again. He reloaded the gun and slipped it back into the glove box.

The air around the car was heavy with the smell of Gunsmoke. His hands were shaking. That was the first time in his life he had ever fired a handgun. He had not put a single shot in the target he had aimed at. It did not matter though, for he intended to be close enough to Annabelle Owens that he couldn't miss. He started the engine pulled back onto the highway and once again headed South toward Tupelo. In just over an hour later he was on the outskirts of Town. He crossed over the Natchez Trace Highway and pulled into the Mallard Motel that advertised weekly rates on its marque. He grabbed a small bag from the ford and went inside and rented a room for five dollars. A bearded caretaker took his money.

"Where can I get a six-pack of beer?" he asked the desk clerk.

"Tennessee or Alabama, the clerk said. This is a dry town. A dry state in fact, he added, though sometimes you'd never know it."

"That's enough reason right there to hate Mississippi," Jason muttered.

"You're welcome to go on to Alabama," young man, the clerk retorted, laying the room key on the counter.

He took the key, went to the room, threw his bag on the dressing table, and stretched out on his bed. There was a television in the room which surprised him. He turned it on, lit a cigarette, and watched the evening news. He needed a beer. He could get only one station and it was not very clear. From the drawer below the phone he found a telephone directory. He had learned from his time at the Medical Center that Annabelle's Mother name was Anna Marie Owens. The phone listed her address as 215 Evergreen. He wrote dawn the address and stuck the paper in his shirt pocket. He would wait until dark and see if he could locate the house of Annabelle Owens. He would eventually get around to punishing her for the trouble she had caused. But first he just wanted to scare the hell out of her. Then she would suffer.

When darkness had finally settled on Tupelo, Jason went to the motel office and picked up a city map. He then returned to the room and studied it carefully locating Evergreen Street. Just after Eight o'clock he left the motel parking lot taking the Highway East. Two miles later he took Main street to the middle of town, He located Evergreen with little trouble and drove slowly until he located 215. He Stopped momentarily in front of the house but saw no movement. He made a block and came back and parked on the street a half block down from the Owen's home in front of an empty house with a for sale sign in the yard.

He watched the Owens house for half hour, but no one came out or went in. He started the car and drove until he came to a phone booth just past the Lee County courthouse. He stopped the car and waited to make sure there were no people around. There was little traffic and no pedestrians on the street. It had turned much colder and was beginning to sleet a little. He paid no attention to the icy pelts to his face. He stepped into the phone booth and put a dime in the phone and dialed the number.

"Hello, came the voice of Annabelle Owens. This is the Owens Home," she said in a happy voice.

Jason said nothing for a few seconds.

"Who is this?" Anna asked after no one had spoken.

"I'm coming after you, witch!" Jason said in a raspy voice

Anna dropped the phone and it hit the floor hard. Her mother, who was sitting at the table finishing her dinner jumped. Anna ran to her face in her hands, tears streaming down her cheeks.

"Somebody just told me he was coming to get me in a threatening voice. I'm scared!"

Mrs. Owens picked up the phone, and shouted "who is this?" The phone was dead. She then dialed the police department and told them what had happened.

"We'll send a patrol to the neighborhood to check for activity. If they call again, we will send a detective over," the officer said.

In a few minutes, a patrol car stopped in front of the Owens home and a uniformed patrolman came to the door."

"Everything ok Maam?" He asked through the screened door. Has he called back again?"

"No, Not yet."

"Probably just a prankster, but do not take chances, keep your doors and windows locked and a porch light on if you can. If you get another call or see anything suspicious, call us. Do you have a firearm in the house, Maam?

"Yes, and I know how to use it, Mary Owens said."

"The patrolman laughed. "Good. Keep it loaded and handy,"

The patrolman said goodnight. He went to the car made a block, driving back by the house a few minutes later heading back toward town."

Marie Owens went to the cupboard and took out her snub-nose colt revolver that was wrapped in an oil cloth and checked to make sure the gun was fully loaded. She laid it on the table in front of her.

Annabelle, although badly shaken by the call, phoned Zack's number. Charlie answered."

"Charlie this is Anna, can I talk to Zack please? I need to talk to him." She said through sobs.

Charlie ran to Zacks room and yelled. "Zack, come quickly, Anna is on the phone and she's crying."

` Zack rushed to the phone. "What's wrong Anna?"

Through sobs Anna explained what had happened. "I'm scared," She said.

"Any idea who would do such a thing?" Zack asked.

"Not sure, but I think it was that Jason Wilbanks. The person disguised his voice, but I feel sure it was him. What am I to do? I thought that he was out of my life for good."

"The guy must be nuts. Zack said. Do you want me to come over?"

"I want you to but that's not something my mother would want."

"Well, let me know if it happens again. I will come anyhow. Maybe it was just a stupid prank."

"I hope that's all it was, but I think it was more than that." Anna said.

"Remember that tomorrow is the grand opening day for the new showroom at the lumber company. I told Pappy you and I would help with the serving of drinks and goodies. They are giving away two new television sets at the drawing. They are expecting a huge crowd for the opening, do you think you'll be ok to help? They have been running ads on the radio and in the newspaper for several weeks now. If you do not feel like it, I'll understand."

"I wouldn't miss it Zack. I will be fine. Just a little shook up now. Momma is coming too."

"I'll pick you up at 7:00. Keep the phone close, and if you need me call."

I was worried, and I was sure it showed on my face.

"Is Anna ok Zack?" Charlie asked.

"Yeah, she'll be fine just an ugly phone prankster!

"I love Anna," Charlie said. I don't want her to be sad.'

"I love her too, Charlie, and I don't want her to be sad either."

"Can I go with you and Anna tomorrow to help with the grand opening? Charlie asked.

"I think we will all be going, including Robert. You will have to help Momma watch out for him. Momma will be trying to help Bonnie in the office, we'll help you to see to him. Keep him from drinking too much and eating too much candy,"

"I went to bed thinking of Anna and wondering if she was right about who she thought had made the phone call."

I picked Anna and her mother up just before seven on the day of the grand- opening of the new showroom. I drove through the big gate at the lumber yard and parked behind the new building. We got out and went to the rear door. Miss Bonnie Purnell was already there and let us in. The showroom walls were lined with new appliances—refrigerators, Stoves, washing machines and New RCA and Philco Television sets. There was hardware bins of nuts and bolts, shelves of small appliances and just about everything a homeowner could possibly want. We walked through the building to the front door and went outside to take our place at the stand where we were to help serve free hotdogs and sodas. We were putting on aprons with the new name of the lumber company on front, when suddenly we heard the sound of a siren nearing the lumber yard.

Dozens of people had gathered around the store awaiting the grand opening and the drawing for new television sets. Everyone was now looking toward Main street and the sound of the sirens. I looked up the street toward Main Street and saw Pappy and Mr. Purnell strolling down the sidewalk back toward the entrance to the showroom.

20

Expanding Business

Pappy thinking of Big Flat

WAYNE PURNELL AND PAPPY stood in front of the newly constructed building of the former Purnell Lumber and supply Company. Workman wer e attaching the giant company logo sign across the front of the new structure. The big neon sign was nearly ten feet in height and more than fifteen feet in length.

Pappy was now half owner of the newly formed company, for it was agreed that Pappy would purchase the new land for the expansion for a fifty percent interest in the existing business. He had put up half the one hundred and fifty thousand in cash and the balance he and Allie financed through merchant's bank.

It was now the *Purnell & Calloway Highway 6 Lumber and Building Supply Company.* It had been over two years in the planning and construction but was now the one largest lumber and supply companies in all North Mississippi, with a showroom of more than fifteen thousand square feet of hardware and appliance showroom space. The company now covered more than twenty acres of land in just about the center of Tupelo. On any given day, the company had an inventory of more than two million board feet of lumber stored in more than a dozen storage barns. The partners had also opened branches in the city of West Point and Aberdeen fifty miles to the south.

Housing construction in Tupelo was lively, and the profits were beyond their expectations. The branch in West Point and Aberdeen were beginning to be profitable too. In addition to the lumber business, the partners had also completed the construction of a thirty-six-unit apartment complex that was near one hundred percent occupied. The company now employed more than fifty workers.

The partners had split the profits for the previous year of more than sixty thousand dollars each while maintaining a cash reserve of more than a half million dollar. Both men were now two of the wealthiest men in Tupelo, but few people knew it. They both were very frugal, choosing to live quietly and without flair and invest much of their income in their employees in pay and benefits. The men had been close friends since their days at Pearle Harbor during the war, and mornings would find Wayne at our table having coffee and, in fact, breakfast most days, while the two men talked business. Pappy continued to manage the yard while Wayne handled the business end of the operation. Momma was helping Bonnie more in the office and seemed to enjoy the work and being with Bonnie and Mrs. McCullough. Sometimes Robert would follow Pappy around and even go on short deliveries with him, while Momma worked.

While Pappy had been financially successful beyond his wildest imaginations, I knew he still longed to be back in Big Flat around his family and his friends. He missed farming tremendously, and the peace and tranquility he had felt when living in the little settlement. The more their business grew, the less time he was able to spend with Momma and Willy and me, and now the young ones, and the more difficult it became to extricate himself from business in Tupelo. "Willy would be graduating from high school in just a few months, and then I would soon follow. I had been promoted a grade after a series of tests and would still finish at the top of my class and then It would just be Pappy and Momma and the two little ones at home. He was having little time to spend with Charlie and Robert—no way to raise kids," Pappy had said.

Although Momma rarely complained about anything, Pappy knew that she longed to be back in Big

Flat too. Momma had become close friends with Bonnie Purnell, and Mrs. McCullough but he knew that she missed her friends and kinfolk back in Big Flat. He and Momma had money and property, but it seemed a poor replacement for doing something you really loved. Pappy often thought of the little Baptist Church where they went on Sunday mornings and the Methodist Church where his mother had taken him as a child. To think of going back now Pappy knew was foolish. He said that he needed to just clear it from his mind. Still he said it nagged at him like an itch you could not reach to scratch.

I knew Pappy loved Momma more than he could ever express, but he had said it, sometimes, seemed his life was sliding away from him and there was an emptiness inside him that nothing could seem to fill. That worried him, and it showed, for he seemed to always carry that furrowed look on his brow. Pappy knew this time would come when the we would be leaving and making our own way in the world but he sure as hell was not ready for it. And now he had two other children depending on him and I knew he dang sure wasn't prepared for that either.

In the back of my mind there are pictures I see
Like words to old songs, they keep coming to me'
Like the smell of a rose or the taste of sweet wine
They are there in the back of my mind.

- RC

21

Disaster Strikes

Shattered

ANNA AND I WATCHED as Pappy and Wayne walked back toward the office. Today was to be the big day that Pappy and Mr. Purnell has been waiting for, the opening of the new showroom and expansion of the Company. It was a sunny but cool Saturday and many people had gathered near the entrance waiting for the doors to open. Flags and banners were everywhere announcing the event. Anna and I had also come to see the new television sets on display and to help serve Cokes and hotdogs to those gathered for the big opening. Other part-time help had been added to help with sales and activities inside the showroom.

Suddenly there was the sound of sirens that were obviously coming east on Main Street. With squealing tires, a car rounded the corner in front of the new building, a high-speed chase in progress. The car crashed into a parked truck on the left side of the street and careened across the street fishtailing and careening off another parked vehicle on the right. The driver tried to bring his car under control but when he accelerated, he lost control and the car powered toward Pappy and Wayne who had turned toward the commotion just as the car bore down upon them. Pappy reacted immediately trying to push Wayne out of the way of the oncoming car. He was too late however: the car crashed into the wall of the store crushing Mr. Purnell between the car and the building.

The policemen who had been giving chase surrounded the scene immediately and the crowd scattered.

Pappy yelled at on lookers for help to push the car off the body of Mr. Purnell. A dozen men, including Willy and myself came forward to help and we were able to move the car. The Driver was unconscious, and a woman passenger was pulled from the car by the police and handcuffed and placed in one of the police cars, she apparently had been unharmed. The driver looked to be in bad shape.

By this time Mrs. Purnell had run from the office to the side of Wayne. She now had Wayne's head resting in her lap who was bloody all over. Wayne had been killed instantly. Bonnie was crying hysterically. Pappy knelt beside her holding Wayne's hand with one arm around Ms. Bonnie. Momma soon came and knelt beside Bonnie and tried to comfort her. That was impossible, however.

Seconds later an ambulance from The Hospital on The Hill pulled in beside the wrecked car. They carefully removed the body of Wayne from the street side onto the gurney and into the ambulance. Mrs. Purnell and Momma climbed into the ambulance beside Wayne for the trip to the hospital. Pappy was crying as he went to the front door of the store and asked the folks gathered around to please go home. The store would be closed for the next few days. He said there would be an announcement in the Tupelo Journal newspaper.

The driver still lay motionless on the street covered in his own blood and glass from the shattered windshield. A Tupelo policeman stood by the man. Soon another ambulance arrived and took the man away. The policeman told Pappy that the two had robbed a supermarket over on Gloster Avenue and killed an employee and were trying to escape. It was no comfort to Pappy, but he was happy the two had been apprehended.

Pappy cleared the store of employees and asked Mrs. McCullough if she would secure the lumberyard while he Went to the hospital to be with Bonnie and Allie. His heart was broken. He had lost the best friend a man could ever hope to have, but he knew that he had to help Bonnie get through this terrible ordeal.

Anna and I had watched helplessly as the tragic event unfolded. Anna had not stopped crying even though she did not know Mr. Purnell very well. She knew that I loved the man and she loved me. She held on to me as tears filled my eyes. It was like she could almost feel my heart breaking as if her own heart was somehow connected to mine. I think she wanted to hold me and comfort me. She knew I wanted to be strong, but she also knew that I needed her.

Pappy got to the hospital fifteen minutes after the ambulance. They had taken Wayne directly to the morgue located on the basement floor of the medical center. Bonnie, Allie, and Doctor Little were in the waiting room just outside the morgue when Pappy arrived. Bonnie was still in a state of shock and Dr. Little had ordered her a sedative to help calm her, she was still sobbing uncontrollably.

Dr. Little advised that they should go home so that Bonnie could get some rest. He doubted, however, if sleep would be possible for her. She had a long and difficult period ahead of her and she would need all her strength. She did not want to leave Wayne, but finally relented at the doctor's insistence. Wayne and Bonnie and Dr. Little had been friends for many years and had coffee together two or three times a week. He was heartbroken too but seemed calm.

Momma told Bonnie that she would stay with her through the night and handle phone calls that were bound to come. Bonnie asked Pappy to stay with them too. She said she needed his help in making funeral arrangements. Pappy led the two women to the parking lot and the three of them got in Pappy's old truck and drove away. Dr. Little watched from the hospital entrance until they were out of sight.

The doctor had never married, and he wondered what it would be like to have a woman love him the way that Bonnie had loved Wayne. Medicine had been his mistress and the love of his life, but now in middle-age he sometimes wished for more.

Pappy. and Momma handled the phone calls that came in once they had made it to Bonnie's home. Momma made coffee, but Bonnie was withdrawn and silent. Zack, Annabelle, and Jesse came by as night was settling. The presence of the young people seemed somehow to help her begin to accept the reality of the situation. She became engaged with the three and ask them about school and other activities and their future plans.

The Journal called and asked if they could send a reporter by for an article to be published the next morning. Pappy agreed that they could come but were not to talk with Bonnie. He explained that she just was not up for that, but that he would try to give the information they needed, the reporter came within an hour and he and Pappy sat in the small office that Wayne had maintained in the home. Momma served them coffee while they talked. Pappy answered the questions and gave the reporter information about +when the business would reopen. The next morning the Journal reported the tragedy in the morning edition.

"Mr. Wayne Purnell a prominent Tupelo businessman and co-owner of the newly formed Purnell & Calloway Highway Six Lumber and Supply Company was killed early yesterday morning in front of that business on Main Street, according to Tupelo police. Mr. Purnell was killed by an out of control automobile.

The driver of the car, Samuel Goodnight of Hindsville Alabama was also killed in the crash and a passenger in the car with Mr. Goodnight, sustained minor injuries. According to the authorities, the driver of the car and his passenger were trying to elude the city police when a high-speed pursuit ensued after a robbery of the Burrows Star Grocery Store on Gloster Street. The passenger in the car, Miss Virginia Hale, also of Hindsville was placed under arrest at the scene and according to a police spokesman, is being detained in the Lee County Jail. Jason McKee an employee of the Burrow Star Grocery was also shot and died in route by ambulance to the Tupelo Medical Center.

Mr. Purnell, a decorated Veteran and his Wife Bonnie were owners of the Purnell Lumber Company for the past fifteen years but had recently joined with his longtime friend AC Calloway and formed the newly Named High Six Lumber and Supply Company, Today was to be the grand opening of the New Showroom. Several dozens of people who hand gathered for the event witnessed the crash. According to witnesses Mr. Purnell was crushed between the car that Goodnight was driving and the newly constructed showroom.

Funeral arrangements have not yet been finalized and will be announced in tomorrow's edition of the Journal. The Lumber Company will be closed until after the funeral and the grand opening will be rescheduled for a future date. Details of the arrangements to be published in this paper as soon as they are known.

The nest morning Bonnie Purnell made funeral arrangements at the Madison-Wilcox Funeral Home in Tupelo, she was accompanied by Pappy and Momma and Doctor James Little, their friend from the Medical center. The funeral would take place in Tupelo at the First United Methodist Church, with burial at the Verona Methodist Church Cemetery in Verona Mississippi, just t few miles from Tupelo and the place where his family lived when he was a child. The Reverend Arthur Wade would conduct the ceremony at 2;00 P.M. Tuesday Visitation would be at the funeral home two hours prior to the service.

The Journal carried a lengthy obituary on Monday morning with an announcement on the front page concerning the reopening of the lumber yard.

Tuesday the Methodist church was filled with friends and business associates and employees of Wayne Purnell. The Calloway family sat with Bonnie Purnell along with Mrs. McCullough and Annabelle Owens and Penelope and Jessie and Doctor Little in the family section. Neither Bonnie or Wayne had any siblings or living relatives that Bonnie knew of. The employees of the Purnell lumber company had been their family for nearly twenty years. Momma had, however, become her closest and dearest friend over the last four years. They sat side by side in the family section shedding tears together.

Pall Bearers were business associates from Tupelo and Verona that Bonnie knew well. When the service ended the processions of cars proceeded South on Highway 45 to the cemetery. Dozens of people stood on sidewalks and paid their respect to the war hero and well-respected citizen of Tupelo. Pappy, Momma, Bonnie, and Doctor Little rode in the Limo with Bonnie.

The Navy presented a Flag to Bonnie at the graveside service, a seaman played Taps as was the custom and flag bearers gave a final military salute to the Veteran, who had been awarded the Bronze star for bravery, and also a Purple Heart for being wounded in the battle.

After the service, the Limo returned to the funeral home, Pappy drove Bonnie home and went in and made coffee. Doctor Little stopped by for a moment to see if she needed anything and they all sat at the table and talked for a few minutes, Zack and Annabelle, Willie and Jessie stopped for a few minutes too.

It seemed to brighten her day a little to have the young folks there. After a while, they realized it was time to give Bonnie some space and they wandered away. Momma hugged Bonnie and promised to call her the next day. Bonnie Purnell was alone.

She went to her bedroom, opened the trunk, and took out the picture album of photos collected over nearly twenty years of marriage to Wayne. There were pictures of their honeymoon trip to New York, and recent pictures of Wayne and Pappy sitting on the front porch, and a picture of Wayne and Pappy and the me and Willy sitting on the tailgate of Pappy's old truck with a string of catfish we had caught from the Davis pond. Sweet memories that would forever be in the back of her mind. Tears began to fall again, and she put the album away, and lay across her bed. She stretched out her arm to where Wayne used to lay beside her. It was a long time before she slept.

22

Jason Seeks Revenge

Jason stalks Anna

JASON WILBANKS WAS PARKED down the street when Anna and her mother came out of the house just before 7:00. He had started toward the two, with the intention of running them over with his car, when an old truck pulled to the curb and the two got inside, Jason sped on by, parked at the curb underneath a giant White- Oak tree, and waited until the driver of the truck pulled into the driveway and tuned the truck around, and in a few seconds passed by him on the street. He started the old Ford and followed the truck until they crossed Main Street and pulled through the double gates at the lumber yard and parked behind the big showroom.

Jason made a turn around and crossed over Main street and parked in the parking lot of the Army Surplus store, and Pawn Shop. There he purchased a heavy Military fatigue jacket, dark glasses, and green military hat. He left his car in the parking lot and walked back toward the lumber yard. A large crowd of people had gathered in front of the new showroom waiting for the doors to open. He lost himself in the crowd but never took his eyes off Annabelle Owens who was serving up sodas in front of the store, until he heard the sound of the siren,

When he witnessed the crash, he hurried away from the scene for he knew reporters would likely not be far behind the police, and they would take pictures. No doubt that the local television station would be on the scene as well. He could not afford to take a chance on being identified in the crowd, so he rushed back to his car and sped back to the Mallard Motel. He would have to wait for another chance to deal with Annabelle Owens.

He called the First Citizens Bank of Tupelo and checked to see if his father had made a deposit into his checking account for his monthly expenses. As usual, the money in the amount of three hundred dollars was on deposit. He got in the car and drove to the bank and went inside and went to the first teller and asked for his balance. He learned that he had a few cents over five hundred dollars on deposit. Using a counter check, he withdrew all but twenty-five dollars.

Outside the Bank he picked up a copy of the Journal newspaper and drove back to the Motel. He went to the office and talked to the day clerk. He wanted to buy beer and did not want to drive to Alabama to get it. He asked the clerk if he knew where he could buy beer. He knew that there were dozens of bootleggers in North Mississippi and you could buy any kind of liquor if you had the right price. The clerk said he could arrange to get him a case of beer for twenty dollars. He turned on the television, and as expected the local station was all over the incident at the lumber yard. Cameras scanned the crowd of onlookers and the crash in front of the lumber company. The cameras even scanned the crowd and he spotted Annabelle the beautiful Annabelle Owens. His anger was stirred again.

What a beauty she was, but she would not be after he got through with her. He would find his chance to destroy her one way or another. He imagined how would take her body, then he would take her beauty and then her life. He would find a time when she was alone, and he would continue to watch her until that time came. If he needed to, he would also take care of her boyfriend, Zack Calloway if he interfered.

He drove back to the Mallard Motel asked the desk clerk to order him more beer and rented the room for two more nights. He went to his room and waited for the bootlegger to bring the beer. He turned on the television and the local news reporters were still covering the disaster at the lumber company.

Jason did not know exactly what Anna's connection was with the owner of the lumber company, but he knew at the present time he would have to wait until things settled down, for those who were connected to the lumber company would be under extreme scrutiny. Thirty minutes later the bootlegger came with his beer. He paid the man twenty dollars and opened a can and drank his first of the day. For an hour he drank beer and smoked cigarettes until his mind was completely numb and he finally slept.

He awoke three hours later and stumbled to the bathroom and held his head under the sink and let the cold-water help wash away the alcoholic fog that clouded his mind. He then pulled on his hat and green fatigue jacket and left the motel. He drove to the street where Anna lived and again parked in front of the vacant house a block down. For the next two hours he waited and watched, but Anna made no appearance.

Tired and restless and craving more beer, he drove back to the motel. He decided to call his father in Nashville. He knew his father would be calling the hospital to check on him if he did not check in on a weekly basis. They exchanged small talk, his father asking how things were going at work and when he was coming home. Spring break was coming in three weeks and he promised to be there, but told his father that he needed an extra two hundred dollars for he was going to have an additional week of more classes and training at the medical center before he could return to the Medical School in Nashville. His father agreed to wire the money to his account the next day. His father handed the phone off to his mother and they talked briefly, and he finally said goodnight. He opened a beer and drained the can and lay across the bed and slept.

23

The Locket

Charlie and Anna

THE DEATH OF WAYNE Purnell had taken Anna's mind off the threatening telephone call she had received from the person she believed to be Jason Wilbanks. Now however, she was worried again that he was still around and might try to harm her.

She wished she could just stay with Zack for she felt safe when he was with her. She knew she had to get over that for Zack would not always be around to protect her. Today Penelope had walked with her from school and stayed until her mother came. Penelope was worried too. Jessica and Anna had started to school together in the first grade and had been like sisters ever since. Anna was thankful that they were her friend.

The next afternoon Zack drove Anna to the Medical Center and promised to pick her up at 7:00. Her mother agreed for Zack to do that and it was a chance for the two to be together for a little while. Her mother however, had decided that this would be Anna's last day to work at the hospital on school days. She did not want her out until she was sure there was going to be no more threatening phone calls. She would be able to work only on weekends when she could drive Anna to work and pick her up. Anna understood her mother's concern for she had been sleeping with the snub-nose pistol under her pillow every night since the phone call. Anna had no doubt that her mother would use the gun if she or her daughter were threatened.

Anna had promised that Charlie could come and stay with her Saturday afternoon. She and Charlie were both excited about that, but she was unhappy about not being able to work during the week at the center. She had promised Charlie they would go to the Drugstore for a root beer and that she would take her to the jewelry store where Zack had bought her the heart-shaped locket the first Christmas after they had met.

Charlie had, of course, wanted to see the necklace, so she took it from around her neck and opened it for her to see Zack's picture.

"My goodness, Charlie said, that's beautiful! Zack bought that for you?"

"Yes, he did," she said. Gave it to me the first Christmas I knew him, taking the locket and kissing it and returning it to her neck.

"Why did you kiss it Anna?"

"Because it's the most precious thing that I own. I will always wear it."

"Charlie said, "I love Zack and I am glad you love him too. Just don't tell him I said that."

"I won't have to tell him Charlie," Anna said.

'Why not?"

"Because he knows! It shows every time I see you two together, plain as dirt," Anna answered"

"I like Willy too, but not like Zack, and I don't know why that is though for Willy is kind and really watches out for me."

"Zack told me that some bright, wise little girl once said you can't help who you love, and I believe that is true. I cannot help loving Zack any more than you can. My trouble is loving that boy too much."

"I hope someone will give me a locket like that, someday," Charlie said.

"Don't worry, Charlie, that will happen, but it's not the gift that's really important but rather it's the person who gives it to you."

'Billy Davis at school told me he liked me," He said I had foxy red hair. Is that good or bad?"

"Well if he told you he liked you he probably meant it as a compliment. Boys don't always seem to know the right things to say to a girl, Anna smiled."

"Billy asked me if he could hold my hand going to lunch and I told him no, but I might let him if he asks me again."

"If you like him really well, you might just go and take his hand."

"Yeah, I might do that" Charlie said, smiling. He doesn't smell very good though. He's always sweating,"

Anna Laughed.

24

Pappy Needs Help

Anna and Charlie face trouble

I DROPPED CHARLIE OFF at Anna's house on Saturday afternoon after I got through running errands at the Webb Law Firm. Anna and her mother met us at the curb, and they walked Charlie hand and hand to the porch. They waved goodbye as I drove away. I drove to the lumber yard to see Pappy.

Pappy was having a rough time dealing with the death of Mr. Purnell and Miss Bonnie was unable to do much more than get out of bed in the morning. It had only been just over a week since the accident but the weight of it all was bearing down on Pappy. He had taken over the inside work of Mr. Purnell and with

Bonnie in mourning and not able to help, Momma had been coming in a few hours a day to help with the sales, but with Robert Lewis at her heels and into more trouble than two sore tail monkeys, she had about all she could handle. Pappy was sitting behind the big desk in the new office with a stack of invoices in front of him.

"Got something I want to run by you, Zack, he nodded for me to sit down in one of the padded chairs,"

"What's up?" I asked.

"I need some help. I need Willy too, but I will get him later."

Your mother has her hands full with the two kids and trying to run the household. Willy will be graduating in a few months and will be leaving for flight training and Officer Candidate School as soon as school is out. We are, he continued, just getting the expansion started in West Point and Columbus, and I will be busy helping to get those stores off the ground. Wayne was the business brains of this operation and I need trustworthy help now until we can get back to a full staff. I do not want to interfere with your schooling, but I really need you to spend as much time here at the lumber yard as you can for now and through the summer. The McCullough boys can take care of the farm operation along with Joe Webb."

"Sure, Pappy, if you need me then I want to help. Mr. Webb is a good man and will understand. He and Wayne were good friends and would want me to do what

I can. I can load and drive trucks and make deliveries. I'll also ask Anna if she could give Momma a hand watching the kids after school so Momma can spend more time doing the office work, Anna is also good at office work, she's been doing most of the billing for Dr. Little and keeping his financial records. I will ask her if you want me too.

Pappy scratched his chin, indicating deep thought. "I'll think on that some tonight, he said. Don't know it it's a good Idea for you two to be spending that much time together."

"When do you want me to start," I asked.

"You already did, go help Mrs. McCullough load that flatbed out there with twelve bundles of shingles. She'll tell you where to deliver it."

"how much am I getting paid, I panned."

"Supper! he said. Willy will be here in a few minutes to help. Make sure you stack those shingles neatly when you unload them at the site. Do a good job and you get breakfast in the morning, he laughed, nodding for me to take the door."

"Pappy didn't overpay his sons," I thought, but kept my thoughts to myself.

Anna and Charlie left the drugstore and walked down Court Street toward the Owen's house. The sun was bright at their backs, but it was cold, and a North wind caused them to draw their collars tight and don their scarves around their ears. Anna knelt in front of Charlie to put in place her scarf and tied it tightly around her head. They then hurried down the street.

"Let's run Anna! It's so cold," Charlie shouted breaking into a trot. Anna ran to catch up. They were a block from the house when she noticed that her mother's car was not in the drive. She then remembered that her mother had told her she was going to pick up a few groceries and would leave the door open for her and Charlie for she would be just a few minutes, and for her not to answer the phone until she returned. It was just about time for Zack to pick up Charlie and she hoped that the three of them could sit in the porch swing under a blanket until her mother returned. She was still apprehensive at being alone in the house after the threatening call. She hoped that Zack would be there soon.

She ran and caught up to Charlie and then noticed the old Ford sitting in front of the vacant house just up the street. She suddenly realized that she had seen that car sitting there before and it bothered her for there was someone sitting inside the car. She suddenly had a chill down her spine. Her every sense told her that she and Charlie were in danger. She called for Charlie to stop running and took her by the hand.

Charlie realized something was wrong when Anna held her hand to keep her from going forward.

"What is it Anna? What's wrong?" She yelled!

Anna was looking directly at the car up the street when it pulled away from the curb and headed in their direction, Anna and Charlie were almost to the house, When Jason Welbourn stopped the car got out and ran toward them with a gun in his hand.

Run for the house Charlie!" Anna yelled She prayed her mother had left it unlocked. It was.

Zack had just turned the corner onto Jefferson when he saw the man running toward Anna with a gun out and his arm extended, he stomped on the accelerator of the old truck, it coughed and sputtered but then it lurched ahead. He drove for the man as the man fired the gun toward Anna who had turned and was getting ready face her attacker when Zack slid the truck to a stop a few yards from Jason. Jason turned the gun toward Zack and fired two shots wildly at the truck. Both shots hit the windshield and splattered glass into the truck cab, but the small caliber shot did not pierce the windshield of the truck. Zack ducked down and slid out of the cab of the truck and pulled his Louisville Slugger bat from under the seat.

`Anna lay on the porch, blood oozing from beneath her body. He had to get to her. He reached in and restarted the old truck, and staying behind the driver's door, he jammed the old truck in gear and the ancient vehicle eased forward with him behind the door and walking beside the slow moving truck, Jason fired the pistol emptying the cylinder toward Zack and ran for his old ford. He knew he had hit Anna with his first shot, but now he had to get away. He floored the old Ford, not realizing the pistol was empty, he was planning to shoot Zack when he could get a clear shot. However when he drew even with the truck, Zack stepped out with the Louisville Slugger bat and came down with all the power he could summon, across Jason's extended arm, Jason screamed in pain and swerved to the left, but gained control of the old car and sped off down Jefferson, and turned toward the highway at the stop sign. Neighbors appeared on the scene after hearing the shots and commotion, Zack yelled for them to call the ambulance and police as he ran to Anna. She had been hit in the chest, but she was breathing, but loosing lots of blood. He ripped away her coat and blouse she was wearing. He could see the bullet had hit her just below her bra under her right breast. He wadded the blouse and pressed it over the wound. Charlie had come to the porch now and was crying and yelling for help, obviously scared witless.

"Charlie, go in and call the lumber yard and tell Pappy to come over here quickly, Zack yelled at her. Be strong girl, he told her."

Neighbors were now gathered in the yard, and the lady who lived next door to the Owens came and knelt beside Anna and brought a towel to place over the wound. Minutes later the first police car pulled up to the house with the siren blaring, and an ambulance right behind.

Zack stayed beside Anna and held her hand until medics took over. She was groaning and sobbing but alive. Seconds later they had Anna on a gurney and in the Ambulance ready to go to the Hospital. He and Charlie were about to climb into the ambulance with Anna when Pappy pulled in behind Zack's truck.

Pappy ran to the ambulance and asked what had happened, but all I had time to tell him was to wait for Anna's Mother and tell her we were at the hospital. Charlie could tell him what had happened, I told Charlie to go with Pappy.

Emergency room doctors met the ambulance at the emergency entrance and took her directly into the surgical unit. They would not allow me to go into the area but told me that someone would update me on Anna's injury as soon as they could access her condition. I bowed my head and prayed for God to save her. That was all I knew to do. Moments later Pappy and Mrs. Owens came through the door to the surgical waiting room. Pappy had Charlie by the hand. Mrs. Owens was crying and begging me to tell her what happened. Thirty minutes had passed When Doctor Little came from the surgery unit. Mrs. Owens ran toward him for information. Very calmly Dr. Little quickly took charge of the matter.

"Your daughter is going to be alright, Mrs. Owens. Anna was shot with a small caliber Gun just below her right breast, She was very lucky, the bullet apparently partially hit the gold necklace she was wearing and ricocheted away from her vital organs to the rib cage and lodged there against the rib. We have removed the bullet and stitched the wound. She lost a good deal of blood, so we gave her a unit and antibiotics for infection. We also gave her a sedative to help her sleep. She will be very sore from the wound for several days, but the good news is she is going to be just fine."

Minutes later two policemen came in and questioned me about what had happened. I explained what I had seen and told them that I had hit the man with my baseball bat as he was speeding away. I felt sure his arm was broken. They asked if I knew the man that had fired the shots. I told them that I had seen him once at the drugstore but had no idea why he wanted to harm me. I did not mention the trouble that he had with Anna. That would have to be her decision. I also told him it was the man that Anna thought had made the threatening call to her a week or so before.

"We have a good description from neighbors of the vehicle, and we have an APB out for the man and the car he was driving. Other officers think they have located the car he was driving at the Mallard Motel just west of town. The clerk at the motel told the police that he registered as Gene Durant but showed no identification and has been registered for several days—paying his rent daily. More officers and the State police are on his trail."

25

Jason on the Run

Cornered

JASON HAD MADE IT to the Mallard Motel with his left arm shattered and bleeding from the wound; a compound fracture, the bone sticking through the skin, from the blow from Zack's Louisville Slugger bat. He thought about heading into the backwoods along the Natchez Trace but knew he had to tend to the wound. Going to the medical center was out of the question and he had to get the bleeding stopped. He knew he did not have much time, but he had a few medical supplies in his travel bag. He had driven the old Ford behind the motel between two Semi-trailer trucks that were parked on the big parking area. Unfortunately, for Jason, the state police had spotted the car within minutes and had the motel surrounded.

Sirens blasting from every direction, Jason hobbled himself to the window, drank a warm beer, lit a cigarette, and featured a peek out the window from behind the musty curtains.

Police cars were everywhere; he was trapped; this was the end of the line. How had he gotten himself in such a situation, he wondered to himself. He knew he was a sick person but refused to admit it and ask for help. He had embarrassed his family and friends and now there was no way to salvage himself. He reloaded the small pistol with extra ammunition he had dropped in his shirt pocket. He then went to the nightstand and took a note pad and pen. He scribbled a short note to his father. He sat down on the edge of the bed, put the barrel under his chin, and pulled the trigger.

Hearing the shot, the state police rapped on the door and then kicked it open and went inside. The room smelled of gun smoke. Jason lay dead on the bed, the pistol still in his hand. Soon the ambulance came and carried Jason Wilbanks body to the Morgue at the Tupelo Medical center. Doctor Little brought word to Pappy and Mrs. Owens in the waiting room. Marie had a feeling of sorrow that the young man was dead, but relieved that Anna would not be bothered by him again.

Anna was sleeping and the doctors did not want visitors, so I told Charlie and Pappy I wanted to leave for a few minutes. He seemed to study my expression, cocking his head to one side, and biting his lower lip.

"Ok son, but don't be gone long, you can take my truck, Anna will want you near when she wakes up and don't forget to pick me up. I'm going to call your mother and let her know where we are and what's happened."

"I won't be gone long I said, but there's something I need to do."

"Can I go with you Zack? Charlie begged. I do not like this hospital! "Please?"

I hesitated but said "sure, come on kiddo."

Charlie took my hand and we left the hospital. I drove across town to the old First Presbyterian Church on Jefferson Avenue, where I often went when I was troubled by some issue and needed a quiet place to study on something.

I sat down on the broad steps that led into the sanctuary, with Charlie beside me, I bowed my head and said a silent prayer of thanks for Anna once again being spared from death. I didn't understand much about God, and his ways of doing things, but I had the feeling that it was no coincidence that Anna's life had once again been spared. Pappy always told us that there was a plan for us all and a reason for everything under the sun and we did not always know what that plan was, but it would be revealed to us at some point in time. I hoped that was true. I knew I was tired of bad things happening to Anna, but what did God have planned for

Anna? Spiritual matters were always a mystery to me. Charlie bowed her head sitting un-lady-like beside me, her elbow on her knee and her chin cupped in her hand and her other arm resting on my knee.

When we raised our head there was a man standing before us smiling. It startled me. I had not heard him walk up. He wore a black suit with a minister's white collar around his neck. His hair was snow white and his eyes were ice blue. He spoke to us in a very soft but clear and calm voice.

"Don't let me disturb you two from your thoughts, I was just walking over the grounds and thought I'd come by and introduce myself. "Pastor Luke Jackson he said, extending his hand to me and then to Charlie.

"No problem, I said, I often come here when I have a problem and just need a quiet place to think; I hope it's ok. I'm Zack, Calloway, I said, and this is my sister, Charlie."

"Good place to come isn't it. Peaceful here in the afternoon. Kind of makes you feel closer to nature doesn't it?

"Yeah, something like that," I answered.

"You look familiar, I said shading my eyes from the evening sun. Have we met before? I asked."

"Perhaps, he answered. I am here and there. I've seen you here before."

"You a preacher?" Charlie asked, shading her eye from the sun as I had.

"Kind of, he answered. Why do you ask?

"You look like a preacher to me. I don't much care for preachers though, she proclaimed."

"And why is that young lady, what do you have against preachers."

"A preacher told me once that God answered prayers and I prayed and prayed for my mother and my daddy when they were sick, and it didn't do a lick of good. Not a flipping lick! Charlie answered. They died anyhow."

"Preachers don't always understand God's ways either, he said, but I trust his purpose for everything. Although his plan often causes us pain and sometime confuses us."

"I wonder if God even likes me, Charlie said. Sometimes I feel like he is mad at me for something. You think he is?"

"I'm Sure God is not mad at you, Charlie," the man said.

"Well he needs to lighten up on me and Robert some, she said without a smile, we haven't done anything bad to be punished for."

"Did you pray for Anna?" the man asked.

"Yes, I did, hard as I could."

"If you had not prayed for her, she may have died."

"How do you know Anna anyway," Charlie asked, shading her eyes again.

"In my business, he shrugged, I know lots of people. I just came from the hospital."

"You two have a good day, he said and walked away.

I looked at Charlie and she shrugged her shoulders. When I looked up the man was nowhere in sight. I shook my head in dismay. "How the heck does he do that." I wondered. "He's spooky!"

"It was strange, but I felt like I should know the man, but I shrugged it off.

Charlie and I left the old church and drove back to the hospital. Anna was still sleeping. I sat down in the waiting room with Mrs. Owens and Pappy. Mrs. Owens was much calmer and she put her arms around me and gave me a hug, and then hugged Charlie. She laid her head against my shoulder and in a few minutes, she was sleeping soundly. She was exhausted. Pappy said he needed to get Charlie home and left with her holding his hand but looking back and waving goodbye to me.

Pappy spoke with Doctor Little as he was leaving, but I was unable to hear the conversation, and then he and Charlie left through the double doors to the waiting room. Mrs. Owens aroused from her sleep enough to tell me to go on with my father that she would call me when Anna was awake. I caught up with pappy in the lobby and the three of us climbed in his old truck. He dropped me off in front of the Owens house to get my truck with the shattered windshield. Pappy followed me home.

Momma Willy and Robert Lewis was sitting at the table having supper when we came through the door. The day had been so hectic that I had forgotten that it was supper time. Momma kissed Pappy and followed him to the bedroom. That was a sign they wanted to talk in private. Charlie and I sat down with the rest of the family.

How was your day? "Will asked," looking at Charlie. Weird," she answered.

Willy look at Charlie then at me. "Weird, How?"

"We met this preacher at the church, and he was spooky weird, but I liked him though," Charlie shrugged. "I think he was an Angel or something," Charlie said, her eyes rolling.

Willy laughed. "An angel huh? Did he have wings?"

"No, don't guess he could fly, but he was just different somehow. His eyes were so blue, when he looked at you it seemed like he could tell what you were thinking.

That ended the conversation on pastor Luke. Willy looked like he had plenty more questions to ask but let the subject drop.

I had not thought about it before, but what Charlie said was true. It felt like when Pastor Luke looked at you, he was reading your very thoughts.

26

Anna Recovers

Back in school

MRS. OWENS DID NOT call me until the next morning, just after seven. She said she had slept in the waiting room, and that Anna had just woken up and was asking to see me. I quickly dressed and told Momma I was going to the hospital. It being Sunday, Pappy was drinking coffee in front of the Television watching cartoons with Robert Lewis sitting in the rocker with him,

"Call me, Pappy said, and let us know how Anna's doing," as I was leaving.

Anna was awake and smiling when I was ushered into the intensive care unit by Mrs. Owens and a duty nurse. Anna was beautiful even though her hair was trussed, and she wore no makeup. I went to her and she tried to raise her arms to touch me but could not. Her hands were bound to the bed to prevent movement of her right arm. I reached over and took her hand and kissed her forehead.

"Are you hungry? I asked. It has been a long time since you've had food."

"Would like a milkshake, she said. I don't know what I can have though."

The nurse, overhearing our conversation said she would see if she could find the doctor and see if Anna could have a milkshake. But, related that her chart said only liquid diet. She left to find the doctor.

I didn't know what Anna knew, if anything, about what had happened to Jason Wilbanks after she had been shot, so I didn't mention anything about his demise, until I had a chance to discuss it with Mrs. Owens. I had read the short article that was in the Journal that morning but did not mention it to Mrs. Owens or to Anna. The headline read.

"FORMER MEDICAL STUDENT ATTEMPTS MURDER THEN COMMITS SUICIDE

A medical student, who formerly was in training at the Tupelo Medical Center, was found dead in his room at the Mallard Motel on the Natchez Trace Highway by State

Police yesterday, after witnesses said he shot and injured a local high school student and attempted to shoot another, before leading police on a chase to the motel. A Police spokesperson said he died of a self-inflected gunshot wound.

The student who was shot, and the other person, both residents, were not identified. Police spokesmen said the incident was still under investigation and that more details would be released later. The shooter, however, was later identified as Jason Wilbanks of Nashville Tennessee. The son of a prominent Nashville Banker. Motive for the shootings has not yet been clearly established.

A few minutes later the duty nurse returned with a vanilla shake for Anna. Mrs. Owens Took it and held the straw to Annas lips and she took several long swigs.'

"That's good," she said.

Her mother continued to hold the shake until she finished.

Still groggy from medication, Anna slept again.

"Let's go get a Coke in the waiting room and talk for a few minutes, Mrs. Owens whispered to me."

I followed her to the vending machine area, and she put in change for drinks. We then sat down on a padded sofa and talked about what had happened and what to tell Anna. She asked for my opinion, which I though was a positive thing for our improving relationship, although I figured she already knew what she was going say. Most women, I had already figured out, were born half lawyers. They ask you a question, they already know the answer to. Men are foolish enough to think that they are giving input, when they're, actually, just getting their ego stroked.

"Why not just let her read the article in the newspaper? I asked. She is going to find out what has happened sooner or later,

"She's going to ask questions, Mrs. Owens offered."

"Answer honestly; the best you can," I said, "Anna is really smart and will see right through any attempt to keep information from her. Jason was a sick person, obviously."

"You are right about that she said. I just don't want her to feel, in any way that she's responsible for any of these things that have happened," she said.

"Well, Pappy always tells me and Willy that truth and honesty is always the best policy. Anything else just leads to more problems."

"Mrs. Owens nodded—agreeing with me in a non-committal way."

Dr. Little came into the waiting area and sat down beside Mrs. Owens, he was in his OR scrubs." Just got through delivering twins, he said. "I also looked in on Anna, and she is doing fine. The wound is healing and no sign of infection. I am going to keep her another night but if all goes well, you can take her home tomorrow. I'd like to see her at my office in about a week," he said. He handed Mrs. Owen a prescription and told her that it was for pain medication if she needed it. She will have to miss a few days of school and will need someone to stay with her and change dressings every day. We do not want too much movement. "Keep her in bed for the next few days if you can."

Anna was discharged the next morning and her grandparents came from Columbus to stay with her while Mrs. Owens returned to work. Anna was pale and week from the surgery, but otherwise she was in good spirits. And happy to be going home.

I was back in school but stopped by every afternoon to sit for a little while with her but could not stay but a few minutes or Pappy would be complaining, and Willy even worse. We were swamped at the lumber yard. Baseball season was in full swing and Willy and I were playing two games every week and sometimes three, but the games started usually at noon and players were excused from class which took me an Willy away from the lumber yard on days we played out of town. It was hard time for all of us for it seemed everyone's time was stretched to the limit. Weather was beginning to warm up some and demands on all the workers at the lumber company was taking its toll, but Pappy was working hard to hire new employees, and was making weekly trips to Columbus and West Point to make sure those operations were running smoothly. Miss Bonnie Purnell had finally returned to work and seemed to be doing better. Wayne had been gone for over a month now, and she was trying to move forward.

<hr>

It had been four days since Anna had been discharged from the hospital, Doctor Little sat at his desk with a stack of patient folders in front of him scanning each and making notations as he did his review. Pappy had sent me by his office to drop off a new Television set for the doctors waiting room I had finished hooking up the Antenna and was getting ready to leave. His pretty receptionist Debbie Archer came in and spoke quietly to the Doctor.

"Doctor Little, there's a Mr. Gordon Wilbanks in the outer office that is asking to see you and the hospital administrator. As you know Doctor Bell is in Chicago at a hospital administrators conference and won't return until tomorrow."

"What's the nature of his business?" Doctor Little asked. Did he say?"

"Yes, He said he was the Father of Jason Wilbanks, and that he wasn't leaving here until he could talk to you. He seems very angry."

Pull the employment file on Jason Wilbanks, Debbie, and then tell Mr. Wilbanks to come in.

"Zack, step into the examination room there and leave the door open, you might need to hear this,"

I did as the doctor instructed and sat on a stool beside an examination table. I could clearly hear every word of the conversation. Between Debbie and the Doctor and then the conversation with Gordon Wilbanks. I could see the doctor through the door that was slightly ajar, but I could not see the man who entered.

Minutes later Debbie returned with a blue folder marked confidential and placed it in front of the doctor. The doctor scanned the folder quickly for there was very little information, I would learn later, in his records.

Debbie ushered Gordon into the office and asked if she could get him coffee. He refused the offer. Doctor Little stood an offered his hand. That was when I caught a glimpse of the man for a few seconds before he moved away from my view. The man made no offer of his hand when the big man entered the office. He was an impressive fellow. Well over six foot, with wavy grey hair, he had the broad shoulders of an athlete. He wore an expensive pin striped business suit; he carried his black fedora in his right hand.

"Doctor, my name is Gordon Wilbanks, father of Jason Wilbanks. I'm sure you remember the name."

"Yes, I do Mr. Wilbanks. I'm sorry for your loss. What can I do for you?

Well, to begin with, I have learned from the police here that Jason was discharged from his training program here and I want to know why. And why he would shoot a sixteen high school student?"

''The first part of your question I can answer, Doctor Little began. The second part, I cannot. He was removed from the training program for violation of Hospital Rules. A rather serious violation I'm afraid; Fraternization with an employee who was a teenage employee and a minor. We talked to Jason Before he was let go and he admitted that he had violated Hospital Rules but that he meant the young lady no harm. Any further information on the matter will have to come from the police who are investigating the death of you son.

"Who was the young lady that he was fraternizing with, Doctor?"

''You know I can't tell you that Mr. Wilbanks. All I can tell you is that she was a minor,"

"You may as well tell me, for I'm a very wealthy man Doctor and have many connections. I will find out who she was, one way or another."

"Mr. Wilbanks, I know you are a wealthy man, but my advice to you is to let the police do their work. Contrary to popular belief by outsiders, our State Police are very good, and if you go poking your nose into their business, you may need a plastic surgeon to fix it. You may also find out things that will only bring more heartache to you and your family."

Gordon, Wilbanks got up to leave, but had to get in a few more choice words before he left the office.

"You haven't heard the last of this from me Doctor, and for your information, I don't have the least bit of confidence in your State Police, city police, or any other law enforcement agency in the state of Mississippi.

"Guess that means they don't need to come to your bank for a loan, huh?"

"Funny Man! Real funny Doctor! Mark my words, you haven't heard the last of this."

Gordon Wilbanks turned and told the Doctor that he was staying at the Blue Moon Motel on highway 45.

"If you change your mind, I'll be there for a few days until I get to the bottom of this." I'm not leaving until I get answers."

"Don't wait by the phone, Mr. Wilbanks."

When Gordon Wilbanks had left the building, Doctor Little called his friend Justin Webb to let him know that Wilbanks was there asking questions about his son, and he wondered if he should call the state police to let them know what was going on.

"I think that would be a good idea, Doc. You should give them a heads up."

Two hours later Gene Edwards. Chief detective for the Mississippi State police knocked on door 114 of the Blue Moon Motel. Wilbanks opened the door in just his pants and undershirt, a half-smoked stogie in his mouth.

"Mr. Wilbanks?"

"Yes, who's asking?"

"Gene Edwards, Mr. Wilbanks. Pulling his credentials to show Wilbanks his Mississippi State police badge.

"What do you want detective. Am I double parked? Wilbanks grunted."

"Would like to talk to you down at our office by the courthouse."

"Can't we talk here."

"Could." But would rather do it at the office." You can come voluntarily, or I can place you under arrest. I don't think you want that and neither do I. We are currently investigating the apparent suicide of your son and we very much want to finish our investigation without interference from you or anyone else. Interfering with a police investigation is a serious charge."

"Ok, he said, let me grab a shirt."

Ten minutes later the two men entered the offices of the Mississippi State Police. Gene Edwards offered Wilbanks a chair and asked if he would like something to drink.

"No thanks, let's just get to the matter at hand," Wilbanks said.

"Very well, Mr. Wilbanks, let me get my assistant in here and we will get to the issue at hand."

In a few moments Angela Winston, a tall blond woman came into the room and took a seat in a padded chair beside Lieutenant Edwards. She handed him a thick file.

"Angela this is Mr. Gordon Wilbanks, from Nashville. He's the father of Jason Wilbanks, the young man whose case we've been investigating."

Angela nodded with a slight smile, as Gene opened the file.

"Mr. Wilbanks, Edwards began, we know that you have spread word around the Tupelo Police Department that you are willing to pay a substantial reward to anyone who would furnish you the names of the students that Jason shot. And just in case you may doubt that Jason did it, you can forget It. The victims knew their attacker and there were neighbors who witnessed the crime. We have also done extensive background work on this case and we know this is not the first time Jason had taken advantage of minors. In at least two of those cases we have substantial information that you may have been complicit.

"That's a damn lie. Where did you hear such slander, he shouted?"

Wilbanks, red faced started to stand but was told to sit by Detective Winston. Wilbanks sat.

"Further, Detective Edwards added, we have more young women who may come forward and if so, that would not be a pretty picture for you or your family. Jason has a sibling and how about your wife and, I might add, your own standing in Nashville. I doubt that the bank would want to keep a CEO who had been charged with a felony."

"You have suffered a terrible loss Mr. Wilbanks. I am advising you not to make it worse by stirring the waters. Leave Mississippi today and don't come back. Go home to the rest of your family. We are prepared to release a statement saying that the case was a suicide, most likely from pressures from his studies, and the case is closed, unless further evidence comes to light."

Gordon Wilbanks left the office. He was angry but didn't want to get in trouble with the two law officers. They seemed plenty tough, and not people to get sideways with. He returned to the Blue Moon Motel, packed his travel bag, and took the highway north toward Tennessee.

An unmarked Ford sedan followed his car until he left Mississippi and crossed the state line into Tennessee. The Ford sedan stopped and watched until the taillights of the Wilbanks car disappeared into the darkness. Teardrops ran down his face and his heart ached for his son, but for the first time in many years he realized how wrong he had been to try and protect his son, rather than help him get psychological help for the boy. Now it was too late

"I sure hate to see a man like Wilbanks get away without being punished, Detective Angela Winston said. He knows he was complicit in how his son ended up. My daddy had an old saying that trash flows downstream from the source. "Like father, like son," she added.

"He's suffered plenty, already, Edwards said and will carry guilt with himself for a very long time, and the teenagers here won't have to worry about the Wilbanks. Everyone here has suffered enough, Edwards said closing the file, and handing it to Detective Winston. Anything you want to add to the file?"

"Nope, sounds about right to me. I don't trust the arrogant Ass, but the case can always be reopened if we need to."

"Detective Edwards smiled when Angela left his Office. He knew that Wilbanks did not want to cross her for she e was not only very pretty and smart, she was also a master of Martial Arts, and could bench press Wilbanks with one hand, He was glad to have her as a partner,

*"Patience is a virtue, I suppose, but when does
too much patience just become cowardice?"*

-RC: From my notebook

27

Doctor Little Likes Bonnie

The bus is running

DOCTOR LITTLE, WHO USUALLY stopped by to have
coffee, at least once a week with Pappy at the lumber
yard, asked Pappy one morning if he could have private
words with him. He and Pappy had become good
friends and liked to josh with each other. The Doctor
was an educated man and Pappy hadn't finished high
school, but the Doctor valued Pappy's opinion on just
about everything that didn't have anything to do with
medicine. Pappy told him sure. Pappy had a feeling that
the doctor had something important on his mind, and
the two men walked outside the showroom and strolled
down the street toward Main.

"What's on your mind Doc? You been fidgeting like girl on her first date."

"AC, the doctor said, you know what close friends Wayne and Bonnie and I were through the years, and I would not want to do anything to tarnish my relationship with Bonnie, but I've been thinking of asking her if she would consider having dinner with me some night. You know, kind of like a date or something. What do you think? Too soon for such a thing? Am I trying to get on a bus that ain't running? I sure do like that woman, but I've got no idea about how she feels about me. I haven't had much time for romance in my life and know nothing about how women feel about such matters the doctor said."

Pappy looked at the doctor with cocked head and a little grin.

"A date or something? he said. There is no such thing as a date or something, it's a date or its not, and you say you don't understand how women feel about romantic matters huh? Well join the damn no-clue club, where every other man on the face of the planet is a full-fledged member," Pappy told him! He said, "I never knew a man that understood a woman. If one told me he did I sure wouldn't loan the fellow ten cents. But the only way I know to find out if the bus is running is to ask the driver, Pappy told him. She's the only one who can say if it is or if it's not. Personally, I think it would be a great thing for you both. Bonnie is a fine lady and neither of you are kids anymore. Why don't you go in the office there and just ask her flat out? She's by herself. If I hear shots, I'll call the ambulance," Pappy grinned.

"What if she does reject me? the doctor asked.

`"Well, I reckon you just keep at it or leave town, Pappy said, grinning.

"Thanks a lot, you've done a world of good for my confidence," the doctor groaned.

"Glad to help," Pappy said, grinning. The two men then turned and walked back toward the office. Doctor Little went inside the office with Bonnie and closed the door behind him. Pappy was smiling.

"Don't matter how old you are, AC thought, asking a woman out on a date for the first time is plumb damn scary. The fear of being rejected by someone you care about weighs hard on a man's confidence." That first night he went to see Allie he had walked up to her house only to find her whole family on the front porch. He had thoughts of taking to the woods. He was sure glad his courage had held.

Pappy remembered too how pretty she was that first time he went to Allie's house to ask her out. He nearly backed out two or three times on the way over there to her place. He also remembered how he felt when she had said yes. It was like a huge weight had been lifted.

He didn't hear any shots when the doctor entered the office. Ten minutes later the doctor emerged and waved at Pappy as he was leaving.

"The bus is running," he, said grinning at Pappy as he left the store.

Anna was still very sore from the gunshot wound but the bandage was now gone, and she was looking forward to the outing. Charlie and Robert Lewis were ecstatic. Anna seemed to be getting past the trauma of the ordeal that she had gone through with being shot by Jason Wilbanks and the experience of the attempted rape. She was getting back to normal. Charlie, on the other hand had not. She was still having nightmares and would often cry out in her sleep.

Most mornings I would wake up with Charlie cuddled beside me with her favorite bear. She sometimes would be sobbing. I would put my arm around her, and she would soon be sleeping peacefully. It concerned Momma some that Charlie did not come to her bed for comfort rather than coming to me. All Charlie would say about it was that being close to me made her feel safe. That made me feel good, that Charlie cared that much for me but Momma worried that she was becoming too attached to me, for I too would be leaving home in just another year. My plans were still to attend school, and Law school at Ole Miss which was only fifty miles away and I would be able to spend weekends at home. I could still help Pappy some at the lumber yard and get to spend time with the kids.

Willy was getting ready to graduate from High school in a few days and would be leaving for Officer

Candidate School at Lackland Air Force Base in Texas the fifteenth of May. Willy had finished at the top of his class and had College scholarship offers from all over but had heard nothing from the Newly formed Air Force Academy in Colorado Springs. He still held out hope though. If he was accepted, he would be a member of the first graduating class at the newly established Military School. He had recommendation from U.S. Senator Johnson Carter who was a Tupelo resident. Dr. Little and his High school administrators had given him glowing recommendations too.

When Easter weekend came, Pappy decided to close the lumber yard and give the employees Saturday and Sunday off and Pappy wanted to go to Big Flat to See Grandpa and Aunt Zula. Grandpa had not met Charlie and Robert, and Willy would be leaving for Officer Training School in Texas soon, so Pappy and Momma wanted us to all get together before he left.

Grandpa was not doing well according to the letters Aunt Zula had written Momma and that was bearing on Pappy some though he never complained. Aunt Zula thought a visit from Pappy and the boys might do the old man good. Charlie and Robert were disappointed that we were not going to the farm for a picnic, but Momma promised she would pack them a picnic lunch and they would stop along the way to Big Flat for lunch.

Momma Suggested to Pappy that He should let Willy and me drive my truck to Big Flat and invite

Anna and Jessie to go over and spend Saturday. She said
If we left early, we could have lunch at Grandpas and the
boys could have the girls back in Tupelo at a reasonable
hour in the afternoon. Pappy agreed that was a good
idea. He thought Grandpa would enjoy having all the
young people in the house—especially- Robert Lewis
and Charlie. Pappy even agreed that the kids could take
Squat along too. Squat liked to ride with Pappy in the
old truck.

> *"Down a dusty old road to a dry creek bottom'*
> *By fields of sage grass where we used to grow cotton*
> *There stands an old homeplace back*
> *there in the shade of the trees*
> *It used to be home for my Momma and Pappy*
> *my sisters and brothers and me."*
> *- RC*

28

Trip to Big Flat

Anna and Jessie meet Grandpa

MRS. OWENS AND JESSIE'S parents agreed for the girls to go long if we could have them home on Saturday afternoon before dark. Anna was excited to get to go to Big Flat, because I had talked so much about it. Charlie and Robert Lewis were overjoyed to get to take any road trip.

We picked the girls up just after seven that morning, Both Anna and Jessie were dressed in jeans and black and white loafers, high collar white shirts tied at the waist They could have been sisters for they were both beautiful and about the same size, Annabelle only slightly taller. "How lucky could two brothers be," I wondered.

Pappy had given both Willy and me ten dollars for our work that week, so we treated Anna and Jessie to breakfast at the Natchez Trace Restaurant before taking highway 6 West toward Pontotoc. We stopped at the Texaco service station, in Pontotoc and put five gallons of gas in the old truck. It cost Willy and me fifty cents each. Willy grumbled about having to put in his half, but Jessie told him to pay up or she would. Willy turned red.

We topped the ridge overlooking Big Flat just before nine thirty in the morning, but we knew it would be a good while before Pappy made it, since he never drove over twenty miles per hour. For most folks it was an hour's drive but for Pappy it would be two hours before they made it to grandpa's place. We drove the girls through the little village of Big Flat, showing them the old school and where some of our Aunts and Uncles lived, Grandpa's store, and the two other mercantile, the tiny post office and pointing out anything that we thought might be of interest to them. We drove them down to the river showing them the Parker place that we used to farm. I drove up by the ancient necropolis on the ridge above Big Flat where most of my ancestors were laid to rest. The cemetery was surrounded by huge oak and sweetgum and tall pines it was quiet beautifully peaceful setting for a cemetery. We drove by grandpa's and Uncle Otto's old store, where I had spent many hours. The windows and door were boarded over, and grass and weeds grew on the dirt floor beneath the portico, The old *Lion Oil* sign still stood as a landmark as it had for many years. I supposed it would only be a short time before it was in someone's antique or junk store but did not express my thoughts.

"I guess some day that's where I'll be, but I'll be among some great people."

"They may not let you in Willy," Panned. We drove away,

When we figured the girls had seen about all of nothing they could stand, we headed back toward Grandpa's house and parked the old truck under the big oak trees to the East side of the old house. We barely had the engine turned off when Grandpa and Aunt Zula came out the side door. Aunt Zula drying her hands on her apron tail and grandpa right behind her on his cane and the old crooked stem pipe in his mouth. Grandpa didn't look much different than the last time I had seen him. I suspected Aunt Zula might have been exaggerating his detreating health just to get Pappy to come for a visit. They both welcomed the girls with open arms, hugging them both like they were long lost kin folk.

Aunt Zula was talking ninety to nothing, herding us all toward the house where she had tea cookies and lemonade waiting. She had lunch on the table waiting for us, but she insisted we eat cookies and drink lemonade while she set the table. The girls took to grandpa and Aunt Zula right off for the two liked to pick and jest and grandpa had them rolling in laughter in no time.

The old house hadn't changed too much. Pappy had paid to have indoor plumbing and had installed a new bathroom in the old room where Willy and I had slept and called our room. That addition was more for Aunt Zula than for grandpa. Pappy had also sent over a new refrigerator for the kitchen and had ceiling fans installed in the kitchen and the bedrooms.

Aunt Zula had fried chicken for our lunch along with creamed potatoes and gravy and fried okra. She also had made banana pudding for dessert. Anna and Jessie ate small servings of everything, but Willy and I ate like starved porkers.

When we had finished eating, we all went to the big back porch and Grandpa lit up his old pipe and we sat and talked until we heard Pappy's old truck pull into the yard. Everyone went out to greet Momma, Pappy, and the kids.

"You finally made it, Grandpa grinned, was about to give up on you."

"If we'd driven any slower, we would have been backing up, Charlie panned. I could have made better time on Robert's tricycle."

Pappy just laughed.

Squat didn't want to get out of the truck, but with Pappy's coaxing finally jumped out and started peeing on every bush in the yard. It wasn't long until he was roaming and investigating everything on the place. Grandpa had a few chickens in a pen behind the house and Squat checked it out. When he stuck his nose through the wire fence, the big Rhode- Island Rooster fluffed his wings and ran toward him. Squat nearly had a heart attack running backward and howling at the big Red. We all had a good laugh at Squat's expense. Me and Willy knew a lot about big red roosters though. They were means as a Braham Bull and we had been chased more than once by the critters. The only time I had any use for the Reds was when they were cooked and on a dinner platter with Momma's cornbread dressing.

Grandpa had to hug the children and Anna and Jessie. Grandpa had a way with strangers and always made friends easily. He soon had them by the hands leading them around. Grandpa had aged some and was noticeably more feeble. He had always used a cane as far back as I could remember but now, he had to use it to push himself up when he stood. His acritude was still positive and he love to laugh and tell stories. Charlie and Robert took to him right off.

Aunt Zula carried on about the children like she had never seen a child before. She completely forgot that she had other guests. She wanted to know if they were hungry, and of course Robert Lewis said he was, so she took him by the hand and led him toward the kitchen. Charlie joined Anna and Jessie and headed to the back porch. Robert dove into the fried chicken. He ate everything except the tablecloth. Charlie ate a little banana pudding but was in a hurry to get back with Anna and Jessie. Girls!

"Grandpa's Barn"

29

The Piglets

Baby chicks

AFTER A WHILE, GRANDPA told Charlie and Robert he had something he wanted to show them and told Anna and Jessie to come along too. Grandpa led the way down the high steps, to the pathway by the well and through the gate that led to the old barn. Squat following close behind, sniffing everything in sight. He smelled things a city dog had never smelled before.

Beside the barn was a hog pen with four large black and white Hampshire shoats and a dozen or so smaller pigs. It didn't smell like a flower garden, but the pen was clean, and the pigs were fat and slick. We walked on past the pen into the barn and Grandpa opened the door to the first stall.

"Watch where you step," Grandpa cautioned.

A huge mother, black and white Hampshire sow lay stretched out on fresh hay and ten baby pigs were suckling. There were ohs and ahas from the girls and Charlie and Robert Earl. Grandpa stepped over the threshold and knelt beside the big sow and rubbed her head and scratched her back. Grandpa took a half ear of corn from his jumper pocket and hand fed the big sow and rubber her all over her back. She made no attempt to move.

"Who wants to hold a piglet," he asked.

Charlie's hand shot up!

Grandpa picked up one of the piglets and handed it to Charlie. The pig let out a loud squeal when he was taken from the sow and his feeding.

"Hold him tight now, grandpa said, he is gonna wiggle some-- not used to being held.

"Charlie took the pig and held it firmly. It squealed again.

"He's a squealer ain't he, Robert offered."

"Yeah he don't like us taking away his dinner. You can stick your finger in his mouth and let him suck on it and he'll settle down. Scratching his back will help too."

The piglet settled down quickly, and Anna and Jessie asked if they could hold one. Grandpa handed each one a piglet they cuddled the piglet on their back and rubbed their stomach and let the babies suckle their finger,

"You want to hold one, Robert?" Grandpa asked.

"No, but can I come in with you and pet the big hog?"

"Sure, come on in, she's just a big old pet; follows me round like a hound dog."

I had to hold Squat to keep him from going into the pin with Robert. He was whining and wanting to check out the piglets.

Robert had no fear of anything and was soon rubbing the big sow all over.

"I bet I could ride that hog," Robert said.

"You're an idiot, Charlie, said. You can't ride a hog.

"Could if grandpa put a saddle on her," he retorted.

The girls laughed at the thought, and how quick-witted Robert was.

After a while grandpa took the piglets from the girls and placed them back with their momma, stepped out of the stall and walked down the barn hallway to the tack room. There was a heavy smell of cow manure, but the girls did not complain, they just followed Grandpa. Aunt Zula had a brooder house set up with a hundred baby chickens. The children were wide eyed. They had never seen baby chicks before.

"That's a lot of damn chickens Robert said, shaking his head. Ain't never seen that many chickens in one place before. They stink too, don't they,"

"Yeah they do." Grandpa said. Want to hold one?"

"Yeah, they don't bite, do they?"

"They don't bite but they might peck a little.'

"They got peckers?" Robert asked.

"I looked at Willy and grinned,"

"They're called beaks." Grandpa smiled."

Charlie held one too,

"They feel so soft," she commented.

Grandpa took the baby chicks and put them back in the brooder and we all returned to the house. Pappy was stretched in the porch swing with his hat over his face, he was sound asleep. We ate more tea cookies and drank more lemonade It was getting late and we had to get back on the road back to Tupelo. I sure didn't want to get sideways with Mrs. Owens.

When Anna and I were alone for a minute she said, "I wish we had more time. I love this place. I see now why you love this so. I hope someday we can live in a place like this she said." She put her arm around my waist and pulled me close. This was the first time in a while she had suggested a future life with us together.

We said our goodbye's to Grandpa and Aunt Zula and took the dusty road over the ridge with the sun at our back until we reached the Dogtown road. The old road was half blacktop and half gravel. A project that had been started years before but never finished. I never heard anyone complain about the road though. Folks around Big Flat were used to making do with what they had and never seemed the worse off for it. Pappy had said that a bad road was better than no road and riding was better than walking.

On the Shiloh cutoff road, an old man in faded overalls flagged me to a stop. He was big around the middle and obviously wore nothing under the overalls. He had a bush of grey hair and a weeks' worth of whiskers.

"I got me a flat tire, and ain't got no jack that works. Wouldn't happen to have one would you?" he asked.

The girls looked a little worried until the man said, "aren't you boys AC Calloway's sons? I'm Jake Russell, he said, offering his hand.

"We are, I answered, taking his calloused hand. Do you know our Pappy?"

'Yep, he said, I farmed some cotton land down there in the river bottom next to his place a few years ago. I heard he had moved to the city."

"yeah, we been in Tupelo, near 'bout four years. I said taking the jack from under the seat of my old truck. Willy helped me change the old man's tire on his flatbed truck. He took two crumpled dollar bills from his bib pocket and handed it to me.

"I couldn't take your money, I told him. Pappy wouldn't like that. Supposed to help people on the road when they're in trouble."

"Well, many thanks," he said, as we climbed back in the old truck and continued toward Tupelo. Anna put her arm around me and pulled me to her. In the rear-view mirror, I could see the old man getting in his truck in a cloud of dust we were leaving behind.

I could not help remembering the day we had left Big Flat and moved to Tupelo. It had only been four years, but it seemed like a lifetime. I loved the little hamlet but didn't figure I would ever live there again. My future, I believed would be with Anna in Tupelo.

30

Charlie Falls Ill

Doctor Little helps

PAPPY SENT SQUAT BACK to Tupelo with me and Willy, for he didn't want to tie him up and didn't want to take a chance on him getting into someone's chicken house. Squat was a city dog and did not know country manners. Squat didn't seem to mind. He liked to ride and didn't much care who the driver was. He stood in the back of the truck with his head around the cab and saliva streaming from his long tongue as we traveled along.

We pulled into Tupelo just after five o'clock, with the evening sun rays coming through the back window of my old truck. The girls said the trip was great and wanted to go back sometime soon. I was glad that Anna enjoyed the farm animals for she had been raised a City girl in Tupelo. Life in Big flat could be a shock to the system if you didn't have an open mind. I was happy that Pappy had put in the indoor bathroom. City girls were known to get the hives from having to use an outdoor facility. Some even fainted from the smell.

Momma and Pappy and the kids got back to Tupelo on Sunday afternoon just before dark. The kids had really had a good time and Robert couldn't stop talking about the baby pigs. Charlie, however, came home not feeling well. Momma thought she had some sort of a virous and made chicken soup. I think Momma thought chicken soup would cure the black plague, for she made it any time one of us was sick with a cold or a virus. During the night Charlie had started throwing up and was having chills and fever. She also had a serious cough. Momma and Pappy were clearly worried about her. I called Anna to let her know that Charlie was very sick. Mrs. Owens answered the phone and told me that Anna was also not feeling well, but was not throwing up, but was nauseated and was running a fever.

The next morning, Charlie's condition had not improved, so Pappy called Doctor Little to see if he could see her. Pappy was told by Doctor Little's housekeeper that the Doctor was with Bonnie Purnell. Pappy rang her number. Bonnie confirmed that the Doctor was there and handed him the phone.

Doctor Little asked Pappy several questions and after a short conversation, Doctor Little said he would come by in just a few minutes, that he was Just getting ready to leave Bonnie's place. Pappy hung up the phone and sat down at the table with Momma and me and Robert Lewis. After a while. Momma got up and put on a pot of coffee and then sat down and waited for the doctor.

The doctor pulled into our drive ten minutes later. He came straight up the steps with his medicine bag in his hand. He was dressed in jeans and a sport shirt. Unusual for the doctor I thought, but since he had been seeing Miss Bonnie, he had started dressing more casually.

Charlie was sleeping now but her fever was high. The doctor examined her, listening to her heart and lungs with his stethoscope. Next, he took her temperature, and shook his head.

We better get her over to the hospital. Her temperature is 106 and I want to get blood sample. Probably a virus but I want to be sure."

The next morning Charlie's condition had not improved, and her breathing had become labored. She was placed in the ICU Unit at the hospital Her condition had become critical. I had driven Robert Lewis over to stay with Bonnie Purnell who would watch after him until after I had opened the lumber yard for Pappy. Pappy had been allowing me to take on greater responsibility since Mr. Purnell had passed. Mrs. Purnell was also spending less time at the company since she and Doctor Little were seeing each other. Pappy had hired more help, but the new employees had not learned the ropes very well, and we were all stretched thin. Mrs. McCullough was a God send to Pappy. She had practically taken over the daily operation of the Tupelo business. I had just opened the doors and was preparing the cash register when the phone rang. It was Mrs. Owens, Anna's mother.

"Zack, Anna is very sick and I'm taking her to the emergency room at the Hospital. She has a high fever and I can't seem to get it down, and she is also having some trouble breathing."

"That's the same symptoms that Charlie had," I responded. I can't come over right now but as soon as we can get some extra help, I'll be over. I said.

"Hurry," she said.

I was really worried now. I remembered the conversation that we had once had about God and what his plans were for our lives and how worried Anna was about that. I asked Mrs. McCullough if Naught could help with delivers for a few days. There was only a month left in school for the year. She said his grades were very good and he could take a couple of days to help until we could see how Charlie was going to do. She promised to call Naught's principal at school and explain what was going on. He was over at the store in half an hour. He had become a great friend and he would do just about anything to help Pappy. He would help with deliveries and loading and unloading supplies. Mrs. McCullough would take over in the showroom.

It was mid-morning before I could get to the Hospital to see about Anna and Charlie. I reached the parking lot just as Mrs. Owens was pulling into the emergence room area. I parked and headed toward her car when Mrs. Owens got out of the car and went to the driver's side to help Anna. Two nurses came out with a gurney and wheeled Anna into the Hospital. I parked Mrs. Owen's Car for her and then followed them into the Emergency Room. Mrs. Owens was very distraught. Tears running down her face. I went to her and put my arm around her. She was scared, and so was I.

"What is wrong with Anna? "I asked.

"I don't know she answered. She stared feeling bad last night, and just kept getting worse," She said. Started throwing up about two hours ago."

31

Doctors Await Diagnosis

Girls isolated

MRS. OWENS FILLED OUT papers to get Anna admitted while the nurses began giving Anna oxygen. Minutes later the Nurse in charge told Mrs. Owens that they were taking Anna to the ICU area, until they could determine the cause of Anna's illness. They would not permit me into the ICU area, but Momma and Pappy were sitting in the waiting area. They had been told nothing until this point. They were both obviously distressed. I sat down beside them and then Mrs. Owens came into the waiting area,"

"Any news, she asked Momma as she sat down beside her."

"Nothing yet, she said, but Doctor Little said he would be out shortly. It was, however more than an hour before he came into the area."

"What's going on," Pappy asked. What's wrong with the girls."

"Not sure, he said, but the symptoms are like the Polyimides virus.

"What's that?" Pappy asked."

"Polio, "The Doctor replied. Now that's how we're treating them as a general precaution. The girls are going to be isolated from the rest of the hospital population until we can be certain of the diagnosis. We should have a firm diagnosis before the end of the day, the Doctor said.

"Are they going to die? will she be paralyzed?" Momma asked.

"I can't answer those question, Mrs. Calloway. But just because she has the virus, doesn't mean it will actually be fatal, but you know, this disease is epidemic, and can be deadly, but just recently there has been some hopeful results with new serums. But contracted at the present time there is no cure. I urge you not to grieve. The girls will get the best of care and both are healthy and strong.

Right now, regardless of the diagnosis, the girls are very sick. We are working to reduce their fever and making sure they get plenty of liquids and nourishment. We will notify you of the test results as soon as possible.

During the day there seemed to be little change in their condition. Dr. Little recommended an Iron lung for Charlie's breathing difficulties were much worse than Anna's. Iron lungs filled one wing of the hospital due to the epidemic nature of the Polio disease. Only one patient, to this point, had been diagnosed as having the disease. Tupelo had not been spared, but the survival rate was very good due to very good diagnosis and treatment. Family members were not allowed into the Polio Ward.

Only Nurses and medical staff wearing special clothing were allowed in the ICU. Waiting rooms were nearly empty, which was a good sign that the disease had not spread through the city. The thought of Anna and Charlie being perhaps crippled, or dyeing scared me, and I wondered why Willy, and Jessie and I had not contacted the disease, since we had all been together so much.

I called the Lumber Yard to see if Willy was OK and if he had talked to Jessie. Willy had been called to go by the National Guard Armory and was to be gone for about an hour, so I called Jessie directly and asked her if she was ok, She said that she was fine but wanted to know if she and Penelope could come and see. I told them that they had better wait, for they would not be allowed to see Anna. I told them that the doctors said they would have a firm diagnosis by the day's end and that I would let them know what they said as soon as I knew something.

I then told Momma and Pappy that I was leaving for a little while and would be back to stay with Momma so that Pappy could check on things at the business. Pappy cocked his head and then nodded his accent. I drove straight over to Jefferson and once again walked down the tree shaded sidewalk to the steps of the old church. I prayed for Charlie and Anna, not really knowing how to pray but just asked God to make them well. For some reason I felt a chill on my neck even though the weather was very warm. In a few moments I raised my head from my prayers and Pastor Luke stood before me.

"Back again," he said,

It was not like a question, just a statement, like he wanted me to know that he was paying attention to my actions.

"Yeah, I said, I didn't know what else to do. Two of the people I love the most in this world are very sick—maybe dying and I can't do nothing about it."

"Maybe by being here, you've already done something very important."

"Yeah, and what would that be Preacher?" I asked.

Pastor Luke didn't answer directly but asked; "Mind if I sit beside you, Zack?"

"I nodded for him to sit."

Pastor Luke was a tall man, a good four inches taller than me, but he had a very kind demeanor and an easy manner about him.

"Maybe you've already done a lot more than you know" he said.

I kind of let out a soft laugh. "And what, exactly, have I done."

"By just coming here you have shown that you believe that there is a power beyond yourself, that is in charge of human events," he said, placing his big hand on my shoulder. None of us mortals can ever know, with certainty, what tomorrow will bring. But rest assured, that God knows your thoughts and hears your prayers. Not even angels know God's plans."

"Continue your thoughts, Zack, it is time for me to go, but I'm usually around if you need me just come here and I will know."

He raised his long body off the steps, dusted off the seat of his black suit and started toward the street.

"See ya, Preacher," I said as he walked away.

He never looked back but raised his hand in an indication that he had heard me. Soon he went into the shadows once again. I liked Pastor Luke, but he was plum dang spooky.

I returned to the hospital just before five o'clock to relieve Pappy. The doctors had not yet been by to inform us of the diagnosis. I took a seat by Momma and waited. An hour later Willy came through the door with Robert Lewis. Robert ran to Momma's arms and she pulled him to her. He clung to her like he never wanted to let go.

No doubt that Momma and Robert Lewis had bonded more than Momma and Charlie, but I kind of understood that, for a long time Charlie had essentially been like a mother to Robert, calling all the shots, but now that Momma was in charge Charlie had been feeling she was losing Robert.

I saw that Momma knew all that, but Charlie was an independent, but scared little girl who was strong willed, and was not going to relinquish her relationship with her brother to anyone. Together they had shared their loss of their father, their mother, and their foster parent, I understood how she felt. Because of their losses, nothing was permanent except her and Robert. Whatever happened in the future Robert was her brother and she would always look out for his interest no matter who their guardians were.

"How is Charlie", he finally asked. She still sick?"

"Yeah," Momma answered but she's going to be Ok. The doctors and nurses are going to take real good care of her."

"Can I see her," he asked with those big blue eyes glistening with tears. "Maybe tomorrow," Momma answered. We don't want you to be sick too, so we're going to have to wait until the doctors tell us it's alright. He then laid his head across Momma's shoulder and in minutes he was sound asleep. Momma held him for a while and then laid him down on the couch beside her and covered him with her shawl. He slept peacefully until the doctors came in to announce the diagnosis.

32

Good News

MOMMA TALKS

Doctor Little and his Nurse came into the waiting area just after seven 0'clock. The doctor sat down on a chair in front of Momma and Mrs. Owens the Nurse stood beside while he talked.

"I've got some good news for you Mrs. Calloway and Mrs. Owens. The virus is not Polio, as we thought it might be but rather a strand of influenza called type B. Some of the symptoms are similar, and that's why we were so cautious. This strand of flu is a very dangerous virus but fortunately we can treat it. We have contacted the Medical Center in Memphis and a carrier will deliver the serum before morning. We have been watching both girls carefully and their breathing has improved somewhat, but they are still very sick. Like most strands of the flu, we believe it will run its course in a week or so. Until their fever subsides, however, we are going to recommend that the girls be kept in isolation and have no visitors. I recommend that you go home and try to rest tonight. I have given instructions for the nurse on duty to call you if there is any change.

Mrs. Owens, however. Refused to go home for the night and asked me if I would stay until she could go home and pick up some personal items. I said that I would and told her to grab her a bite to eat while she was out. Momma wanted to stay too but Mrs. Owens urged her to go home and take care of Robert. Pappy picked up Robert and carried him out to the truck. I watched from the window as he and Momma climbed into the old truck and headed for home. I stayed until Mrs. Owens returned and we sat in the waiting room together and talked for a few minutes. Anna was a mirror image of her mother, both beautiful and smart and straight forward in their manner, and prone to speak their mind. Their trust of others never came automatically or easy, it had to be earned. I liked Mrs. Owens a lot but how she really felt about me, I was not completely and firmly sure. I had disappointed her once, and like a dog that had once been prone to bite, you are not quite convinced that they won't it again. I felt I had made some progress and that she wanted to trust me but was not yet ready to pat me on the head. I was surprised when she began to open to me.

I have been wrong about you Zack, she said, looking right into my eyes. I believe your motives toward Anna have always been honorable. You have proven your love and dedication to her. She loves you and I know you love her. When she comes through this illness, I have decided you and Anna can carry on a normal courtship without interference from me. She then reached and took my chin in her hand and stared at me and smiled, "but watch your step with my daughter. Buster."

"Please don't worry Mrs. Owens, Anna is the only girl I have ever wanted. I will always do right by her. Someday I want to marry Anna—when the time comes and if she wants to marry me, I promise that you will be the first person we tell. I don't know when that time will come but I hope it won't be too long. We both want to go to college. I want to be a lawyer and Anna wants to be a doctor so it may have to be a while."

Dr. Little came to the waiting room just before seven and told us that the girls were doing better now, but was still very sick, but that Charlie's breathing had improved enough that she was being taken off the assisted breathing machine.

"The Iron Lung, you mean?"

"That's right, but she will remain in isolation. We do not want the virus to spread. In addition to the flu virus, however, Charlie has also contacted Pneumonia.

We have been treating her with antibiotics and she is responding well. As I said, she is now breathing on her own, and her fever is down. I will check her again around ten tonight and will let you know when she might have visitors."

Doctor left to continue his rounds and I left Mary Owens and went home for some much-needed rest. Pappy had dropped Momma and Robert Lewis and went back to the lumber yard to catch up on phone calls and other business. I could tell by Momma's demeanor that she was plainly worried. Not just Charlie but Pappy too. She fixed me a plate of fried eggs and hot biscuits while I took a quick bath and then she sat with me while I ate. When I finished, I stood and was getting ready for bed, Momma stood up and came to me and hugged me."

"I love you Zachery. I haven't told you that lately, and you have grown up so fast and we have had so much happening that I feel like I've neglected you and Willy and your father."

She was crying now, and tears were also in my eyes. I didn't know how to comfort my own mother, and she had spent her life-giving comfort to her whole family. I just hugged her and turned and went to my room without further words. Sleep was a long time coming, however, for my mind was filled with thoughts of Annabelle Owens, Charlie. Pastor Luke, Mary Owens, and the worry of what tomorrow might bring. Willy was still at the Guard Unit and finally I heard Pappy come through the door and talk to Momma in low whispers. He then came to the door of my room and looked in.

"You ok son?" He asked.

"Good Pappy, I said. I turned out the light and slept.

33

The Girls Recover

School year is over

ANNA AND CHARLIE REMAINED in isolation until Thursday, and then were assigned private rooms and could have visitors. I went to see them the first thing Thursday morning. Kissed both of them and they clung to me, and I didn't want to leave them, but Pappy needed me at the Lumber yard. I promised Charlie I would be back after work and would bring a book and we'd read it together, Charlie liked for me to read to her and comment on what I had read.

Pappy told me that evening that we were moving into the new house on Monday, and Willy would be graduating in a week. Pappy had hired movers to move the furniture into the new house but with the girls he hadn't had much time to help Momma do much packing so he wanted Me and Willy to get our possessions packed and help momma all we could. It was a difficult time with the girls in the hospital and Robert Lewis hanging on to her like a wood tick. Mrs. McCullough sent her boys over to help Momma load boxes of clothes and other items to Pappy's old truck.

Willy had finished at the top of his class and had to give a short speech at graduation. It was plain that unless Charlie and Anna made a fast recovery, they would miss the graduation ceremonies. Willy had earned top athletic honors and had been recruited by several top school but had not heard a thing from the Air Force Academy. He was disappointed but he had been accepted to Officer candidate school and would begin the three-month training program in less than a month.

Thursday afternoon I ran by the City library and picked up a couple of books that I thought Charlie would like and headed to the hospital. They had placed both girls in the same room, so I pulled up a chair between them. Charlie wanted me to get her a Root Beer, but they had none in the vending machines at the Hospital, so I promised I would bring her one the next time I came to see her. I told them that Willy was going to graduate Friday night. They were both disappointed that they would not be able to go. I also told them that we would be moving into our new house over the weekend.

SHATTERED DREAMS

When Friday night came, Pappy, Momma and Robert Lewis drove to the High School auditorium for graduation ceremonies Jessica met us at the entrance and sat by Momma through the exercise. The place was packed and there were more than a hundred students in his graduating class. It seemed like everyone of any importance in Tupelo had to talk. Finally, the droning ended, and Willy gave his speech and accepted his honors. Willy had received scholastic offers from more than a dozen schools, which included Ole Miss, Tennessee, Vanderbilt, Texas, and Michigan. I could tell that he was very nervous, but he made a good talk, giving credit to Momma, Pappy, Grandpa Calloway, and to many teachers and coaches. I was very proud of my brother and so was Momma and Pappy.

I would miss my brother when he left for Texas, but I knew he was following his dream, like we all must do, so I was happy for him. Momma and Jessie cried some, but I knew that they were happy. Pappy showed not much emotion, just winked at me when Willy took his diploma. Pappy would say "Life goes on."

After graduation, visiting hours were over at the hospital, but I picked up a bottle of Root Beer and a milkshake for Anna and took them to the waiting room. Mrs. Owens was there and greeted me with a hug and kiss on the cheek. She told me I was spoiling the girls, but promised to get the drinks to them, I said goodnight to Mary Owens and headed for home. Pappy and Momma were still up and waiting on me when I got home. Momma poured me a glass of milk and I sat with them until Willy came in and sat with us. Robert Lewis was asleep in his bed but woke up when he heard us talking. He went to momma, and she held him to her. But he didn't ask for milk. In minutes he was asleep again.

We talked about Willy's speech he had given and complimented him on how well he did. Willy told us that the date for his reporting to Lackland AFB been changed and he would be leaving a week earlier than first told. He would be leaving on May 15, and would graduate, if thing went according to schedule on August 20. He would start flight training in Biloxi the first of September. He would be on Active duty during this period and if he completed his training successfully, he would be commissioned an officer and remain on active duty if he chose to. Flight training would last at least dix months and maybe longer, depending on the type of Aircraft he was training to fly.

Pappy finally told us that we needed to get some sleep, that movers would be there in the morning at 8 o'clock to move us into the new house. I had mixed emotions about moving to a new place. A lot had happened since we moved to Tupelo—four years had seemed like a lifetime and change was never easy, but I knew that Momma wanted a bigger place for the family. Money and prestige meant nothing to Momma and Pappy, but they had both and all they really wanted was to be close to their family and friends.

Saturday morning, the movers came and had everything loaded and hauled to the new location before noon. Momma had dishes and glassware packed in boxes and me and Willy hauled it over to the new place. We took squat on the last load over and we watched him as he got acquainted with the new place. He didn't seem impressed. Momma showed the workers where she wanted furniture placed and by late afternoon the house had taken pretty good shape. There were still drapes and curtains to hang but the place was livable, and we had beds to sleep in. Momma had bought new living room furniture and a new cook stove and refrigerator. It was a very nice place. I couldn't wait for Charlie and Anna to see the new house after it was furnished. Momma said Bonnie and Mrs. McCullough were going to help her hang curtains on Sunday afternoon after church.

Pappy took us to the City café for supper after the move, so Momma didn't have to cook. Dr, Little and Bonnie joined us. Robert Lewis said that was the first time he had eaten in a café. He wasn't timid about it though and ate everything on his plate and drank two glasses of milk. The boy ate like a hungry wolf, but never gained on ounce. Pappy said he had a hollow leg.

Momma and Pappy had taken to attending Services at the Methodist Church, and occasionally I would go to preaching at the Episcopal church with Anna and her

Mother. Willy usually spent his Sundays at the Armory although Momma pestered him to go to church, Willy resisted, and Pappy told Momma that Willy was old enough to find his own way.

Although I didn't mind going to church, I always felt better just sitting on the steps of the old church and saying a silent prayer. I didn't ever know for sure that God heard my prayers or if he cared one way or the other what I prayed for, but it made me feel better anyway. If God knew what was in my mind and in my heart, what good was telling him, I often wondered. It seemed like a waste of time. Preachers carried on about that a lot, but I wondered if they really knew any more about prayer than I did, or that Squat did, for that matter. I knew that Anna was different about spiritual matters. It was if she was really connected to God and knew that he was watching over everything I did. I hoped that someday I would make that connection for I believed that there was a higher authority than ourselves, and if I could, and I sure wanted to stay on his good side.

> *"If there are no dogs in heaven when I die, I want to go where they went"*
> *-Will Rogers*

34

Squat Leaves Home

Jumping fences

SQUAT WAS PART OF our family: he had been with us since the first day we moved to Tupelo. He had been living under the house by the lumber yard when we moved in, and it was apparent that he was not pleased with our new digs. He missed his old lair under the house behind the lumber yard and he also missed going down to the lumber yard with pappy and following him around all day. That had been his home for five years and although he loved us all, he just couldn't seem to make the new place his home. Some folks say dogs are just stupid critters and can't think. Well, they don't know Squat. We had not been in the new house but three days when Squat got it in his head to go back to the old home.

Squat was a big dog now, black and tan in color, for a hound, he was sleek and pretty. He jumped the five-foot fence around our yard one morning and followed Pappy's old truck to the lumber Yard.

Pappy didn't realize that Squat had followed him until he opened the big gate to the yard. There was Squat right behind him. Squat followed Pappy around until he went inside and then the big hound headed down the road toward the old home place.

Halfway to the old house, Squat stopped and sat down on his haunches and looked toward the old house and whimpered. The house wasn't there! Workers were tearing the old house down and the only thing left standing was part of the floor and foundation. They were making more room for expansion of the lumber yard. Pappy said that Squat sat in the middle of the road for a long time, and watched the workers destroy his old home. At times he would stretch out and lay his head on his front paws and every now and then he would raise his head, look toward the old house, and let out a low growl. Pappy said he tried coaxing him back to the yard, but Squat would just look at him with sad old eyes, look toward the old place and back at Pappy, and bark, as if to say, "Do Something, Dammit, they're tearing my house down!"

Eventually, Squat came to the realization of what was happening and went to the yard and curled up on his old rug that lay beside the office. Mrs. McCullough saw Squat, heard him whimpering, and went out and took him a piece of her ham sandwich that she had brought for lunch. She bent down and patted Squat on the head and scratched his long ears. But Squat was in no mood for condescending behavior.

The next day Squat jumped the fence again, but Pappy was watching for him and pulled over to the curb and let the big dog in the cab with him. From then on, Pappy just took Squat with him when he went to work. Charlie and Robert Earl both missed the old dog, and sometimes Momma would take Robert over to the yard and let him eat lunch with Pappy and Squat. Dog, Boy, and Pappy, would sit on a stack of two by fours and laugh and talk, sharing lunch with the big hound; happiness happening!

Squat soon became accustomed to Pappy's work schedule and never jumped the fence again. Pappy would just say to the dog "We're not going to work today, and the old dog would just wait by the door until one of us came out. He finally made him a new lair underneath the porch that spanned the front of our house. At night sometimes we would hear him bump. We knew he was just making his bed for the night. Pappy said dogs were probably smarter than humans, but God had used good sense in not giving them the ability to talk about it.

35

Charlie is Released

Danger for Anna

CHARLIE WAS RELEASED FROM the hospital on Wednesday. She and Anna had shared a room since they were moved from isolation. She liked for me to read to her and I had gone every night and read to her from Jack London's '*Call of The Wild*.' I would sit on the side of the bed with Anna and she would hold my hand as I read. She would allow me a kiss on the cheek when I said goodnight. I wanted more. I wanted to hold her in my arms and feel the warmth of her body next to mine.

Momma and I picked Charlie up in my old truck just after nine o'clock the next morning, but they did not release Anna. That troubled me some, but she said she was feeling good and hoped they would let her go home later in the day. That didn't happen though. She called me just after noon at the lumber yard to tell me that they were holding her for another day and that two police detectives had been by to ask her some questions, but didn't say what it was all about, but felt like it had to do with the problem with Jason Wilbanks and his suicide.

I didn't have to wait long to get more information on the situation, for ten minutes later the two detectives came through the door of the lumber yard showroom. They asked if there was a place that we could talk in private, and I nodded toward Pappy's office. They went in and took seats beside Pappy's desk, and I sat down behind the desk in Pappy's chair.

"I am detective Gene Edwards, and this is detective Angela Winston, we are with the Mississippi State Police. We investigated the shooting by Jason Wilbanks and his subsequent suicide. This call is a follow-up to that investigation. I'll let detective Winston explain why we're here."

"This morning I received a call from the FBI field office in Nashville. The agent said because of an ongoing investigation in Nashville, that they had developed information they felt that we needed to know. This was not related to our investigation but they felt the information that they had received was very creditable and felt they needed to inform our office, They had information that indicated that Miss Annabelle Owens and yourself might be in danger from a person hired to do you harm. We have not yet been able to verify the information but we're taking no chances. We want you to know that you may be in danger.

I was stunned. "Who in the world would want to harm Annabelle? She would not hurt a sole!"

"'We have some leads that we're looking into, and we have asked Doctor Little to keep Annabelle in the hospital for one more day while we dig deeper. We have posted guards at the hospital and the City police is adding extra security and we will be installing surveillance equipment at her home if Mrs. Owens agrees. That will be a few days though. We believe the focus is mainly on Annabelle and not you, but we want you to call us if you see anything suspicious. We will keep you and your family posted as we look into this matter." Detective Winston said.

"This is all about what happened with Jason Wilbanks isn't it?" I asked.

"Looks that way, but we're not sure at this point. We have sent an agent to Nashville to talk with Jason's father and the FBI agent who called. We want to see if Jason's father may know anything about this," the detective answered.

The two detectives made a few notations in their notebooks and then left the office. I followed them to the door. "Don't worry about me," I said, "Just take care of Anna."

Angela Winston turned and smiled. "Your girl huh?"

I nodded. "Yeah, She's my girl!"

They climbed into the police car and left. I watched until they made the turn on Main street. My heart was racing; worry controlled my thoughts. I couldn't grasp the fact that someone would harm Anna. Pappy always said that good and evil are brothers, born of the same blood with both love and hate coursing through the same veins, "You can never know what might cause a person to go one way or the other."

I went back to work but couldn't think of anything but Anna. I went to the hospital as soon as we closed for the day, but I called Pappy who had been in West Point all day. I told him what had happened. He said for me to be careful and to come home early so we could talk more about it. I was greeted at Anna's door by the largest Police officer I had ever seen in my life. I told him who I was, and he checked on his clipboard for my name and then motioned me in. Anna and her mother sat side by side on her bed. They both smiled when I came in and her mother moved to a chair and motioned for me to sit on the bed by Anna.

"Any news?" I asked, looking at Mrs. Owens.

"Nothing new, except that they are releasing Anna to go home tomorrow. Her grandparents will be up from Columbus tonight, and will stay with us for a few days. I just have to get back to work, I cannot afford to lose my job at the bank."

I nodded that I understood, and asked Mrs. Owens if I could come see Anna while her grandparents were there. She smiled and said it would be fine and added that she thought it was time that they met me. She told me that she had informed the grandparents about the situation with the Police and their concern for Anna's safety.

"Anna's Grandpa is a retired Marine Military Police veteran and I will be glad to have him around for a while," Mrs. Owens said. He's in his sixty's now but he's not someone you would want to tangle with."

"That made me feel much better about Anna's safety. I stayed until visiting hours and then left for home.

36

Advice from Justin T. Webb

Business decisions

WHEN I PASSED BY the Webb Law firm, I noticed that the lights were still on, so I turned at the next street, made a block and parked in front of the building. I went inside, the outer office was empty as expected. I could smell the Cigar smoke as I walked to his office door and knocked.

"Who's there?" came the voice from inside. If you're looking for money, I don't have any. If you're bringing whiskey, come in and visit."

I opened the door and went in smiling. "Don't have any whiskey and don't have any money either. Just wanted to stop and see if you could spare a minute."

Mr. Webb got up and came from behind his usual stack of law books and took my hand and patted me on the back.

"I've always got time for you Zack." he laughed, "You're not one of my better paying clients, but we've sure missed you around here. I know you have been helping your Dad since Wayne died, and I respect you for that. Is there anything I can do to help?" He asked.

"No, don't guess there is but I wanted to let you know what's going on with Anna."

We both sat down, and he laid his cigar aside and we talked for maybe a half an hour.

"I know the police chief well, and the detectives too. They are good dedicated folks and will do their best to keep Anna safe." I'll keep an ear open and let you know if I hear any news."

I stood up to leave, and the lawyer took my hand again. "You still studying for the Bar exam Zack?' he asked.

Yes, I said, when I have spare time. It looks like I might be able to finish my High School credits for graduation by the end of first semester and could enter Ole Miss if I choose, but I haven't decided if I want to do that. Pappy needs my help and I would miss my friends."

"That's a decision you'll have to make Zack, but it would be my advice to stay in high school with your friends. You're seventeen. Plenty of time for college and law school. Enjoy your senior year and all that goes with it, you won't regret it, he smiled.

I said goodnight and headed for home. The lights were still on and Bonnie Purnell's car was at the curb. I pulled in the drive beside Pappy's truck. Parked and went inside. Pappy, Momma and Doctor Little and Bonnie sat at the kitchen table, coffee cups in front of them. Charlie and Robert were already in the bed. Willy was away as usual.

"We've been waiting on you Zack. Pappy said. Why don't you pull up a chair and mom will pour you a glass of milk?"

I sat down and Momma set a glass before me. "What's up, I asked. Looks like a board meeting., I laughed.

"Well, you're not far off, Pappy said. This concern's the business and it therefore it concerns us all. I'm going to let Bonnie tell you what we've been discussing."

Miss Bonnie took a sip of coffee and Began.

"Yesterday, she said, I got a telephone call from a law firm in Jackson that represents a group of investors in the timber and lumber business that are interested in buying our company and our stores in Columbus and West Point. They have made a cash offer which is substantial. We have practically no debt on the Columbus and West Point stores and only a minimal amount on the business here in Tupelo."

"What about the farm and the apartments, Pappy?"

"They're not interested in the apartments or the farm, he said. Only the lumber business and supply business."

"What about all our employees," I asked. Would they lose their jobs if you sold?"

"Haven't got that far yet, but you can't run a business without good employees, however, if we sold, we would have no control on who they retained or let go. We want your opinion and Willy's opinion on the matter. They want an answer within the week, he added."

I didn't know what to say, Pappy and Mr. Purnell had put more than four years of mighty hard work into building the business, and Bonnie had put many years into building the company."

Bonnie said, as you know the doctor and I plan to be married in November, and whether we sell or not, I want to be a housewife and mother if we can adopt a child and I know your father longs to be back home in Big Flat. This is a chance that we may not have again, so we must consider carefully how we proceed. Wayne and I were well off when he was killed and so is the doctor. The doctor and I will have no financial worries. Your father is also a wealthy man already, and this would ensure financial security for your whole family. They have offered five and a half million for the buildings and real estate and will pay twenty-five cents on the dollar for retail inventory. That means that your family's portion would be north of three million dollars after everything is settled. It is, I believe a very fair offer.

I was speechless, I couldn't imagine that the business was worth that kind of money. Pappy acted as if it was no more than selling a bale of cotton. Pappy and Momma seemed to care little about the money.

Pappy nodded in agreement. And added, that he would try to negotiate at least a year's guarantee for all our workers, "but, he said, I don't know how they will feel about that. I know that we have a fine crew working for us and I expect that they know that already, so we'll see how it goes, if we are all in agreement to proceed with the sale"

Pappy and Momma agreed with Bonnie, and I said I thought it sounded good if that's what they wanted. I had lots of questions but didn't think it was appropriate for me to say too much. Pappy would do what he thought was best for the whole family.

Doctor Little didn't comment on any of the discussion but listened intently. Bonnie said that she would contact the investors the next day to tell them that the offer was accepted. They could begin inventory when they were ready. Pappy knew what the inventory was within a few hundred dollars for Mrs. McCullough was masterful at tracking and providing weekly inventory numbers. Bonnie said she would ask for a sit-down talk with the investors to discuss employee retention and closing details. She and the Doctor finished and got up to leave. Pappy asked if they had set a specific day for the wedding. Bonnie smiled and said they had decided on Thanksgiving Day.

I was glad that Pappy seemed happy that the investors didn't want to buy the farm, for I was hoping that someday Anna and I could build us a home on that place. I knew that Pappy and Momma would go back to Big Flat if everything worked out with the sale of the lumber Yard. I had no Idea what Willy would want to do but figured he would be a career military man. Charlie and Robert would have to go where Momma and Pappy settled. I had to ask Anna how she would feel about living on the farm. I wanted to practice law in Tupelo, and I knew that Anna was set on being a family doctor, like Doctor Little.

When Bonnie and Doctor Little left. I sat and talked with Momma and Pappy about what had been going on with the police and their help for me and Anna's safety. Momma was shocked, but I knew I had to tell her the whole story. I had always looked to Momma and Pappy to solve my problems, but this was something that they had no answers for. I had to get through this without their help. I felt better that it was all out there now. I had learned that keeping things from my parents was not a good idea. I did not tell them, however, that I might also be in danger.

I went to Charlie's room to check on her before I went to my bedroom, who was sleeping but woke up when I kissed her on her forehead. I sat down beside her on the bed, and she gave me a hug.

"How you feeling Kiddo? I asked.

"I feel better, but I was wanting you to come home so you could read to me and Robert. She said.

"Tomorrow night, I promise I'll read to you. Gonna cost you a kiss though, I grinned.

"Mighty big price for a little reading, she said rolling her eyes.

"Well, that's the price," I said as I got up to leave. I tasseled her head and then went to my room. I crawled into my bed, but it was a long time before I slept.

37

Willy Leaves for Officer Training

Naught leaves for the Marines

WILLY LEFT FOR OFFICER Candidate School on Saturday. Our whole family gathered there to say our goodbye. He would take the flyer to Memphis then South to San Antonio. I would miss my brother terribly, but I knew he was on the pathway to fulfilling his dream of being a military pilot. There was no doubt in my mind that he would succeed.

We had watch Naught McCullough leave for Paris Island and Marine Basic Training the day before. My whole family was there to see him off. He seemed happy that we were there. Anna was there too. Penny was not.

"Where's Penny? I asked.

He shook his head, and just said "It didn't work out. Guess I can understand that: he added. I ain't much of a prospect. I shore did like her though."

"Maybe she'll come around someday, I said. I know she likes you a lot."

Naught just shrugged and said, "Maybe."

Mrs. McCullough hugged her son and kissed him and handed him a sack of sandwiches she had prepared for his trip. Nate hugged his brother too. I hated that Naught had decided to drop out of school, but he was already eighteen and could make his own decisions. I begged him to stay for his senior year, but his mind was set, and he promised he would study to get his diploma. I believed he would.

Nate took my arm and led me away from the others, toward the steps of the depot.

"You remember the day you and Will crushed my balls with that Louisville Slugger bat?" He asked, speaking in low tones.

"I sure do, I said, my balls hurt every time I think about it."

"Mine too," Naught laughed'"

"I'm sorry about that," I said.

"Don't be, he said, that was the luckiest day of my life. You saved my momma's life, and me and Nate too," he added. You have been a really good friend, and I want ever forget that."

I took his hand and shook it and told him I was sorry about Penny. I patted him on the back and watched as he stepped upon the platform and then into the passenger car. I wondered when I would ever see him again. We had sure had our differences when we first came to Tupelo, but we grew to be good friends and I knew I would miss him. Life is what it is, as Pappy would say, and we all must adapt to ever-changing circumstances. Friends come and friends go but the good memories will stay with you. I knew he was right about that.

Willy had been gone so much the last month, it was almost like he had already left home, but I hated to see him go. Momma and Daddy both shed tears but Jessie cried like a new-born baby and hung onto him like a wood-tick. I think Willy was a little embarrassed, and I know Jessie's daddy was. I figured he'd give that girl a good talking to when he got her home. Charlie allowed that she needed her ass whipped with a hickory limb for carrying on so. Robert Lewis didn't like trains and held on to Pappy's leg the whole time.

Things were changing fast in our lives now, but it seemed like we were treading water. I knew that Pappy wanted to go back to Big Flat but that was not in my plans and yet, I knew if Pappy made his mind to go back, then Charlie and Robert Lewis would have no choice but to go too. I didn't like the thought of them not being a big part of my life. The next few weeks were going to be unsettling,

The next week I went back to work at the Lumber yard, but Pappy agreed to allow me to work at the Webb Law Firm on Saturday mornings. Saturday's was the busiest day of the week for the firm, except the times when Mr. Webb was in court. I continued to run errands, delivering documents here and there, but Mr. Webb always found time to tutor me in the law and would sometimes talk to me about cases and ask my opinion. He loved the law and being a lawyer in Tupelo and that made me even more determined.

On Saturday, a week after Willy had left for Texas, I left the law firm just after noon. When I pulled into the drive Charlie was sitting on the front steps and a boy with a mop of blonde hair and freckles was sitting there beside her. He was twirling a basketball and when I pulled to a stop, he got up to leave.

"It's just my brother, Charlie said, you don't have to go."

"You a basketball salesman?" I asked him as I walked up. "We don't allow basketball salesman around here,"

"I ain't no salesman of any kind. I ain't selling nothing, he stammered. I'm Billy Davis from down the street."

"What are you doing talking to my crazy sister, I asked? You ain't thinking of courting and kissing and stuff like that are you?"

"No. I ain't courting. We were just talking, he stammered again. I like her though."

"You like that red headed fireball? Why?" I asked. She's a delta heathen you know.

"No, what's that? What's a delta heathen?" Billy asked.

"She beats up people she don't like, and she has a foul mouth. Why do you like her?" I asked again.

"She don't neither, Have no foul mouth. She ain't hardly cussed any since I came over. Billy said, his lips pooching, face red. He shrugged his shoulders and said, "Don't know why I like her, I just do."

Charlie had heard enough. She stood up with her hands on her hip, her face red with anger.

"Don't pay this idiot and my brother no attention. He's a lying dog, Billy, he is as dumb as a pine stump, and likes to rub people the wrong way sometimes just because he likes to aggravate people,. You can come by any time you feel like it."

I smiled at Billy. "Sorry Billy, I was just giving you a hard time. Trying to get your goat. She's ok. I kind of like her too." We've got a basketball goal out back if you want to shoot baskets with Charlie sometime. I might even join you."

"Yeah that would be great."

I left the two knuckle heads and went inside. I peeked out the window and Billy was still there, and they were sitting closer. "Gonna have to watch that boy, I thought to myself."

38

Gordon Wilbanks Seeks Revenge

Nashville, Tennessee

GORDON WILBANKS SAT IN a small room in the bowels of the Mercury Hotel in Nashville. The hotel was a four-story half-century old building, just off music row, that he had bought for almost nothing ten years before and renovated the place and made it into a popular haunt for musician, singers, and songwriters seeking to make their fortune in Music City. The rooms were small but clean and adequately furnished—but most of all they were cheap.

He had kept the key to the basement room of the place for just such a meeting that might require extreme privacy. He had made a small fortune off his investment.

Being the president of one of the largest Banks in Nashville had given him opportunities for other equally profitable investments; he had become very, very, rich.

The loss of his son, however, had made him a bitter and angry man. He had been warned by police in Mississippi to stay out of their business and leave the matter alone, but his bitterness had ate at him like a cancer and he had made up his mind that he would, at whatever the cost, finish the job that his son had started. Unlike his son, however, he had money, and other resources at his disposal, and would have people who would do the deed for him. He had connections everywhere in Nashville and beyond, and tonight he sat in the dark little room on a folding metal chair at a laundry table awaiting the person he was to hire to take care of his problem. Before him, on the table, was a shoebox filled with stacks of twenty and fifty -dollar bills. It had been agreed that he would pay four thousand dollars up front and the balance of six thousand whenever the job was completed. He had already paid a thousand dollars to a "Handler" to find a person to do the job he wanted. He also carried a brown envelope with other materials for the man he was hiring.

Gordon wore dark glasses and a Brown fedora, pulled low over his eyes. He had been there but minutes when there were five raps on the door and then two more knocks. Gordon got up and unlocked the latch opener and the man entered.

"I'm Gilbert Short, the man offered, extending his hand for a shake. Who am I doing business with?" the man asked.

Wilbanks ignored him and turned his back to the man. "My name is not important, Wilbanks said. On the table you will find the money as per our agreement, and a picture and the address of where the person lives, and where she works part-time. Also, there is a picture of her boyfriend, from their High School Yearbook. If the boy gets in the way, take care of him too; there will be a thousand-dollar bonus. The girl lives with her mother. Take her out too if you need to.

"When the job is done leave a note in this room. Just drop it in the slot on the door. Say nothing in the note but *finished*. I will check daily for the note beginning in three days. Give me a number where you can be reached for final payment."

Short shuffled through the papers and finally looked up and said, " these are just kids," shaking his head. I ain't never had to take out a kid before."

"Well, do you want the job or not? If not, tell me now, don't waste my time.""

"A job is a Job. I'll do the deed. Should take no more than a week. But I'll be dropping no notes. Just meet me here with the rest of the money a week from today, Same time. Same place. The job will be done.

Short left the room walked up the steps to the sidewalk above and down the block to a Chevy Panel truck parked midway of the block. He climbed inside, put the shoebox in a compartment under the upholstered side bench. He then took up watch from the rear window of the van, where he had a good view of the side entrance of the hotel. He waited for the man who had paid him the money. He waited for twenty minutes before the man emerged. Short took pictures with his telescopic camera through the rear window. Although it was dark outside there was enough light around the hotel to get clean pictures, that he wanted for insurance.

He watched as the man crossed the street walked south past the van and climbed into a Lincoln Town car. With camera ready, Short took more pictures and wrote down the license plate number as Wilbanks pulled away from the curb. He made note of the color of the car, then climbed into the driver's seat of the van and drove away. He made no stops until he was well west of Nashville, there he stopped at the small town of Dixon and rented a room for the night,

He made a phone call from a pay phone from the motel office to confirm to his handler that initial payment had been made. He said he expected to be in Tupelo after noon the next day and back in Nashville in one week, He paid for his room took a soda from the vending machine and a pack of chips, went to his room ate his snack and went to bed. He considered just taking the five thousand dollars and heading for Mexico. He could live five years on that amount of money down there, but there was still six thousand on the table to be had and maybe more. No, he would fulfill the contract as agreed, collect his money, and then head South for a good long vacation.

Short slept till ten o'clock the next morning, got up and dressed and headed West again, stopping at a diner for breakfast. He had his thermos filled with black coffee, climbed into the panel truck, and headed South again. He arrived in Tupelo late in the afternoon. He took a room at the Skyline Motel at the edge of the city and settled in for the night. He flipped on the Television and picked up the evening news. The TV was snowy, and there was only one channel that was watchable.

The newscaster was carrying on about the Supreme Court's decision on the case involving school desegregation. There were protest going on all over the southland, but thus far, none in the City of Tupelo. Short just grunted and laughed. He didn't give a damn about what the Supreme Court said. In his job, he was color blind. If someone wanted a negro killed, he would oblige if the price was right. Black or white, yellow, or brown, it didn't matter. From his night case he took out a new nine-millimeter Ruger nine shot semi- Automatic pistol. With a cleaning rag he oiled and checked the mechanism, it was a beautiful handgun and he was an expert marksman. He expected to make quick work of the job.

The next morning Short studied the pictures and information give him. He decided he would locate the home where the girl lived and find a way to get into the house without being seen. Doing this kind of job in the open and in the daylight, was stupid. He wanted no witnesses. It might take a little longer, but caution and patience were essential requirements in his line of work."

He left the motel and drove to the address he had been given. Schools were not in session and he had no way of knowing if the subject was at home or not. He stopped the van and took out his New World Encyclopedia Brief case with business cards and went to the door. He knocked several times, but no one came to answer the door. He made note of the locks on the door which he could pick in two seconds. He was about to leave when the next- door neighbor, a grey haired, older lady, came out on the front porch. She was a heavyset woman wearing an apron and carrying a sweeping broom and a dust scoop.

"Can I help you mister?" She asked.

"Well maybe, Short said stepping off the porch and taking out a business card. "I was hoping to see a Mrs. Owens. I was told she had a daughter and might be interested in a set of our New World encyclopedias, but it appears there is no one home."

"No, Mary works at the bank and Anna is working at the hospital. They usually get home around five."

"Would you like to take a look at our newest edition, Mrs.____?

"Flora, Thomas, and no. I have no children or grandchildren to use them and my eyes are no good for reading."

"Well, I will try to catch Mrs. Owens at another time, he said, doffing his hat and walking quickly to the van.

Short climbed into the van, started the engine, and slowly drove down the street, turning right at Cross Street, he then took another right that was a narrow alley that ran behind the row of houses on Jefferson, Then, he could tell was rarely used except for trash pick-up. There were metal trash cans beside the rear fences, but the left side of the alley was covered with honeysuckle vine and Crepe Myrtle bushes—just what he was looking for. When he came to the back of the Owens House, he noted that there was a low roe of hedges that enclosed a back yard of about fifty feet in depth. He noted that the back door was a plain wood door and there were four windows across the back. No air conditioners and the windows were covered with louvered slats. Probably an attic fan. He estimated. There was no security lights or dogs in the yard. "Piece of cake," he thought to himself. He drove through the alley, turned left when he came to Broadway. A block down the street he found what he was looking for-- a used car lot. He then drove back to the motel, paid for another night, and retired, and waited for darkness.

39

Anna Gets Med School Invitation

Anna's life is in danger

MARY OWENS HER OFFICE at the Merchants Bank and Trust Company, where she worked, at four thirty, drove to the Medical Center to pick up her daughter, who had been working full time since school had been out for the summer. Anna was waiting under the portico of the building with a book bag across her shoulder when her mother drove up. Anna had been learning to drive but they could not afford her own vehicle. She was trying to save her money so that she could get her own car when she graduated in the spring.

"How did it go today babe," Mary asked as Anna slid into the car.

"O, wee! We were sooo busy today. I must have filled out a hundred insurance claims for patients, and the phone never stopped ringing. Dr. Little looked exhausted by the time he saw his last patient. He is so good with people though. Most of his patients love him. I hope I can be that kind of doctor."

"You will be sweetie. You will be, Mary Owens said smiling. But doctoring doesn't leave much time for family. You do want a family, don't you?"

"Oh, my goodness yes, Anna replied. Zack is going to be a great father. You ought to see him with Charlie. He loves both of those kids."

"So. You're sure it's Zack you want for a husband huh?"

"Nobody else for me. I can't hardly wait to see him every day, and when I'm around I can barely keep my wits about me. And he is so darn handsome, and he don't even know it."

"He is handsome, smart and a charmer to boot; Dangerous combinations for a husband."

"What do you mean, Momma?"

"Men like Zack and his brother attract women like bees to honey. And they don't even know their own appeal."

"Well, I've thought of that, and I aim to give him so much attention he won't have time for anybody else."

'Good luck on that, kiddo."

245

Mary pulled into her driveway just before five o'clock. She was getting out of her car when Flora Thomas yelled for her.

Anna went to the mailbox on the porch and pulled letters from the box without looking at the mail and waited on the porch for her mother to unlock the door.

"Flora said to Mary Owens, a man stopped here this morning looking for you, he left a card for you." She handed it to her from the porch. Was selling Encyclopedias, or so he said. He said he knew you had a daughter and might be interested in a set. I told him that you didn't get home until around five. He said that he'd try to catch you later."

Mary took the card and looked at it and stuck it in her pocket. Her warning system was awakened. She would call the number on the card later. She had never heard of the New World Encyclopedia company, and how would they know that she had a daughter. She would sleep with her 38 under her pillow tonight though.

"Thank you, Flora." Did you happen to notice what he was driving?"

"Well, yes I did, he parked in front of your house. It was one of those panel- truck vans. It was a brownish color, she said, with writing on the side. Couldn't read what it said though."

Mary said goodnight to her neighbor and went inside. Anna followed close behind. She changed from her work dress into a pair of jeans and Ole Miss tee shirt.

She went to the kitchen and prepared to start dinner for her and her daughter.

"Soup and Salad tonight, Anna. Is that alright with you?"

"How about a grilled cheese?"

"You got it."

Anna went to the kitchen and began preparing a salad as her mom made the sandwiches.

"You look worried Mom, what's wrong?"

"That man that was selling encyclopedias. There's Something about it that doesn't feel right to me. Keep Zack's Louisville Slugger bat by your bed in case of trouble."

"You think we should call the police?" Anna asked.

"I don't know what we would tell them. That a book salesman stopped at our house? They would just probably laugh at us. Think that we're just two crazy women."

"Yeah, it's probably nothing,'"

"Mary Owens picked up the stack of mail and began shuffling through it. "You've got a letter here Anna, she said, handing the letter to her daughter. It's from the University of Mississippi."

Anna grabbed the letter and quickly opened it and read it.

"Oh my God!" she cried. I've got an invitation to visit the Med School in Jackson."

Her mother took the letter and read.

Dear Miss Owens:

I am happy to inform you that your application to The University of Mississippi School Of Medicine has been received and reviewed by our board of directors, and the board has conducted interviews with your school administrators, teachers and your references, I am happy to say that our board is anxious to meet you in person, and has asked me to schedule a personal interview as soon as possible.

I have enclosed a business card with my direct number. My assistant, Mrs. Sarah Williams will work with you on a date that would be acceptable. We will provide lodging for you and your Mother for two nights stay on our Jackson Campus. We want you to tour our campus and facilities and will provide you with a personal guide during your visit. We look forward to welcoming you to our program of future doctors in the 1955/56 school year. Of course, you will be expected to keep up your current level of excellence during your senior year of high school. And your Pre-Medical schooling at the University. Your Pre-Med Classes will, of course be on the Oxford campus. Please give my regards to your mother and my old friend Doctor Jackson Little.

Best Regards
Richard R. Brooks, MD

Anna was beside herself. "I've got to call Zack and tell him the news. This is my first acceptance letter and it's the one I wanted most." Mary hugged her daughter.

Anna had another year of high school left, but Mary Owens was dreading the day when she left for college. She would be alone. She was glad that she had made friends with Allie Calloway and Bonnie Purnell. At least she would have friends to spend time with. She had thought little about dating since her husband was killed, even though she had been asked out many times. She was happy with her life just the way it was.

Anna telephoned Zack with the news and asked if he could come over for a while. He was there in ten minutes. He had run the whole way over. Anna was waiting in the porch swing with the letter from Dr. Brooks in her hand. Zack sat down beside her and read the letter.

"When are you going to go to Jackson?" Zack asked.

"I'm going to call tomorrow, and I want you to come with us if you can,"

"I don't know if I can. Will have to ask Pappy. See if he will advance me enough to pay for my expenses. I've never been to Jackson before, and if you're going to be there, I want to know how to find you."

"We've got to talk about that, don't we? Anna said. What are we going to do when we must be separated? When I'm in Jackson and you're in Oxford."

"I've been thinking about that a lot and sometime when we can talk, I'll tell you what I have in mind," Zack said.

"Ok. How about tomorrow after I call Dr. Brooks?

"Sounds good, Zack said. Give me a call.

40

Anna is in Danger

Louisville Slugger

GILBERT SHORT LEFT THE motel just after ten o'clock and drove to the alley behind the Owens house. He pulled into the alley and turned his lights off and drove slowly down the dark backstreet. Lights were still on in the Owens house. He drove until he came to Cross street, drove two blocks, turned right, and drove to the car lot on main.

All the lights were off, and he watched until he was sure the car lot was deserted. The streets of Tupelo were deserted. He then pulled onto the parking lot and parked his van between two used trucks, eased out of the van and keeping to the shadows made his way on foot back to the head of the alley. He was dressed completely in black as he kept close to the crepe myrtles until he was even with the Owens house. The place was now dark, and it was nearing eleven o'clock. He continued to wait until every house on Jefferson was dark. He then eased his way across the alley to the shrubs behind the Owens house.

Silently he made his way to the back door. He took out the Nine MM Ruger automatic, screwed on the specially made silencer. From his belt he took a set of lock picks. He first put his ear to the door to see if he could hear any movement inside. It was silent. He inserted the pick into the deadbolt, and seconds later the latch was open. The door opened into the kitchen, dining and living area. There was a hallway that led off the living area to bedrooms. He had no Idea which room Annabelle Owens occupied, so he would just have to kill both the mother and the daughter.

Short moved down the hallway like a cat, his Ruger at the ready. When he came to the first door, he noticed that the door was slightly ajar. Good, he thought. He pushed the door open and eased inside. There was a small night light on in the bathroom adjacent to the room, it provided just enough light that he could make out a woman with dark hair that covered her pillow. He stepped within a step of the bed and raised his pistol, to fire. He never got to pull the trigger. From behind, Annabelle crushed his head with the Louisville slugger.

He fell like a sack of rocks to his knees groaning. Anna hit him again in the back of the head and he fell flat on the floor. The noise awakened Mary Owens who threw back the covers and was now holding the thirty- eight on the man who was bleeding from his right ear. He was unconscious.

"Go call the police Anna. Tell them to get over here.

Minutes later three Tupelo police cars and a state police car was in front of the Owens home and an ambulance came a minute later.

Anna drew on her night robe and met the police on the porch. When they entered the house, they told Mrs. Owens to put the 38 away but she told the policeman she would put the gun away when they had the man cuffed. They handcuffed the man's hands behind his back. He checked the man's pulse and then called the EMT's to bring the gurney. Minutes later two of the policemen climbed into the ambulance and they took the man away. He was groaning and in bad shape, but at least he was alive.

The police questioned Mary Owens and Anna for nearly an hour, taking pictures of the house and the bat and the Ruger pistol that still lay on the floor. Anna and her mother were badly shaken from the events of the night. Anna wanted to call Zack, but it was well after midnight, so she decided to wait until morning. She was glad that he had given her the bat after she had been shot. He had taught her how to hold it to get the most power from her swing. It had worked. Her mother was alive.

The police rode to the hospital emergency room with the ambulance driver but kept the prisoner cuffed while medical personnel checked the man over. He was coming around but still couldn't talk coherently. The Emergency room doctor said he probably had a concussion and might not be able to be questioned until morning. The two policemen cuffed the man to the examination table and then took a position just outside the exam room and waited.

It was nearly nine o'clock when State Police Detectives Angela Winston and Gene Edwards came to the hospital. They could hear the prisoner cursing and yelling as soon as they walked into the emergency room.

"Sounds like your prisoner is not too happy with his situation, Detective Winston said to the guards."

"About ready to shoot the Bastard, the guard, panned. He's been yelling like that for an hour." Said he wanted a lawyer. Told him he could have one when he was charged with something."

"Guess we'll have a little talk with him. Might let you shoot him then," Edwards said.

The two detectives went into the exam room and stood by the bed of the prisoner.

"Who are you two, and what do you want." Short asked.

"Not much. Just the name of the people who sent you, to kill Annabelle Owens," Edwards said.

"I don't know what you're talking about, Mister. I'm not telling you anything. I want a lawyer"

"Oh, you know all right. We've got your truck that you left on the car lot, the money and your camera. You might save yourself from the electric chair if you cooperate. Otherwise you'll be charged with attempted murder, conspiracy to commit murder and other charges. You'll fry for sure. If you cooperate and help us get the person who paid you to do the job, we might be able to keep you out of the electric chair. If you don't then you will most certainly be a candid for old Sparky. We are going to eventually find the person who paid you, but it may be too late for you then. The FBI is involved now, and they already are working the case. By the time we get the person, you could be on death row at Parchman."

"You've got an hour to think about it, Edwards said, as they turned to leave. You'll get the Lawyer when we charge you with attempted murder and conspiracy to commit murder."

"Wait! don't leave, I want to make a phone call."

"You'll get your phone call when we have you in the jailhouse."

The two detectives left the hospital and returned to the office. FBI agent, Sam Watson, had left a message, that the Bureau had taken possession of the money, the camera, and an envelope with other information. Gene

Edward knew that the FBI lab would soon know where the money came from and would know if their prisoner was who he said he was. In the meantime, his agency was looking the place where Short had been staying. The panel truck had a Tennessee license plate and they were running that through the system.

Three days later, Detective Gene Edwards walked into the Break Room of the Mississippi Highway State Police, where Angela, his partner, was pouring herself a cup of coffee. He tossed her a copy of the Nashville Banner newspaper. She spread it out on the table before her and read the Headline *"Prominent Nashville Banker Arrested: Charged with conspiracy to Commit Murder"*

She then read the details of the arrest aloud.

"Gordon Wilbanks, prominent resident of Nashville and President of the First Commerce Bank and Trust of Nashville, was arrested this morning by agents of the FBI and local police and charged with several crimes, including conspiracy to commit murder of an unnamed minor in the State of Mississippi. Wilbanks was also charged with other unspecified crimes. He will be arraigned later today.

"Where did you get the paper?" Angela asked.

"Agent brought it down with him last night. Thought I might like to show it to our prisoner. Heading over to the jail now. We've got a camera set up for questioning. He was told about the arrest of Wilbanks last night and they said he was singing like a mad canary.

"I'm going to drive over and tell the Owens ladies. Maybe they'll sleep a little better tonight. Edwards said. You want to come?"

"Guess I better. Those ladies are just too dang pretty to let a single man like yourself go over there alone," Jessica kidded.

"Yeah, I'm sure they'd really be interested in a middle-aged police detective, Edwards responded."

"I don't know, some young women are attracted to middle age men," Jessica responded.

"How about you, Jess? Are you attracted to middle age men?

"I'm not saying, "she said smiling."

They drove up to the Owen's home fifteen minutes later. Mary Owens was in the driveway washing her 1950 model Chevy. She was dressed in jeans and a T-shirt. She shaded her eyes when they stopped at the curb.

"Morning, Mrs. Owens, Edwards said, walking up the drive. Don't know if you remember us or not, but we were at the hospital when we talked to your daughter, Anna.

"Yes, I remember you. Why are you here now?"

"Just to bring you up to date on the case and to let you know that you and your daughter are no longer in danger. The FBI has arrested the person who hired the man who tried to kill you and your daughter, Edwards said, handing her the Nashville newspaper.

Mary quickly scanned the article.

"Gordon Wilbanks? The father of Jason Wilbanks?" Mary asked.

"Yes Maam, looks that way. He could spend the rest of his life in jail if he doesn't get the death penalty for his crimes. The man we arrested her has agreed to a plea deal to stay out of the electric chair."

"Thank you, detective, Mary Owens said, I will tell Anna and Zack."

"Are you doing ok? Edwards, asked. I know you've been through quiet an ordeal."

"I'm getting there, Mary responded. It's been a tough few day.

"I know, he said. If there's anything I can do to help just call, he said handing her a business card."

"Thank you. I will."

The two detectives got into their car and drove away. Mary Owens watched until they were out of sight. She turned off the water to the hose and called for Anna. Her heart had been relieved of a huge burden. She would say a prayer tonight and thank God for saving her daughter and herself. She liked detective Edwards, and he was very handsome. He had a certain look in his eye when he talked to her. "I bet I see him again," she thought to herself. She looked at the card he had given her and on the back was his private phone number. She smiled.

Mary Owens had been happy with her life and had thought little about dating. Her husband James and Annabelle had been the loves of her life and when James was killed in the war, she had focused her entire world on Anna. She had married James at sixteen, and Anna was born a year later. He had been called to duty two months after they married, and he never saw their daughter. She was thirty-five now and, in a year, Anna would be leaving for college and she would be alone. Maybe she would think about going out. The thought of dating, however, scared her to death. When she had sexual dreams, it was often of AC Calloway or Zackery, that were vivid in her thoughts. She would wake up angry with herself for having such dreams.

Mary had always found AC to be a man that appeared to be extremely family dedicated and a gentleman. Forbidden fruit, she knew. And why, was she attracted so much to Zack. She understood completely why her daughter felt the way she did. She looked at the card again and sighed.

She would call Gene Edwards the next few days and find out more about him. She had noticed that he did not wear a wedding ring, and that he was very tall and handsome, but knew little else. She knew it was not proper for a woman to be calling up and asking a man out, but she would find a reason to call him, and see what more she could learn about him. She had to stay away from AC Calloway though, for Allie had become one of her best friends and she wanted nothing to damage that relationship.

Mary finished washing her car and went inside where Anna was sound asleep on the couch, she didn't bother to wake her for she knew she had been through a lot the last few weeks and she surely needed to rest. She went to the shower, stripped off her wet clothes and showered off, and went to the closet for a clean pair of jeans and a T-shirt. She was in just her panties and bra when she stopped to look at herself in the door length mirror. That was not something she did very often. She was still very thin, and her body was firm, but there were a few places that needed work. If she was going to put herself out there again, she needed some fine tuning. Anna loved to walk, so that was a good way to get in shape. She was not a person who had to watch their weight. She guessed it was genes, for she had never been overweight. She worried more about being too thin. Thin was "in" she knew, and she and Anna could wear the same clothes, but she was not about to dress like the teenagers did.

She slipped on her jeans and T and when she turned, Anna was watching her from the doorway, her arms crossed smiling broadly.

"You are one hot chick, Mom, 'Anna laughed. "First time I've ever seen you looking at yourself, you got your eye on somebody?"

Mary threw the wet shirt at her daughter. "What if I did?"

"I think it would be great, Anna Responded. It's time you started going out. Past time, in fact. I have to meet him though, and give my approval,"

41

Anna Sets Visit to Med School

Zack and Anna make plans

ANNA PHONED THE MEDICAL Center in Jackson Just after nine o'clock the next day and talked with Doctor Brook's assistant, Sarah Williams. She learned that the board of directors only met once each month to interview prospective students. The last Thursday of the month. The first available slot was in January of the next year. Anna thought that was mighty late in the year but accepted the time. She would meet the board at nine in the morning and would begin touring the campus after the meeting. She would be furnished lodging at the Medical Center Hotel. Meals would also be furnished in the hotel restaurant or in the Medical Center Cafeteria.

She would meet her guide at the board meeting, who would be a teaching Doctor.

Anna was excited and called Zack as soon as she got off the phone. He was busy at the lumber yard but asked her to meet him on the steps of the Old church on Jefferson at noon. She said that she would and would bring a sandwich and a soda for lunch.

A little before noon, Anna made two peanut butter-jelly sandwiches and took two Cokes from the fridge and walked over to the old church. Zack was not there yet. She sat down on the steps and waited.

Five minutes later, Zack pulled up to the curb in front of the big church. He was smiling as he walked toward her. God! He was a handsome thing. "No wonder why her mom said he was a dangerous combination of good looks and intelligence. He walked tall and straight and was filled with self-confidence, she thought to herself."

Anna stood when Zack walked up. She put her arms round him and kissed him full on the lips for a long moment. Zack picked her up and held her to him.

"Wow! He said. We need to come here more often. finally releasing Anna".

Anna Smiled. "Yes, we do". She said.

Anna opened the bag she had brought and handed Zack a sandwich and a soda. She had also remembered to bring an opener for the bottles. They sat on the steps to the entrance of the church and talked as they ate.

"Why did you want to meet here?" Anna asked.

"I don't know exactly; it's just a place I like to come to when I have something really important to think about. What I want to talk to you about is really the most important thing I have ever thought about. This seemed like the place for me to come to."

"What do you want to talk about Zack, that's so important."

"I want to Marry you Anna. And I want to do it *before* we start to college. I have checked with the University and we can get a small apartment on campus. Will you marry me Anna? Will you be my wife, Anna?"

Annabelle was shaken. She had expected that Zack would asker to be his wife at some point in time, but she had not expected it to be before they finished high school. "She wanted to be his wife, but was this the right time, she thought to herself"

"Yes Zack, I want to be your wife, but are you sure this is what we should do?"

"As sure as I can be. I do not want to be separated from you when we start to college and we both will be eighteen when we must leave for school. What do you think?"

"Zack, I would marry you today if you said it was what you wanted to do. I love you and want to spend my life with you, but Your Law school is in Oxford and Medical School is in Jackson. How can we make that work?"

"I talked with Mr. Webb at the law firm and he has a part-time job awaiting me with a law firm in Oxford, when I get to Ole Miss. I'm saving all the money I can, that I earn at the lumber yard, so we will have money to get started. We can finish our undergraduate work at the Ole Miss campus and I can attend law school in Jackson while you are in medical school. I can work, maybe teach, until you get finished, then I can get my law degree. I know it will take at least six years for you to complete Medical school, and I just don't want to wait that long for us to be together. I'm ok with waiting until you finish school to start a family, and I really want a family, but what I want most of all is you."

"Oh Zack, I don't know what to say. Looks like you have been doing a lot of planning and given it a lot of though. I don't want to be separated from you either. But what if I should get pregnant while I'm in school. I don't know if they would allow me to stay in school, and should that happen, would you be willing to give up your dream of law school in order to support the family."

"Yes. My family would always come first, but I really believe we can make it work," Zack said firmly. I believe you can become a Doctor and I can be a lawyer, and we can do it together.

Anna took Zacks hand and looked deep into his eyes. She expected to see some doubt but saw none. Ok, she said, but first I want you to talk to my mother and your father about what you are thinking. Then, if this is what you want, I will be your wife."

The two lovers embraced there and kissed there on the steps of the old church. When they broke their embrace, Pastor Luke stood before them, smiling.

"Back again, I see, the pastor said. Been kind of expecting you."

"Dadgum, Preacher, you're going to cause someone to have a heart attack someday, sneaking up like that, Zack stammered. Anna was clearly red-faced and embarrassed."

"Saw you two during my noontime stroll around town and thought you two might have something you wanted to discuss with a minister.

Zack looked at Anna, and she at him. They both shrugged and nodded.

"We're thinking on getting married Pastor, before we go off to college."

"Figured as much," Pastor Luke smiled.

What's your thoughts on the matter, as a preacher?" Zack asked.

"That's for you two to decide, but I know God will bless your marriage. Some people are just born to be together. Like your momma and pappy, Zack. I believe you two were headed down this path since the day you were born. Other details will take care of themselves. Be true to yourself and to each other. Luke then turned to go."

"Wait, Zack, called after him, as he walked toward the big trees that shaded the street. How did you know Momma and Pappy?"

"Know a lot of folks, he said, raising his hand as he walked away."

''What a strange man, Anna said as they watched the pastor walk away. He looks familiar, but I just can't seem to figure out where I've seen him before. It's weird."

"Yeah, it's plumb dang spooky, that he seems to know every time I'm coming here," Zack offered.

Zack dropped Anna off at her house on his way back to the lumber yard and told her that they would talk more later. His mind was filled with a thousand questions. He dreaded talking to Mary Owens and his father about his plans, although he knew, in the end, his father would give his approval, for he really liked Anna and would accept her into the family just as he had Charlie and Robert Lewis.

Mary Owens would eventually give her approval too, for he knew she loved her daughter and wanted her to be happy. And when all was said and done, that's what everyone wanted. Zack realized that happiness was a pursuit, not a goal, an exploration, not a destination, for what made people happy was forever changing. Happiness was not something that could be measured, only felt.

42

Summer Passes

WILLY RETURNS HOME

I worked at the lumber yard the rest of the summer putting in ten-hour days Monday thru Friday and working for the law firm on Saturday mornings. Pappy had opened the new building for truss fabrication, and orders were coming faster than we could fill them, for new house construction in the city was brisk and we had the only truss building facility in the county.

Pappy needed me at the yard but knew how much I wanted to work at the firm and had relented. The sale of the company was taking much longer than expected, and we were all putting in long hours. The investment associates that were buying the company were pouring over the books and had staff taking their own inventory. Pappy was only forty, but the last five years had taken its toll. His hair was getting grayer and the wrinkles in his brow were deeper. His piercing blue eyes were still bright and clear though, and it seemed he could read my every thought.

Pappy had raised my pay to a dollar an hour, for he knew I was saving to go to college. I had not yet told him my plans of marriage. I had managed to save most of what I earned and had put away nearly five hundred dollars. I had opened my own bank account and made deposits every week. Pappy could always read me and Willy like a cheap novel and sensed that something was going on in my life but wasn't quite sure what it was. Finally, he asked.

"What are you doing with all that money you've been making Zack? Is there something going on that I need to know about?" Pappy asked.

"Nothing I want to talk about right now, but I want us to have a good long talk before I graduate from high school next year. I'm just trying to save my money for school," I said.

"Well, I think there's more going on, but when you are ready to talk, I'll be here.

"Thanks Pappy!"

"I want to pay my own way through college if I can. I know I'm in line for academic scholarships and may even have a baseball offer. But I may still have to have help."

"Your mom and I have always intended to help you get through school. We feel we have that responsibility to you and Willy and the kids Charlie and Robert too. We do want you to work for your education. We believe you'll appreciate it more if you do.

I was getting ready to leave the yard to make a delivery when Pappy said, "Wait a second. I meant to tell you that Willy called from Texas. He is to graduate next week and will be coming home for ten days before he reports to flight training in Biloxi. He expects to be there for at least six weeks, and then go back to Sen Antonio for more flight training. He will be on active duty once he has his commission. Thought you'd want to know. He said he might catch a hop to Columbus on a military plane, and would want us to pick him up there,"

"Yeah, it'll be great to see him. Was about to forget I had an older brother. Guess that means he won't be going on to college now."

"Guess not, Pappy said, a little dejected. Maybe later."

TWO WEEKS LATER

"Willy called as he was leaving San Antonio. Said he would be in Columbus just about noon and wanted us to pick him up at the air base. He wanted us to bring Jessie if she could come. I called and told her I would pick her up about ten thirty for the trip to Columbus."

"Is Anna going with us?" Jessie asked.

"I don't know if she can, I haven't called her since I heard that Willy was coming home."

I called and asked Anna, after I had talked with Jessie, if she wanted to make the trip to Columbus. She said she could not, that she had already promised Doctor Little she would work at his office that day, for his regular receptionist was going to be out for a few days, and really needed my help. I told her that I had called Jessie and that she wanted to go. I could sense that Anna did not like the idea of me driving to Columbus alone with Jessie, but she just said, "don't you two set too close going down there."

"Don't worry, I won't put my arm around her or anything," I laughed.

Anna slammed down the phone!

Minutes later Anna called back. Said she was sorry for slamming the phone but that there was something she really needed to tell me.

"What is it?" I asked.

"Well, I'm angry at Jessie. I've been seeing her riding around Tupelo with that new Pharmacy trainee at the drug store. I think they've been going out."

"What's wrong with that girl, I asked? I thought she was crazy about my brother.

"I don't know, she's changed, but you've got to tell your brother, as much as I know you hate to do that," Anna said.

"Good grief," I said, Willy will be devastated. He loves that girl, but you're right. He must know.

I called Jessie as soon as I got off the phone with Anna and asked her if the rumor was true that she was seeing someone else.

Jessie hesitated a second before she answered. "Yes, I've gone out with a boy a couple of times. But it doesn't mean anything", she said.

"Yes, it does mean something too. It means you do not really love my brother the way you said you did. I'm withdrawing my offer to allow you to go to Columbus with me." I hung up the phone."

I drove my old truck to the Air base at Columbus on Saturday morning, and stopped at the front gate for a visitor pass and directions to the flight line security office, where I was supposed to meet Willy. He was standing by the gate when I pulled up. He was in dress blues, and I could see the gold bars on his shirt collars. He stood straight and tall. He was an impressive soldier. He threw his duffle in the back of the truck and then climbed into the cab and I turned the truck toward home.

"Where's Jessie? "he asked.

"Didn't come with me," I said. And there is something else that you need to know.

"She's seeing someone else isn't she, Willy looking straight ahead, his mind apparently trying to deal with the matter. Figured as much, she hasn't taken my calls the last times I called her house. Oh, well I don't have time for romance now anyway. Will be in flight training for at least six months and then on active duty to who knows where; sure did like that girl though."

We made small talk on the trip back to Tupelo about all the things going on with the family and the sale of the business, and all that had happened with Anna. He wanted to know if Pappy and Momma would move back to Big Flat after the sale was complete. I told him that I thought that it was their plan to do so, but that was not my plan.

As much as I loved Grandpa and Big Flat, I did not plan to go back there to live. I told him that my plan was to practice law in Tupelo, and I was pretty sure that someday I would build a home on the old Davis place and live there.

"Dang, he said my life has been a piece of cake compared to yours. You and Anna ok now?" He asked.

"Yeah, we're good, I said."

Willy slid down slightly in the seat, crossed his arms, and closed his eyes, the roar of the old truck had him sleeping in minutes. He didn't awaken until we pulled into the lumber yard. Momma had brought the kids with her and they were waiting for us sitting on a stack of lumber with Squat right there with them. Squat recognized Willy and jumped down to greet him, his long tail wagging and howling to announce his homecoming.

Willy spent most of his ten days leave at the lumber yard with Pappy. He was clearly enjoying being away from the rigors of basic training. He would usually go by the Guard Armory for coffee each day. He was antsy, though, and talked at the supper table each night about his new assignment and what he would be doing. He also spent time with Charlie and Robert Lewis. Twice we took them to the drug store for root beer and burgers. Only once did he see Jessie that I knew of and she tried to get him to talk to her, but Willy was having none of that. One kick of the mule was enough lesson for my brother. Pappy always said that if you got kicked twice, you deserved what you got.

Willy left the first day of September on the Express to Memphis. We were all there to see him off. In a year I would be saying goodbye to the family too. My high school senior year would start in a week, the day after Labor Day. Anna and I both had mixed emotions about setting out on our own after graduation. Pappy said that uncertainty is what causes people to either move forward or backward. Change never comes easy, he would say, no matter what age you are. If men don't challenge uncertainty they will never marry, for there ain't no way a man ever can be certain of what a woman is thinking.

43

Lumber Business is Sold

Pappy unemployed

PAPPY AND MRS. PURNELL closed out the deal on the sale of the lumber business on the last day of September. The new owners took possession on the first day of October. The new owners had agreed to keep all salaried employees on for a year and hourly employees for three months, but it was a cordial arrangement and Pappy felt like the new operation would want to keep all the workers that he had on the staff now. They were good, hardworking people. Pappy was now a wealthy man by most any standard, and he and Mrs. Purnell gave each of his workers a nice bonus when the deal was settled.

Mrs. McCullough was given enough to purchase a new home in Tupelo and the managers at Columbus and West Point stores an amount that was equal to three month's wages. The Webb Law firm, as usual, handled the legal matters and with making sure Pappy's money was invested wisely. Mostly in government bonds. Pappy had agreed to give advice when asked, but he knew that with Mrs. McCullough on their staff, they would not need his input very much. For the first time in his married life Pappy didn't have a job to go to, but he had the farm and that would do for now. There was always work on the farm to be done and he enjoyed working with Joe Webb. It wasn't long until he and Joe were like brothers and Joe would sometimes come to the house for supper.

Joe took to the kids too, he had a grown son, Wesley, in the military somewhere in Germany. His wife had left Joe and the boy when the boy was eight and Joe had left the New York Banking firm to raise the boy in the country near Tupelo. Joe was well off financially, but lived very simply, and just seemed to enjoy working on the farm. That too, was Pappy in a nutshell. He loved the Farm work. He was free now to go back to Big Flat if he wanted.

Pappy said that Joe told him the two happiest days of his life was when that no-account woman left him, and the day he moved back to Mississippi. "I got rid of a pain in the ass and a train ticket to Tupelo with my son the next day. Won't ever leave," Joe said. It wasn't easy raising the boy by myself, but I don't regret a minute of it. I hope someday he'll have the good sense to come back here to live."

Mr. Webb at the Law Firm advised Pappy that he should buy some new equipment for the farm for tax purposes. Pappy took his advice and bought a new model 420 John Deere two-cylinder tractor and a new 1954 Chevrolet Pickup. The truck was the top of the line with chrome grill, side vent windows, a radio and heater. Pappy would not think of getting rid of his old truck and had the Chevrolet dealership put a new coat of paint on it, and new tires. He kept it parked in the barn at the farm for what he called, The rough work.

Momma and the kids went to the farm with Pappy whenever they were not in school. Momma loved for Pappy to hitch up the mules to the wagon and to ride around the farm with Pappy. She loved riding the horses and soon had Charlie and Robert Lewis riding too. Robert also loved the big pond and would spend hours fishing off the levy. He got good at catching the catfish and sun perch. Pappy would usually make him turn them back in the pond, but occasionally Pappy would skin two or three good sized ones and Momma would skillet-fry them for supper. Charlie and Robert were both getting well-tanned from being outside in the sun, and it seemed Charlie ad grown two inches. She was slim and was not yet starting to take on much shape, but she was a real beauty, nonetheless. Robert was shooting up too, he was in school now and had picked up plenty of bad habits. He was caught cussing on more than on one occasion, but a hickory switching from Pappy taught him quickly the error of his ways and he became mighty careful about what he said around the house. I don't know if a hickory switch whipping ever cured anything or not but speaking from experience, it sure was a deterrent around Momma.

We had started fall football practice the week before the start of school and I was going to be a running back on a team that didn't pass the ball much. That was ok with me, and Pappy and Momma would be able to come to my games since Pappy no longer had a regular day job. Pappy liked football alright, but baseball was what he really looked forward to. When, in the Spring, the high school games would start he would be there.

Pappy and Momma had never taken a vacation that I knew of, but Pappy always said he wanted to take Momma to Saint Louis to watch the cardinals play. They began making plans and calling around for information, on what they could do on the way up and back. They planned to go as soon as school was out in May and get tickets for the Friday and Saturday games, and start back home on Sunday. Pappy had not been out of the state of Mississippi since he was discharged from the Navy, and Momma had never been farther away than Memphis. Pappy said he had seen most everything he wanted to see, and big city folks just made him nervous. Momma on the other hand, loved to go to new places as long as Pappy would go with her. She had already made him promise that someday they would go to Florida so she could swim in the Ocean.

When School started, Rock and Roll had hit Tupelo like a blue plague, and a boy named Presley was the talk of the whole country, They said he had attended Milam Jr. High in Tupelo, the same school where I had started five years before. His record of *"That's Alright Momma"* was playing on nearly every radio station in the country and Jerry Lee Lewis, the blond headed crazy piano player from Ferriday Louisiana, was driving parents' crazy all over the Southland, even in Tupelo. Fats Domino, from New Orleans was topping record charts across the nation. We were in the midst of a Cosmic Music revolution like nothing the world had ever seen before. Even more disturbing to a basically puritanical southland, we were also diving headlong into the abyss of a sexual revolution as well. Hugh Hefner's *Playboy* magazine's hit nearly every newsstand in the country. Nudity, no longer taboo, the magazines were available to anyone who wanted to buy. Girls and boys openly talked about sexual matters and television and movie too were becoming much bolder. Teen Pregnancy's skyrocketed, but it was never clear the true cause of the spike, but many wanted to attribute it to the "revolution."

While Nashville, long the center for country music, resisted the new wave sweeping the country. The east and West Coast music producers did not, and they came to the Southland calling. From New Orleans to Memphis, talent scouts combed the Juke joints and honky-tonks along the river for musicians and singers, and they found the mother lode. Mississippi, Arkansas, and Louisiana were hotbeds of talent, and nearly every TV station in the country featured dance party programs in the afternoon and on Saturdays that featured many Southern boys unleashed. *The Bop* was the dance that swept the nation.

Anna picked up the new dances in no time, but I was a complete and hopeless oaf when it came to rhythm and couldn't dance a lick. I hated that for it made me jealous when she would dance with other boys at parties. I finally talked Mrs. Owens to teach me how to do a two-step slow dance so that at least I could dance with Anna at least once if we went to a party. I especially wanted to be ready when prom night came, for I wanted to be the one dancing every dance with Anna. Mrs. Owens was a fine dancer, like Anna, and I had to admit that I enjoyed holding her close and looked forward to practicing on Sunday afternoons. Charlie would always tag along with me and I would dance with her too. I soon felt I was capable of not embarrassing myself or Anna, which was all I really wanted.

Charlie and Robert were back in school and doing well, Charlie was exceptionally bright and pretty and had all her teachers wrapped around her finger. She was far ahead of her grade level in every course. Robert Lewis was bright enough, but he loved basketball and baseball. Every afternoon he wanted Pappy to play catch and shoot baskets. Billy Davis had become almost a permanent fixture around our house, he was over nearly every day, to see Charlie. Billy, Charlie, and Robert would shoot baskets until it was too dark to see. Billy's mother finally came by and told momma not to feed the boy, so that he would start coming home for supper.

These recent developments weighed heavy on Pappy. I had always assumed that if he was ever able to return to Big Flat to live, he surely would. However, Pappy was a practical man and he most of all wanted to do what was best for his family, and his family had changed dramatically since we had moved to Tupelo. Pappy and Momma had changed too.

Momma loved her close friendships with Bonnie Purnell, Mrs. McCullough, and Marie Owens. Pappy had made friendships with Joe Webb and Dr. Little and with the people that had worked so hard to help him and Wayne in building the huge lumber and supply business. He was also well known in the Tupelo business community although he was never interested in being a member of any of their organizations. He missed Grandpa, of course, but he and Momma had made a new life for themselves in Tupelo and so had his Children.

Momma always said you can't go back, for what you go back to, will not be the same place that you left. It's never what you expect it will be. Willy was gone and I had no Idea where he would settle. I expected he would be in the military once he started flying, for that was his greatest love. Love, however, can be very fickle, but I knew Tupelo was where I wanted to be. The farm was five miles from town, and I could practice Law in a town that really had become a part of my fabric and Tupelo was Anna's town.

44

Bonnie and the Doctor

Willy gets a leave

BONNIE PURNELL BECAME MRS. Jackson Little on Thanksgiving Day. It was a private ceremony with only very close friends invited. They were married on the steps of the First Episcopal Church of Tupelo. The Reverend Joseph Hinds officiated. Pappy was Best Man and Charlie carried flowers. Robert Lewis was the Ring Bearer; a job I felt was way too important to trust to that knucklehead, but he carried it off without falling or dropping the ring pillow. I was relieved when Doctor Little finally took the ring. Anna and I along with Doctor Little's Nurse, Martha Reed, and his receptionist Janie Bell were the only other invitees.

It was the first time I had ever seen Pappy in a suit and tie, and although he was plainly uncomfortable, and was fidgety the whole time, he was a striking man. Momma stood straight and graceful beside Bonnie in a new frock she and Bonnie and Mary Owens had picked out for the occasion. When it came to beauty, Momma finished second to no one. She was clearly enjoying being beside Bonnie.

Bonnie and Doctor Little left after a small reception in the Church foyer, for a two week's honeymoon in New Orleans. We watched them board the train south to Mobile. Pappy allowed that they'd be back before half that time. That the Doctor couldn't hold up for two weeks with that woman. Momma scolded him harshly for such talk, but grinned and grabbed his arm.

Anna and I looked at each other and she pulled herself close to me. There's something about watching two people marry that seems to bring everyone watching to a deeper love and closeness to the person standing beside them. It's a mystery to me why so many people that seem so deeply in love at a marriage ceremony can be filing for a divorce a year later, and others, like Momma and Pappy never seem to wane in their adoration for each other. Pappy says that marriages last longer when the couples are not too familiar. "It's alright to smell the Rose while it's budding, but don't pick it until it's ready to blossom." Whatever that means. Pappy was just full of old sayings.

We returned to school after the Thanksgiving holidays. Anna and I had finished most of our required courses for graduation, so we were taking a class in Spanish. This was the only class that we had together. We would sometimes walk around Tupelo and speak to each other in Spanish just for practice. Anna picked up the language quickly, but it was more difficult for me. Anna began using her new skills at the hospital, Interpreting for Spanish patients that came to see Doctor Little. There were only a few Latino families in Tupelo, but word got around quickly that Doctor Little had someone who spoke their language, and they filled his office on Saturday mornings.

We took other electives that we thought might help our graduation standing with Ole Miss. Football took a lot of my time in the afternoons, and, of course on Friday nights, so there wasn't much time for romance. I continued working for the Law Firm and Anna at the Hospital when she had any spare time. When the Christmas Holidays came, we were out for two weeks. Willy was able to wrangle a three-day pass from his training and Anna and I picked him up at the Naval Air Station in Memphis on Christmas Eve morning. Me and Willy prepared Santa gifts for Charlie and Robert Lewis after they were in bed and spread them around the Christmas tree. Pappy had cut a live cedar from the farm and Momma had it well decorated –with Charlie's and Robert's help.

Willy and I sat up, far into the night, and talked about old times. We wondered whether Naught McCullough would make it home for Christmas from Paris Island, but we didn't call to ask. He asked about Jessie, and it was obvious that he still had feelings for her, but Willy was no fool, and let the questions about her drop.

Pappy insisted that we go to Grandpa's house on Christmas day. That was a bit of a problem, for Anna wanted to go to Big Flat with my family, her mother wanted her to spend the holiday with her and her grandparents. I told Mrs. Owens that if she would allow Anna to have Christmas Lunch with my family in Big Flat, that I would have her back in Tupelo by two o'clock, so she could have dinner there. She finally agreed and invited me to come to dinner too. It was a great day for the kids. Gifts galore from Momma and Pappy, the Little's and, of course from, Anna and her mother. Willy had brought a transistor radio for Charlie and a Catcher's Mitt for Robert Lewis. They were both ecstatic. I had bought them movie tickets to see Cinderella at the Lyric.

We left early Christmas morning for Big Flat and was there before eight o'clock. It was the first time I'd seen grandpa sense Easter and his health had really gone downhill. He had suffered from a stomach hernia for years, but now he was stooped and frail, and had difficulty just standing. It was a hard thing to see. He was glad to see us all though, and even though his voice was weak and barely auditable at times, he teased and tried to joke with the kids. I could see worry on Pappy's face as he greeted his father. It pained him to find his dad in such a state of poor health.

Aunt Zula was plainly worried too. She said that she had tried to get the old man to go and see a doctor, but she said he insisted that he was all right and would be fine when warm weather came. We all knew better. His problems were not going to be corrected by a change in the weather. Aunt Zula had gone all out in preparing Christmas, though it was plain to see that she was not much better off, health wise than grandpa. Momma and Anna pitched in to help finish putting the meal on the table.

I had promised Marie Owens that I would have Anna home by two o'clock in the afternoon, so we left Big Flat just after the noon meal and drove straight to the Owen's home. Anna's grandparents were already there and greeted us both warmly. Her grandfather was a big man and outgoing. In his sixty's and a retired military man, he still had the bearing of a soldier. Anna's grandmother was a petit woman with the same engaging smile as Anna and Marie Owens.

After dinner, Anna and I walked the streets of Tupelo, taking in the holiday decorated stores and light displays all over the town. Christmas music played over loudspeakers located all over the city. The night was cold, and Anna walked close to me and after a while we headed down Jefferson toward home. At the old Church,

I asked her to sit with me for a while. We sat down on the steps as organ music played from inside the sanctuary. I took a small package from my jacket and handed it to Anna. "Merry Christmas," I said. As she took the package and started opening it.

"What have you done Zack Calloway? We have already opened our gifts," she said.

"I know, but this is something special. I love you, Annabelle Owens. Ever since the first time I saw you when I was thirteen, and I will always love you no matter what happens."

Anna removed the wrapper from the tiny box that held the small diamond engagement ring that I had purchased a week before. I had bought the ring from the same store that I had purchased the locket that I had given her when we were thirteen. She opened it in the lights beneath the portico of the Church. Her eyes widened for a second and then she turned toward me and put her arms around me.

"Oh Zack, it's beautiful, and I love it. But I cannot wear it now. I must tell my mother."

"It's something that we have to do, and you must tell your parents too. I want us to wait until after graduation to do that, she said. I love you more than I have the words to say. I want to be your wife and your lover. I cannot break my mother's heart by not telling her and she has given me her entire life. I promised her I would not marry until I finished high school, and I must keep my word to her. I won't accept the ring until we have done that."

I was disappointed, of course, but I knew Anna was right. Anna was smart and a logical, headstrong woman. She was thoughtful about all those that she loved. I, on the other hand, was very selfish when it came to Anna, and wanted nothing to stand in my way of having her for my wife.

"Ok, I said as we got up to leave the church and headed for home. We walked silently until we reached the steps of the Owens house. There she handed me back the ring."

"Hold onto this for a while, she said. I hope you're not angry with me, I don't want you to be. It would hurt my mother if I accepted the ring now. I hope we can tell her and your parents after graduation in the spring and I know that my mother and yours will want to help plan our wedding ceremony. I love you Zack. Don't ever doubt that."

I swallowed hard and pulled Anna to me and kissed her hard. It was a powerful moment that would never be forgotten. I turned then and walked toward home. The cold wind to my back and a little sleet began to fall, Christmas music playing in my head but wedding bells in my heart.

Charlie and Robert greeted me when I returned home, they had been wrestling with Willy on the living room floor. Toys and books scattered everywhere.

Momma had hot cocoa on the stove, and I sat down at the table and Charlie was astride my knee in two seconds begging me to read to her from her new book. "Sister Carrie," by Theodore Dreiser. I thought it was mighty advanced, for a ten-year-old, but then Charlie was no ordinary ten-year-old.

"You know the price", I said.

"Oh, I know," She said, throwing her arms around me and kissing me on the cheek. She was dressed in her pajama pants and a T shirt. She slid off my knee and headed toward her bedroom, tugging at the "wedgie" in her seat. What a joy she and Robert had been to our family since they had come to live with us. I felt that God really knew his business when he sent them to Momma and Pappy to raise.

I drove Willy to The Air Station the day after Christmas for his return hop to San Antonio. We said goodbye at the front entrance to the base. It was likely that I would not see him again for several months, for he was to be sent to Biloxi directly from his current assignment. We shook hands and embraced. He took his bag and stepped aboard a white, converted school bus for his trip to the flight line. I left the Naval Air Station, working my way from Millington down to Lamar Avenue and highway 78. I crossed the Mississippi State line, just before ten o'clock and was in Tupelo just after Noon. The weather had turned nasty as I drove into Tupelo, the rain freezing on my windshield. Icicles were beginning to form on trees and on roof eaves. Robert Lewis and Charlie were at the window watching the slush fall when I drove up. And there right between them was Billy Davis. "What in the world is that toe head doing at our house in this weather?" I wondered. Oh well, he was only two blocks from home."

The weather had cleared by the morning. The sun was bright, but the temperature had dropped into the teens and few people were on the streets of Tupelo. Pappy and I drove to the farm to check on the pond to see if it had frozen over. The temperature was near single digits now and the pond was the main source of water for the livestock. The pond was completely frozen, and the cattle were standing on the levy when we drove up. Tool pick and sledgehammer from the started breaking the ice. It was a chore for the Ice was four inches thick in places, and it was refreezing almost as fast as we could break it. Joe Webb drove up while we were working and started helping. We finally had cleared a place large enough for the stock to drink after an hour's hard labor. Joe said the livestock would be good for a day or two, but if the cold continued, it would be a daily job.

The next day the temperature was still hovering around twenty degrees, but the sun was bright and the area we had cleared the day before only had a thin sheet of ice. By Friday, the weather had warmed, and the ice was melting all around the edges of the big pond.

Pappy went every day to the farm and he and Joe would saddle the horses and ride over the farm checking the cattle. They had set up a checkers Board, in the tack room, where Joe had fashioned a charcoal heater out of a small oil drum. They would usually play checkers until noon. They accused each other of cheating and lying, but they would laugh like a couple of kids with new toys. It was good to see Pappy so happy again. He was enjoying his newfound freedom. He had plenty of time to spend with Charlie and Robert Lewis.

The school year was moving along, and Anna and I were at the top of our class and it appeared that one of us would be valedictorian, I hoped it would be Anna for I didn't want to make a speech at graduation. I was getting letters every week from colleges and universities with scholastic offers, but my mind was already made up. I would attend Ole Miss and so would Anna. They had offered free tuition and part time job working on the *"Daily Mississippian"* the student newspaper.

Mr. Webb had contacted a small law firm in Oxford and if I took the job with them, I would have access to all their resources including their law library. I wanted to leave all options open until I could visit the campus. I had already checked on housing for married couples and found that Anna and I could get a single bedroom furnished apartment in student housing for about two hundred dollars per semester. I told Anna about the apartment and she was excited that we would be able to get housing on campus and wanted us to drive over and see if we could look at the quarters. We made plans to call the housing director to make an appointment to tour the apartments that were available.

45

Grandpa Calloway

Aunt Zula is worried

GRANDPA CALLOWAY'S HEALTH WAS deteriorating rapidly, and Aunt Zula called Pappy from Big Flat to let him know that the old man needed medical attention, but she was not able to get him to go to the doctor.

Pappy left the next morning for his old home to see if he could get him medical attention. He would like to bring him to the medical center in Tupelo, so he and Allie could check on him daily. Aunt Zula did not drive and was only in marginally better health than Grandpa and could no longer see to grandpa. Pappy made it to Big Flat at mid-morning and found grandpa in much worse shape than he had imagined. He was so frail and weak; he could no longer stand without assistance.

Pappy told Aunt Zula to pack grandpa a few essentials in a suitcase, and a bag for herself, that he was taking them to Tupelo for a few days. He would take Grandpa to the medical center and have Doctor Little see what he could do. They had plenty of room in their new home and he wasn't taking no for an answer. Aunt Zula protested, but she knew Pappy was right and she gathered what she thought they would need, and in an hour, they were leaving Big Flat.

Pappy stopped just past the Baptist church at Uncle Herman Epps and asked him if he would see to grandpa's chickens and hogs for a few days; that he was taking grandpa to Tupelo to the hospital.

Grandpa was too sick to protest much, but he was not happy about being forced to go to a doctor. He was eighty- five years old, and not used to taking orders from anyone. They rode in silence for most of the way to Tupelo, and Pappy drove straight to the emergency room. Doctor Little was not on duty, but he had the nurse on duty to call him. Pappy checked his father in while Aunt Zula stayed by her brother in the emergency area. Doctor Little came into the area in ten minutes and examined the old man. When he had finished his examination, he came out and sat by Pappy.

"Your dad is in pretty bad shape, he said, I'm checking him in ICU, and we will get blood and urine samples, and see what we need to do for him. We are going to start an I -V to make sure he is hydrated, and your aunt said he hadn't eaten anything in two days. We will give him a solution in his I-V to build his strength. We are going to have to address the problem with the hernia, at some point in time, but he is much too weak to undergo surgery right now. You need to take your Aunt and get her settled in. She probably needs rest, and make sure she eats regular meals.

Pappy had not called Momma to let her know that we were going to have house guests, and she was stunned when Pappy drove up with Aunt Zula in the truck.

"Gonna have company for a while, Pappy said, as he helped Aunt Zula up the steps and into the house. Had to put Dad in the hospital. He's in pretty bad shape. Put Zula in Zacks room for now. I'll bring a cot and Zack can move in the room with Robert Lewis. We may have to make room for dad later. We'll have to wait and see. Momma hugged Aunt Zula and led her to the living room and had her sit in the rocker by the fireplace.

"You sit, Auntie, she said I'll get you a glass of sweet tea." I have potato soup on the stove, would you like a cup? It's lunch time."

Aunt Zula accepted Momma's offer and sipped the soup from a big coffee mug. Momma brought a shawl for Aunt Zula to give her extra warmth for it was a cold day.

"That's sooo good!" She said.

Pappy went to the truck and brough in Aunt Zula's bag, kissed Momma and left to go back to the hospital to be with his dad. Grandpa was in the ICU when Pappy made it back to the hospital. They already had an I -V started, and his father seemed to be resting comfortably. Pappy sat in a padded chair by his father's bed.

The ICU ward was a busy place. One of the nurses asked Pappy if he would like a cup of coffee. She said that Doctor Little had given his dad a sedative to help him relax. It was working for his dad was snoring loudly."

I had been in school all day and was surprised when I got home to find Aunt Zula there, and learn that Grandpa was in the hospital. I drove to the hospital to sit with Pappy. We stayed until visiting hours were over at nine. Grandpa was still resting well. Pappy had given the duty nurse our phone number in case they needed us during the night. Momma and Aunt Zula were still up and waiting on us when we got to the house. Momma had the kids in the bed, for she put them to bed at eight on school nights. Charlie, however, heard me come in and asked me to read to her for a while, that she couldn't go to sleep. I didn't have to read long for she was asleep in minutes after I started reading.

Pappy had already left for the hospital when Momma woke me in the morning, I ate my breakfast and drove to Anna's to pick her up for school. Today we were having Senior Pictures made for the school yearbook. Anna was to be featured as *Senior Class Queen*. She was also selected as the" most *likely to succeed."* It was a big day for Anna. Momma had insisted that I wear a sports coat and a tie for the picture taking. Anna carried extra clothes for different pictures, but I was stuck with having to wear the coat and tie until the afternoon. I was very proud of Anna. She was beautiful and smart and the most determined person I knew. She was also the girl I wanted to marry. I told her about grandpa on the way to school. She said she wanted me to take her by to see him when we got out of school in the afternoon. She and grandpa had hit it off good on our trips to Big Flat and he really liked her.

We went from school straight to the hospital to see how grandpa was doing. Pappy was in the waiting room with Doctor Little and his nurse. The doctor had just finished his afternoon rounds. Doctor Little smiled as Anna came in. He gave her a hug and complimented her on how pretty she looked. He didn't Comment on my looks though.

"How is grandpa? I asked.'

"Sit down Zack, and I'll tell you what we know. The Doctor has patients to see and has to go back to his office"

I sat down, Anna beside me, realizing that the news was not going to be good.

"Grandpa is very sick, Pappy began. He has a number of issues, all of which are very serious. He has had the hernia for years and refused to have surgery to repair it. It is at the point now, however, where it must be repaired. His heart is just worn out too and his kidneys are failing. He is too weak for any surgery now, so they are just trying to keep him comfortable as they try to help him recover some strength."

Pappy was deeply worried about his father. His eyes were swollen and the furrows in his brow had deepened. He obviously had been shedding tears, but it was not in Pappy's nature to show his emotions. His pain was inward, but he was in pain, nonetheless.

Grandpa's condition worsened despite the best efforts of the medical staff. Momma went to the hospital to be with Pappy for Doctor Little had told Pappy to Prepare for the worst case, that his father's time was short.

Momma cried when she was told that Grandpa was not going to make it. He had lapsed into a coma and his breathing was now labored. Grandpa was dying and there was nothing we could do about it.

Grandpa died just after midnight, with Momma and Pappy and Doctor Little at his side. Anna and I broke the word to Aunt Zula. She was heartbroken. She had been with her brother for five years in Big Flat and they were close. Aunt Zula had a daughter in Atlanta, and we called to let her know that Auntie was staying with us. She said she would come for her mother when funeral arrangements were made for Grandpa. She wanted her mother to come back to Atlanta with her.

Pappy and Momma made funeral arrangements with the Woodbury Mortuary in Tupelo. They would take Grandpa's body to Big Flat to his old house to lay in state for visitation, and his funeral would be held at the little Baptist Church across from the store he had operated for fifty years. He, of course, would be buried in the necropolis on the ridge above Big Flat where his family and other kin had been buried for more than a century.

Pappy called Willy at his base station at Randolph Air Force Base in San Antonio to let him know that his grandfather had passed, and that they had made arrangements for the funeral to be held on Saturday afternoon, in hopes that Willy could get a weekend pass to attend the funeral. Willy said he didn't have money enough to buy a plane ticket, so Pappy wired him money to catch a flight to Memphis late Friday. We would pick him up there and he could fly back on Sunday after the funeral. Willy called back the next morning to let Pappy know that he had been given a weekend pass and when his flight would arrive in Memphis. There were other calls to relatives and friends in Big flat. Pappy knew that the folks there enjoyed a good funeral about as much as they did a summer revival. It was almost like a big family reunion, with plenty of food and time to visit. People in the community would sit up all night with the corpse. Folks would talk for days after a wake about who all had come and who hadn't. They would talk about this or that and their dealings with grandpa. It was all a very respectful time and very much a uniquely Mississippi adventure.

Burt Knox, Pastor of the Big Flat Baptist church preached the funeral and the little church was packed. He read scriptures from the 23rd Psalms and gave a short sermon on what it meant to love your neighbor. Burt knew that Grandpa was not an overly religious man, but he knew that grandpa loved his neighbors.

Grandpa's neighbors served as pallbearers. They had also dug the grave with pick and shovel on the red clay hill the morning of the burial. The funeral home had set up a tent at the grave site and it came in mighty handy, for a cold rain began to fall as the preacher was reading the final scriptures. The family huddled under the tent until the casket was lowered into the grave and the Pallbearers covered the grave with red clay, hurriedly, before it became a muddy mess.

A row of negros stood separated from white folks in the cold rain to give their respects to grandpa, for grandpa extended credit to everyone without regard for color. There were only three or four Black families in the little settlement, but grandpa knew them all by name and they all came to say farewell.

We left the gravesite and went back to grandpa's old house where Willy and I had spent the first years of our lives. Grandpa's brother Otto, who co-owned the little store in Big Flat, was there with Aunt Dora. Otto was suffering from loss of mental capacity and hardly knew what was going on. Aunt Dora said that the old store had been closed for good. Big Flat would never be the same.

When all the friends and relatives had finally drifted away from Grandpa's old house, Aunt Zula and her daughter Sarah Ann, Pappy Momma and me and Anna and Willy sat at the old pine dining table and talked. Momma made coffee for Pappy. Aunt Zula told Pappy that grandpa had told her that his papers were in the old hump-back trunk at the foot of his bed. Pappy opened the smelly old trunk and took out a stack of papers. There he found grandpa's bank book, his last will and testament, an insurance policy, and a handwritten note to Pappy. The bank book showed a balance of $1124.00. There were two $1000.00 U.S. saving bonds made to Me and Willy jointly, and an insurance policy in the amount of $4000.00 with Pappy as beneficiary. There was a deed to the 160 acres made out to Willy and Me. That was the total assets of grandpa's estate. Everything else 'including the little store building and the old house went to Pappy.

Anna had come to the funeral with me and we drove back to Tupelo in a slow rain. Charlie and Robert Lewis had stayed with Marie Owens, for Momma thought they had seen enough death, and wanted to shield them from the trauma of seeing grandpa laying in a casket. Pappy agreed.

Momma and Pappy stayed the night in Big Flat and drove Willy back to Memphis the next morning. Aunt

Zula left with her daughter for Atlanta When Pappy and Momma left for Memphis. I wondered when I would ever see Aunt Zula again. Pappy and Momma made it back to Tupelo late Sunday afternoon. They picked up Charlie and Robert Lewis before coming home. Charlie was filled with questions, about Grandpa and wanted to know what would happen to the little piglets and the baby chicks. Pappy explained, with tears forming in his eyes that they were being cared for and that we would go the next week and bring them to the old Davis farm, where they could check on them each week. Robert Lewis said he wanted to ride that old sow momma.

Grandpa's death had changed us all, he loved us dearly and we returned his love. He would forever be known in Big Flat as the old man who ran the little country store and extended credit to anyone who asked, but that was far from the sum, of what he was, to his family. To me it was his teaching me to tie shoes, walking with me down the dusty road to the old store, and the smell of him smoking that old crooked stem pipe. It was me and Willy sitting at his feet listening to him play the fiddle while Pappy sang and played the guitar; Special moments in time that are forever frozen in my mind. To Charlie and Robert and to Anna their memory would be the day grandpa introduced them to the piglets and the baby chicks.

I thought that I could write a book of the many ways that grandpa shaped our lives. Pappy would just say that *"life goes on,"* but I knew that Pappy's feeling for his father was deep, and time would only temper the loss, and would never erase it. Pappy had lost a part of his soul that he knew he could never recover.

> *'In times of great stress,*
> *moral boundaries become distorted, even opaque'*
> *Robert Coleman*

46

Anna Visits the Med School

I do the driving

THE TIME FOR ANNA'S Visit to the Medical School came two weeks after we had buried grandpa. She was ecstatic that she was finally going to Jackson, the place that Doctor Little had talked so much about. Her mother had decided that they would drive the 160 miles on Wednesday and then drive back on Sunday.

Highways from Tupelo to Jackson left a lot to be desired and it was a five- hour drive under the best of circumstances. Pappy agreed that I could go along and maybe help with the driving. Marie Owens seemed pleased that I was going with them. I knew that Mrs. Owens was worried about the cost of sending her daughter to Med School, for although she worked at the bank, her salary was modest and even with scholarships, she would have to borrow on her home to get Anna through. She would do whatever it took to have her daughter become a medical doctor.

I had never been to Jackson and was also looking forward to the trip to the State capitol. Compared to Tupelo, Jackson was a large town, but like most towns in Mississippi it had a small- town attitude. They knew they lived in a small city and the people who lived there didn't care if it ever got any bigger. Jackson was not only the medical center for the state, it was also the legal center. It was said that there was a doctor on every corner, and a lawyer right there waiting to sue him.

We left Tupelo just before ten o'clock in the morning and only stopped for gas and lunch in Lewisville. We drove onto the campus just after three o'clock in the afternoon and checked into the Alumni House Hotel taking two rooms on the ground floor. The Hotel was a first- class inn, with a full restaurant, and well- furnished airconditioned rooms. There was a Bell Boy to help with luggage and making other arrangements. I had but a small bag but, Anna and her mother had apparently brought enough clothes and accessories to stay a month. We checked into our rooms and agreed to meet at six for dinner in the hotel restaurant. I lay across my bed and was asleep in minutes. I did not wake until there was a knock on my door. Dang! I had slept past six and Anna was knocking on my door. I apologized and said I would be right down. I threw on a clean shirt, combed my hair and rushed to the restaurant. Anna and her mother had ordered drinks. She ordered me a Dr. Pepper and had it waiting for me.

We had salad from the salad buffet and made our dinner selection from the leather covered menu. The prices were off the chart, but Anna and her mother were eating on the house. At prices like these I didn't know if I'd be able to eat all three days that we were supposed to be in Jackson. The food was good, though and I ate every bite.

After Dinner the three of us strolled around the campus and even ventured to walk to the administration building, where Anna would go the next day, We were back in the hotel by eight o'clock, and Marie wanted to have coffee before they returned to the room, so we sat and talked about our plans to go to Ole Miss in the fall. Anna never mentioned anything about our conversation of marriage, although I thought it would have been a good time. We finally went to our room for the night. It had been a good day.

The next morning, the Administrator sent a car for Anna and her mother just before nine o'clock. I took Mrs. Owen's car and asked for direction to the state capitol. I made it to the old historical building without trouble and parked a block from the South entrance. From any view the building was a magnificent structure, with the dome rising some 180 feet above street level. I walked right into the building without so much as a look from the state police officers on duty. I roamed both floors of the structure viewing display and statutes. Inside the building was just as magnificent as the exterior. It housed both legislative branches of government, and the State Supreme Court, as well as the Governor's offices. There was a short film of the history of Jackson, and the construction of the Capitol building, which commenced in 1903. The film lasted for about twenty minutes. At lunch time I took the stairs to the basement where there was a buffet for serving Capitol staff and visitors. The prices were very reasonable, so I had a meal of fried chicken and creamed potatoes and a dish of peach cobbler.

I then drove back to the hotel when my tour was over. In my room I switched on the television and watched TV until Anna and her mother returned from their first day's tour of the Medical facilities. They were impressed to learn just how many programs the center had for those wanting a career in medicine. Anna intended to study general medicine with emphasis on Family Practice. It would be a long hard slog, she knew, but it had been her dream since the first time I met her.'

That night we again ate in the hotel restaurant, and Marie Owens picked up the ticket for my meal. I didn't feel right about that, but I didn't protest too much, for Jackson was quickly draining my resources. Marie and Anna were tired from walking through the various facilities and after dinner we again sat and talked. It was mostly about the events of the day, and I told them about my visit to the Capitol. Tomorrow would be another long day for Anna, and I asked Mrs. Owens if it was alright if I drove her car to the Jackson Law Library, she said, of course. I wanted to find out as much as I could about what was available if Anna and I were married and I had to take classes in Jackson. We decided we would meet for breakfast at eight in the morning, for they were to be picked up at nine, once again to finish her tour.

When the Friday tour was finished, we decided to celebrate by going out to a nice restaurant that was not far from the Med Center. It was called "Plantation House" and was advertised as having live blues music." "The negro Blues singer, Jimmy Reed, put on a show that night that was absolutely fantastic." Song after song he sang for two hours and we stayed till closing time. There was a dance floor and I had a chance to show my skills with Anna on several slow numbers. It was the first time I had held Anna in my arms in a week or more and it felt good.

It was after eleven o'clock when we got back to the hotel, and we went to our rooms for the night. It had been an enjoyable trip for me and we intended to stay another day, at the University's expense but we were ready to get home to Tupelo and decided to leave after check out time on Saturday and drive highway 51 highway North to Batesville and then go through Oxford to Tupelo.

Sometime after midnight there was a slight rap on my door, I thought at first I must be mistaken, but in seconds, another rap, I went to the door and cracked it open, It was Anna in her cotton robe.

I quickly opened the door, and she came in. "What's wrong Anna? Is your mother ok? I asked.'"

"Everything is fine, she said as she untied her robe and let it fall to the floor. She stood before me in panties and bra. "I just wanted to be with you tonight, like we were at the hospital four years ago. I looked, at her almost in shock, and then took her in my arms, and then to my bed. Your mother will kill us both for this I whispered, caressing her now full breast."

"She knows, Anna said. I told her that I was coming. She didn't even protest. She just said don't you hurt that boy. He loves you. I told her I knew that, and it was why I had to go,"

We made love at a torrid pace and then we lay there, Anna in my arms until exhaustion overtook us. Anna left my bed, dressed, kissed me goodnight and returned to her mother's room. I Lay there with the sweet smell of Anna all over me. It was a long time before I slept.

47

Disaster Strikes

Wreck on the highway

IT WAS NEARING NOON when we made it out of the city and headed North. The day was cold; but the sun was bright. A good day for a drive through the small Mississippi towns along the old highway. On Saturdays, Black and Whites alike, gathered on the squares of the towns to socialize and make essential purchases. Most towns were crowded but peaceful.

Marie Owens said nothing about the night before. If she was unhappy with me or with Anna, she didn't let it show. I didn't know what brought about her change in attitude, but I felt no remorse for what we had done.

I was doing the driving when we left Jackson and the three of us sat in the front seat. It felt good having Anna sit next me. Sometimes she would lay her hand on my leg and her very touch set me on fire inside. Mississippi is a beautiful state and we were enjoying our return home.

Mississippians are, by nature, a gentle and independent people. They love their neighbors but despise interlopers trying to run their lives. Mississippians don't much care what their neighbors do for a living, as long as it is honest work. If their neighbor ran a whiskey still, and they knew it, they would never tell a lawman. Whiskey making was on the same par as an undertaker. while most people didn't want to do either job, they were both viewed as necessary services.

Around two o'clock we passed through Grenada. I stopped there and we bought sodas and candy bars and had the car filled with gas. I pulled back onto the highway and headed North. A few minutes out of Grenada. We were nearing the small town of Coffeeville, the traffic was much heavier, big Rigs crowded the two-lane highway, one after the other. We were a little more than a hundred yards behind a family sedan, when a big rig headed South crossed over the center line and crashed headlong into the family sedan crushing and pushing the car toward us. I swerved off to the highway onto a wide shoulder. The big rig coming, finally, managed to a stop not twenty yards in front of us. The car burst into flames, black smoke boiling upward. We could see that there were several passengers in the sedan and the car was crushed into a horseshoe shape. I told Marie to get out of the car and away from the car and wave traffic down. I popped open the trunk and grabbed a tire iron and ran to the flaming car. I turned and Anna was right beside me. When we neared the car, we could hear children screaming. They were trapped inside the burning car. The two passengers in the front seat were crushed. I broke the rear window and side glass with the tire tool. There were four small children and a girl of about twelve in the back seat of the sedan.

I dropped the tire tool and dragged the smallest of the children through the side window. Anna grabbed up the tire tool and went to the other side of the car and broke out the window, yelling for the kids to cover their heads. Marie Owens took the child I retrieved and moved her back from the burning inferno. Anna had pulled a small child through the window and the oldest had crawled through the window on her own. I went back for another child, and by this time truckers and other passer- by's were stretched out along the road, yelling for us to get back that it was going to explode. I turned to look, and Anna was at the car pulling the last child through the window. She was three steps from the burning car, with the child cradled in her arms when the gas tank exploded, sending Anna and the child flying across the highway, raining projectiles of glass and steel down on Anna and the child. I ran to Anna and knelt beside her. Blood was pouring from a severed artery in her neck, a piece of broken glass protruding from the wound. Seconds later, Marie Owens was beside her, cradling her daughter in her arms, crying uncontrollably. The child beneath her body had been Shielded from the explosion by Anna and was taken by an EMT from the place where she lay; very scared and sobbing but because of Anna, she was alive. I cursed myself for stopping.

My Anna lay dead beside the highway because of me. How would I ever get over this tragedy, and how would Marie Owens ever recover from the loss of her beautiful daughter. All our talk and plans for the future were gone forever. Why did God take her from me? "Why had he caused Annabelle so much pain in her short life? What purpose under the sun, could this possibly serve?" I wanted answers to questions that I knew would not come.

Soon the ambulances and fire trucks came from Grenada and the state police too. They took Anna's body to the morgue in Grenada and Mrs. Owens rode in the ambulance with her daughter. I followed in her car. It would be hours before they could remove the driver of the car and the other passenger from the wreck. I did not know who these people were but most likely there were five kids without a mother. It did not temper my loss.

At the hospital, I called Momma and Pappy to let them know what had happened. They had seen the accident report on television. She said that the tv news already had Anna's picture from the yearbook with a report of her bravery, and what we both had done to save the children in the car.

"I'm so sorry, son, I know how much you loved her."

I hung up the phone and sat down in the waiting room outside the morgue and 'for the first time I cried. Minutes later, Marie Owens came and sat beside me and rested her head on my shoulder. She was still sobbing, her face and eyes red and her hair askew. I put my arm around her and pulled her close, as if it could ease our pain. We sat there for a while until the two State Police officers came and asked us questions about the accident. They took our names and addresses and telephone numbers where we could be reached. A reporter also came by and talked to us about Anna. We asked about the children in the car. The reporter said that currently they were in the hands of Child Services until relatives could be reached. The two adults in the front seat was the mother of the children and her sister.

48

Leaving Anna

The final farewell

WE FINALLY LEFT THE morgue in Grenada, after Marie Owens had made arrangements for Anna's body to be picked up, and transported, by the funeral home, back to Tupelo. We would follow the hearse in Marie's car. I also listened as Marie broke the news to Anna's grandparents. It was the saddest day of my life. I had been sad when grandpa died, but we had been prepared for that. He was eighty-five. Anna was seventeen, my friend, my lover, my future, my dreams of us having children together, of her becoming a Doctor. What would I do? How do people get through such a loss, I wondered? I didn't know if I ever could. I thought about

Charlie and wondered how she would react. She loved Anna too. She had suffered so much loss already, I knew it would be traumatic for her.

It was late in the night when we drove into the drive at Marie Owens home. I called Momma and told her that I was going to stay with Mrs. Owens and that I would bring her to the house the first thing in the morning. Momma asked if I wanted her to come and stay with Marie. I told her no, that Marie was exhausted and just wanted to try and sleep. She had made me a bed on her couch, and we would be fine.

Marie made coffee and we sat together on the divan and sipped the hot brew. Marie had calmed very little; she had lost a husband, years ago and now a daughter. The two most precious people in the world to her. She was a strong woman, like her daughter, and at some point, she would move on, like everyone must. Happiness, unlike sorrow, however, is never a guarantee. I hoped she would not be bitter with me for reacting the way we did at the crash. I wanted her to allow me to be a part of her life.

After we talked for a while, I slipped off my shoes and rested my feet on the ottoman by the couch. I lay my head back and closed my eyes. Marie stretched out on the couch and lay her head on my lap. She cried again and I put my arms around her and held her for a while. After a while we slept where we sat, two broken hearted people, we would wake, tears would fall, our sobs almost silent, and we would sleep again. The morning finally came with Marie Owens standing beside me. She had made fresh coffee and brough me a cup when I awoke. She sat down beside me and curled her feet under her. She finally spoke.

"I don't blame you for Anna's death Zack. It was her choice to go to the burning car. I screamed for her to stay away, but that was not the way Anna was made. She was doing what any good Doctor, or any good human being would do. Try to save the life of a child. That's why Anna died. She loved children. It will be a hard thing for us to get through, but we need each other. We are the two people who loved her the most. I must tell you this. Last night when Anna told me she was going to your room, Anna said that she had a strange feeling that she might not ever get another chance to be with you. I trusted Anna's feelings, and now I think, somehow, she knew her life was coming to an end. That may seem crazy to you Zack, but all her life I felt that Anna had a true and special connection to things spiritual.

"No, I said I don't think it's crazy. I have had those feelings about Anna too. She once told me that she was worried that God had something special planned for us, but she couldn't understand if it was good or a bad thing. Maybe this was what she was feeling. I don't know.

The next morning, Marie and I went to Momma and Pappy's house for breakfast and coffee. Neither of us had an appetite for food but it was a comfort to be with the family again. Marie asked Momma, Pappy, and me if we go with her to the funeral home to make arrangements. Pappy insisted that he pay the cost of the funeral. Marie tried to refuse, but finally relented. She cried again from the gift of generosity of Pappy and Momma.

Late in the afternoon the funeral home called and said Mrs. Owens could come and view the corpse. Anna's grandparents had driven from Columbus, and we all went together to review the remains of Annabelle Owens. Even in death Anna was beautiful. I wanted to touch her, but I knew if I did, I would lose control of my emotions, which were, now, very fragile. Anna's grandfather cried like a baby when he saw his granddaughter. Pappy, as usual, was stoic, but I knew he was feeling great pain, for he and Anna had created a special bond.

Marie and Anna had been attending the Old Church on Jefferson, and I told her that we had met Pastor Luke there and that I would like for him to preach the memorial. I told her I would ask him, since we had talked on different occasions. I also said that I would ask Doctor Little if he would say a few words about Anna. Marie gave me permission to handle those arrangements once the time of the funeral was set. I drove over to the old church and walked down the wide sidewalk up to the steps of the sanctuary. I pushed the big mahogany doors open, and went inside. An elderly Black man was sweeping the hardwood floors with a cloth push mop. There was a strong smell of furniture oil and wilted flowers in the broad atrium. I asked the man to direct me to the Pastor's office.

"At the end of the hall on the right, he said." I thanked him and walked to the office as directed. I stopped before the glass enclosed office with a sign in gold letters above the door that said "Pastor's Office" and below that a sign that said James Van Dyke. I opened the door and walked on. A receptionist greeted me.

"I'm Zack Calloway, and I'm looking for Pastor Luke Jackson, I said."

"Pastor Luke? She asked. Our Pastor is Doctor Van Dyke. He's been our Pastor for five years and I don't know anyone by that name."

"Pastor Luke was a tall man, maybe six four or taller, about fifty."

"Let me go ask Doctor Van Dyke, if he knows such a person, she said rising. Follow me, she said, and I'll introduce you to the pastor."

I followed her down a narrow hallway to a large office on the left. Doctor Van Dyke sat at his desk surrounded by shelves of catalogued sermons and study materials. To the right of his desk, on a slanted table was the largest holy bible I had ever seen in my life. It must have weighed fifty pounds and was bound in leather.

Van Dyke stood when I approached his desk and introduced himself. He shook my hand firmly. "You say you're looking for a Preacher by the name of Luke

Jackson? I know of no such person, he said. Did he say he was pastor of this church," he asked.

No, not exactly. I come here sometimes and sit on the steps when I need a quiet place to think. Sometimes he just shows up."

I then explained to Doctor Van Dyke why I was there. That I had intended to ask Pastor Luke to preach the memorial service for Annabelle Owens.

"Oh yes, he said, I knew Anna and Mrs. Owens well. What a tragedy, he said shaking his head, a lovely and bright girl. I didn't know Anna as well as I knew her mother, but she was really a sweet girl."

"I'm sorry I can't help you with your search for the preacher you mentioned, but if I can be of service, I will be happy to say a few words. They were not members of the congregation, but they did attend regularly, and I know Marie quite well. She is our contact person at the bank, and I talk to her quite often, I know that Marie must be devastated"

I thanked him for his offer and told him I would let him know later in the day. As soon as the funeral home set the time. I left the church, wondering about Pastor Luke. How could it be that they did not know him at the church. Who was that man? Where did he come from? How did he know so much about my family, when no one seemed to know about him. I knew he existed, for Anna and Charlie had both talked to him. It was beyond strange.

I relayed to Mrs. Owens what I had learned, and we decided we would call Doctor Van Dyke, and ask him to handle the memorial, and Doctor Little would also talk about Anna, and her work at the hospital. In the meantime, the funeral home and Mrs. Owens had set the time of the funeral at two o'clock on Wednesday at the Church on Jefferson. Burial would be in Columbus, by her father at the old cemetery on the east side of town. Teachers from the high school would serve as pallbearers and The captain of the Mississippi Highway police would present Mrs. Owens with a plaque honoring Annas bravery, and the Mississippi Governor J.P. Coleman would make a special appearance to bestow Mississippi's highest honor, the *Medal of Freedom* to Mrs. Owens for her daughter's bravery.

The church was packed with standing room only, with students from school and all the political dignitaries from Tupelo. I sat with Marie Owens in an area set aside for family members. At Marie's request Pappy and Momma and the kids sat with the family along with Bonnie and Doctor Little. The church choir sang Anna's favorite hymns and the preacher gave a devotional on Love and courage. "Anna, he said, loved people, and she practiced it every day. Loving was not just empty words with her, but a code that she lived by. She wrote in her diary that "love had no boundaries, and love had no master. You can never help who you love, even when love is not returned." She also wrote that Zack Calloway was the true love of her life and the boy she wanted to marry."

I cried until I could cry no more. When the service concluded, Charlie and Marie Owens rode with me as we followed the hearse to Columbus, which was an hour away. There was not much conversation, but I knew Charlie's mind was filled with questions that she would ask later. They would be questions that I would not be able to answer for her. When we drove onto the cemetery grounds, a small group of family and friends had huddled around her gravesite, beneath a small funeral home tent. The ancient cemetery dated back to the Revolutionary War and beyond. It was not particularly a place of beauty, but the ivy-covered walls gave it a peaceful air. For this reason, many of the prominent citizens of the area had been laid to rest there in Friendship Cemetery. Charlie stood beside me and held my hand through the reading of scriptures and a prayer. Charlie shed no tears, but she trembled and sobbed whenever they Said Anna's name. She would cry later, I knew, for I knew how much she loved Annabelle.

When the prayer ended, I asked them to open the casket so I could see Anna's face for the last time. Even in death, she seemed alive. I reached in and took the necklace that was around her neck, kissed the heart and laid the Heart gently on her chest. They closed the casket and lowered her body into the grave. I leaned on a big tombstone, with Charlie beside me, and watched as workmen filled the grave. The evening sun was casting long shadows when the cemetery was finally empty except for Marie Owens, Charlie, and Me. Marie came and stood beside me and took my hand. I held her close as we walked from the gravesite. Charlie held Marie's hand as we walked toward the truck but would turn her head and look back every now and then. I could almost read what she was thinking. Leaving Anna was hard for her. She had lost another person dear to her. She had prayed and prayed but her prayers for Anna had not done a frazzling bit of good.

We can never know how our lives will unfold. No matter how much we plan for the future, we can only live in today. Storms of life come to us all, but I knew also that they never last. Eventually the sun would shine again. I loved Annabelle Owens more than I loved anyone in this world. I didn't know how I would live without her. I would pray that someday I would love that way again. Today, though, I felt like my life had been poured out. I was empty inside, my heart ached for Anna's smile, that I would never see again, and her touch that I would never feel. As we walked, I looked down at Charlie and over at Marie Owens, I stopped and pulled them close to me and told them I loved them. They hugged me and we stood in that embrace for several seconds before we moved on.

From the shadows of trees along the cemetery boundaries stood Pastor Luke, solemn and as still as a stone. He had watched the sadness of a lost loved one play itself out before him. Tears also rolled down his cheeks. He looked toward heaven and shook his head. He then stepped deeper into the shadows and like a ghost, he was gone. His work there was finished.

Marie had asked me to drop her off at Anna's grandparents. Charlie rested her head on Marie and Marie held her close and kissed her head.

"Can I come see you sometime, Miss Marie, she asked, looking up at Marie, her eyes now filled with teardrops.

"Of course, you can, sweetie, anytime you want to come. I would love that."

"I want to come and live with you, Charlie said. You know, be your daughter,"

Marie and I were taken back, and didn't know what to say, but Marie finally answered.

"I would love to have you for my daughter but that is not up to me, sweetie, but we will talk about it when I have regain my wits."

"I love you, Miss Marie, I don't want you to be by yourself,' Charlie said.

"Thank you, Charlie, Marie said, with tears again welling in her eyes. I will be alright as long as I have you and Zack around close

"I didn't believe Marie, however, would ever be alright again She had lost just too much.

I dropped Marie off at Anna's grandparent's home on 7th street. It was a lovely place on a high ridge, surrounded by huge Loblolly pine trees. Crepe Myrtles formed a hedge row along the long driveway. A soft, Magnolia wind ruffled her black dress as I watched her walk away, rejection in her shoulders, her eyes downcast. She was a very broken woman. I waited until she opened the door and went inside. I then took the highway North and cried again; thoughts of what Charlie had just said stirring my troubled mind. Another page had turned in my life and I couldn't imagine what tomorrow would bring.

Darkness was settling over the city when we saw the lights of Tupelo. a place I would always think of as Anna's Town.

THE END

Printed in the United States
By Bookmasters